SCARY SNIPPETS: CHRISTMAS EDITION

Acknowledgements

To all the readers, family and friends that helped make this book possible; we say thank you. Our story has now become a part of yours. Let's write the next chapter of it together- the Publishers

Edited by: N.M. Brown

Cover Design by: Kyle Harrison

Suicide House Publishing

TABLE OF CONTENTS

14

VEGAN THANKSGIVING

By N.M. Brown

The time of year I've come to dread almost has me in its talons; Thanksgiving. It used to be one of my very favorites! I'd wake up in the morning to the smell of meal prep and plop myself down in front of the TV to watch the annual Macy's Day parade!

All of the floats, heartwarming commercials and witty host banter sucked me in every time! My parents would get me one of those large containers of jellybeans the night before, so I'd have something to keep me occupied during the parade to keep me from stealing kitchen snacks.

However, that was years ago. There have been a lot of changes since then, one of which being my relationship status. My girlfriend Kiki's fantastic beyond measure; beautiful, funny, good with kids... the works. There is of course, one drawback. That's always how it goes, isn't it?

Kiki, as perfect as she is, lives a strictly vegan lifestyle; no exceptions. Now, I admire the dedication but as far as her way of living was concerned, all meat is off limits. I'll be swarmed with the scent of steaming vegetables and quinoa instead of turkey.

There'll be no giblet gravy, no chicken in the cornbread stuffing, no bacon with the green beans.

What's worse, is she's dragging me to a friend couple of hers' house this year for the holiday; also vegan. Ah well, at least we won't have to cook anything.

Randy and Paula were very gracious hosts. Kiki greeted them with hugs and warm smiles.

"Thank you so much for having us!" My girl beamed. "It's so refreshing to visit somewhere for Thanksgiving that doesn't celebrate the killing of animals."

Do not roll your eyes John, I warn myself.

"It's so nice to finally meet you after all this time!" Randy tells us.

Finally meet us? Kiki told me she had acted like she's spent time with these people; face time. She has no idea who these people even are?!?

As we sit down to the table, I notice a large carving knife resting on a platter in the center.

"What's that for?" I asked timidly. "Just curious."

Paula evades my question. "Please John, have some wine. We've been saving it for the holiday."

Kiki's eyes plead with me to graciously accept anything they offer. It's the unmistakable look of warning your better half gives you to remind you to remain on your best behavior. So, I sit back and sip most of the contents of the glass.

Paula uncovers a tray to reveal a gorgeous display of deviled eggs.

"I thought Vegans couldn't eat eggs. Not trying to be rude. I'm honestly relieved to be quite honest." Kiki inquires, her amber colored eyebrows raised in curiosity.

Paula and Randy chuckle like they've heard the funniest joke in their entire life, clutching each other for support through ripples of laughter.

"No silly. You misunderstand. See, there are several different kinds of Veganism. The kind that we practice is called Vegan Cannibalism."

A cold, sweat breaks out on the back of my neck. What kind of joke was this?

"I...I don't understand." I stammer as I struggle to back away from the table.

Paula smiles softly. "See dear; it's simple really."

"Yes," Randy continues. "we eat Vegans."

The lids of my eyes become heavy, and I cannot hold myself upright in my seat. The last thing I see as my head slumps to the table, is the crimson spray of Kiki's blood as they slice through her femoral arteries. Happy Thanksgiving.

ᏟᏌᎡᏦᎬᎽ ᎠᎪᎽ

By Ann Wycoff

"I sure hope this isn't a big fail like last year," Christophs said. He could barely see the Felton Emporium from his place in line. There were maybe seven-hundred people between him and the entrance. The Emporium's annual "Turkeys and Tech" sale attracted throngs of eager shoppers from nearby Santa Cruz, and the rest of the Bay Area.

"It won't be long now, Chris."

He listened through his ear buds to Minerva telling a customer where to find pickled ostrich eggs.

Her idea of infiltrating the store by posing as a temp was genius. Surely their plan to cause a riot or at least a diversion would work this year, and in the ensuing chaos they'd both abscond with shopping carts full of sweet merchandise. Last year would have been epic if zombies hadn't already been done to death. Everyone was so jaded these days.

"You there?"

"Huh? Yeah, sorry, Minny."

"I've injected as many turkeys as I could and --"

"I still think we should have gone with trans-cranial implants. It worked great with the zombies." He was going to continue when she said, "Holy *Kalbsleber* on roller skates, how many times do I have to say these turkeys don't have heads? Wait."

A man yelled at Minerva in what sounded liked Spanglish.

"Ok, hit it, Chris!"

There were some muffled scuffling sounds and more shouting. A lot of static in his ear buds.

"Hey, leggo my arm!" Minerva yelled. "Hit it!"

Christophs fumbled with his phone. Somehow he had both hung up and closed his turkey activation app. He muttered expletives and fumbled around for a minute or so. Something was happening down the street. He took a deep breath and focused on rebooting. A few people were leaving the line. Christophs sent his mini-drone gliding toward the Emporium's front windows.

It worked! Turkeys were running amok everywhere. A few still clambered out of the freezers, but most of the birds were wandering around, hopping in circles or committing acts of general strangeness. A few were attacking people and vice versa. He was surprised. Even amped up with his new peptide and nanobot injections, there was only so much animated poultry could pull off in the way of mayhem. The fact they were walking around at all seemed to defy both anatomy and Newton.

Outside their riot wasn't developing. The mini-drone feed went crazy then died.

Someone must have swatted his flying camera out of the air. Offline. He tried calling Minerva back a couple times but she didn't answer so he started jogging toward the street. Christophs got about fifty feet and ran out of breath. He slowed to a fast walk.

Minvera rung his phone. "Security threw me out. You see what's happening out there?"

"Yeah. What a joke."

There were at least a hundred Christmas trees parading in formation past the Emporium, down the middle of Route Nine. In their van was a tremendous redwood, towering over the surrounding buildings, gilt with twinkling lights, silver and gold tinsel, countless bulbs and other ornaments. The vegetable titan scuttled along on a thick, earthy mass of slithering roots that filled the road all around it. People kept a respectful distance as they laughed and called out.

They hoisted children onto their shoulders, and pointed their cell phones at the spectacle.

Zombified Santa's little helpers, high in the redwood's branches, began singing a hip-hop remix of O Christmas Tree.

"Unbelievable," Minerva said.

"I'm all for 'Keep Santa Cruz weird,' but Christmas decorations before Thanksgiving?

What next?" he asked.

"Disgraceful."

People started dancing. Christophs looked for a shopping cart.

CHE HORROR OUC OF CHE ROASCITRY PAT

by R. C. Mulhare

November 24 th , 1898 – East Manuxet, Massachusetts

"And how is the boy adjusting, after his parents' passing?" asked the boy in question's uncle Bedford West, across the kitchen table; laden with mixing bowls and cutting boards covered in parings.

Esther, younger sister to the boy's mother, glanced to her nephew, now basting the turkey while Emilia, the youngest aunt, held the roasting pan balanced on the coal-fired stove door. "He has been well, aside from some momentary debates."

Bedford raised an eyebrow. "I trust these... moments have had nothing to do with your putting him to work in the kitchen? It is, after all, women's work."

The boy, clearly eavesdropping, peered over his shoulder, his blue grey eyes looking coldly over the gold rims of his spectacles. "Uncle, there's little difference between following a chemical formula and following a recipe."

"And what chemical formulas are you concocting, Herbert? Do you plan to be a cattle doctor?" Bedford asked.

"No, I wish to be a medical doctor and cure human illnesses," Herbert replied, turning back to the stove, reaching to his knee pants pocket.

"The tow-headed little fiend has ears as sharp as his tongue," Bedford said. "I suppose you wish to put his father's legacy toward medical college?"

"His teachers say he has an aptitude for the sciences," Esther said.

"I'd rather he went into law or business than squandered his father's money becoming one of those quacks. It's not like they can keep people from dying."

"Bedford, not so soon after the boy lost his parents. It's Thanksgiving Day."

"I have to agree with Uncle Bedford. Perhaps someone can cure that one illness we all suffer," Herbert snipped, palming a small glass bottle into his pocket.

Around the festal board, members of the West and the Rankstone families had gathered. Ordinarily, some would have gathered in the home of Henry West and his wife Eva, eldest and smartest of the Rankstone sisters. But this Thanksgiving, the two families came to the Rankstone homestead, concerned for their orphaned son, the solemn yet smart-tongued survivor of the fire that consumed the West family home. Esther held court at the table, while Emilia and the boy ferried dishes from the kitchen: candied yams, mashed potatoes with herbs, cranberry sauce flavored with nuts and orange peel, roasted corn, green beans.

The guests glanced toward the door to the kitchen, awaiting the king of the feast, the golden-brown turkey with its cargo of cornbread dressing. At one point, the recently installed electric chandelier – Bedford's gift – flickered, drawing concerned remarks about the safety of such new-fangled notions.

Someone screamed behind the kitchen door and it flew open. Emilia, clutching her apron beneath her face, rushed through, white as a sheet. "The turkey! The turkey! Oh God, what's become of it?!"

The aunts, uncles, and cousins stopped chattering. "Great Scott, what ails you, woman?" Bedford asked.

The door swung open again, propelled by something within. A lumpish form, dripping gravy, stumped across the slate floor on its drumstick legs, clots of dressing dropping in a trail before it flopped onto its side. Herbert followed, holding the greasy serving dish, eyes wide in bewilderment, but smirking at one corner of his mouth.

"What happened?" - "Whatever is in this cherry cordial?" -"Something's bewitched the bird!" - "Mama! Da torkey! Da torkey!" the gathered family cried.

Bedford leaped to his feet, grabbing the carving knife and fork, ready to fend off the beast. "What deviltry is this?

"Herbert, we said you could experiment with some of my rabbits and mice, but this is too far," Esther said.

"I needed a larger and different subject for my latest theory," Herbert said, adjusting his glasses and looked pointedly at Uncle Bedford. "And there's no better audience than skeptics."

REVENGE OF THE TURKEY

By Cecelia Hopkins-Drewer

I couldn't afford to fly home for Thanksgiving, so I accepted an invitation from my best friend to spend Thanksgiving with her family in Iowa. The wine I was offered on arrival had been warmed and developed a strange metallic taste. I sipped from my glass to be polite, attempting to admire the decorations, which were too realistic for my sensitive perception. I like my stuffed turkey nicely cooked, and on a platter ready to eat, not mounted on the wall with the feathers still on.

The ugly turkey stared back, its beady glass eyes reflecting a horrible red in the light from the strange smelling tallow candles that had been placed absolutely everywhere. I was glad that the meal I was offered that night appeared to be cold sliced ham, followed by good old American apple pie.

I lay down in the room I was assigned and tried to sleep, tossing and turning fitfully until I was awakened early

Thanksgiving morning by a strange clucking sound. It seemed to be coming from the dining room. I slid out of bed and grabbed my woolly dressing gown, before tiptoeing downstairs.

The table was fully laid out with steaming cobs of corn, crusty bread rolls, tasty leaf salads and many other vegetative delicacies. I couldn't see the main course anywhere, but the oven held a nice, comforting warm glow. I peered inside and noticed a large platter ringed with baking potatoes. Still no meat.

A feathery pressure thumped up against me, forcing me against the burning oven door.

"What the... is going on?"

"Gobble, Gobble, Gobble."

My assailant didn't seem to be human. Ignoring the pain of my searing flesh, I looked back over my shoulder to see a gigantic turkey, like one on the wall, but on serious growth hormones. It opened its sharp beak wide and dived toward my jugular vein.

"Gobble, Gobble, Gobble."

"You can't eat me!"

"Why not – you were planning to eat me?"

"That's not the same."

"Isn't it now?"

I was forced into the oven by strong wings, and as a clawed foot closed the door, the last thing I heard was the giant turkey chuckling.

"Gobble, Gobble, Gobble."

BLACK FRIDAY SLASHER

By Dan McKeithan

Alex couldn't believe the Thanksgiving feast was almost over. He waited for Jerry and Susan to swing by and pick him up from his grandmother's house. They already knew where they wanted to go this Black Friday.

Jerry beeped his horn. Alex climbed into the back with Dave and Susan sat in the front.

They pulled into the parking lot beside the K-Mart store and waited until the doors opened. Jerry spread his map onto the hood of the car.

"Dave—you do just like you did last year—stay in the car. Susan—take make-up and clothes. Alex cover sporting goods and electronics and I'll take care of any stragglers."

Susan placed her arm around Jerry. "It'll be okay this year. It's a different city."

Jerry flinched. "Still, let's leave this store with no casualty's this time."

"It was a fluke," Dave said. "No one knew that girl would be standing out in the rain. It was dark and she should've been inside with the others."

"Everyone was inside last year," Alex said. "I made sure of that."

"Tell that to that girl's dad," Susan said. "We were lucky no one saw us get away."

Dave watched as Jerry, Alex, and Susan rushed inside. This would have to be a better year. This store was bigger than the last three they'd hit. Bigger items, bigger crowd to steal from.

A dark shape caused him to check the rearview mirror. Was there a person back there? He rolled down his window and peered around the back of the car. Nothing. Just nerves.

Suddenly there was a burning sensation on his throat. Everything faded to black.

Susan hated covering make-up and clothes. She always got that because she was a girl.

One of these days, she'd speak to Jerry about it. Maybe she could do movies/games. She watched as a lady placed her purse in the cart and went to grab a coat off the rack.

It was a snatch. She was in and out of the wallet before the lady turned around. A person shoved her in the back. She jerked around. No one was there. Then a hand grabbed her by the back of the head and slammed it into the end of a coat rack. She didn't have time to scream.

Alex watched an overweight man grab a basketball out of a kid's hand. And people thought what they did was bad? His phone buzzed.

"Have you seen Susan?" Jerry asked.

"No, but we've still got thirty minutes before—" Alex said

There was a bunch of screaming and running from the clothing section.

"Somethings up," Jerry said. "They just locked the front door with an armed guard. See if you can get out the back by the loading dock. I'll find Susan and mee—"

Jerry cut off. Alex could hear a gagging sound on the other end.

"Jerry?" No answer.

Alex raced toward the back and out the loading dock. A shadow passed behind him. He ran around to the front. He ran toward their car. Dave was sitting in the driver's seat. When he jerked open the door, Dave fell forward, blood running from a gaping wound in his neck.

Alex turned around to see a large man with a butcher knife standing behind him.

"It's time to pay for your crimes," the man said.

Alex charged him, knowing this time his debt would be collected.

A DAY TO GIVE THANKS

By Gabriella Balcom

Tom Turkey had no appetite, but ate anyway. Then he forced himself to eat even more. He'd been doing the same thing for days now, trying to gain weight. His mate, Tamara, understood his motivation and sobbed. Their son, Tucker, had been sold for Thanksgiving, and the purchaser would be coming for him soon. She'd begged the other turkeys for help, but none of them knew what to do. They all felt worried and hopeless.

When the day of dread finally arrived, the man who'd bought Tucker came for him. Tom had his son hide, though, and took his place.

As he awaited death hours later, Tom heard the man talking and his stomach lurched. He trembled so badly, his legs threatened to give way beneath him. What he'd overheard was worse than anything he could've imagined.

That sadistic human planned to yank out his feathers, chop off his feet and head, then boil him in hot oil.

Without any warning, a large, glowing turkey appeared in front of Tom.

"The Great Gobbler," he whispered, eyes widening. "I thought you were nothing but a myth."

Sinking to the ground, he lowered his head.

"I'm very real," the being replied. "And, I'm here because of you, my child. Sacrificing yourself to save another is noble. It's the greatest, bravest thing a turkey can do, and I'm rewarding you..."

On Thanksgiving Day, Tom bowed his head, uttering a heartfelt prayer before beaming at Tamara, Tucker, and their relatives and friends who were seated around the long banquet table. "This truly is a time for giving thanks," he said. "Our days of fear are over and we've prepared an extra-special feast to celebrate the occasion."

Standing, he reached for the sharp knife Tamara had prepared for him and studied their main course. The man was baked to a golden perfection and lay on a large platter, an apple in his mouth.

"Would you like white meat or dark?" Tom asked the turkey to his left. "A slice from the chest, maybe? Or, do you want some brain?"

Tamara rose, coming to whisper in his ear. "Do you think one human is enough to feed everyone?"

"Don't worry," Tom reassured her. "If not, we have plenty more."

CHANKSGIVING
WITH THE
WHATELEYS
by R. C. Mulhare

November 26 th , 1925

"Why do you have to invite Lavinia and Will to Thanksgiving every year?" young Curtis Whateley asked, setting out the plates on the front room's long table.

His mother Judith handed the basket of flatware to Ermangarde, their kitchen maid and ward. "Because it's the polite thing."

Curtis set two plates as far from the rest of the settings as he could. "Papa ain't so sure about that."

"Why, are they troublesome?" Ermangarde asked, innocently, unfamiliar with the family, due to her recent arrival in Dunwich from an orphanage in East Manuxet.

Curtis moved the plates back as Judith tried to move them closer to the other settings. "Papa says, if you're smart, you don't ask about Lavinia and Will. They do witch-things in the hills about Dunwich. No one's ever seen Will's father."

"They're still family and they pay handsomely for the cows your father sells them. We can afford to send you to college in Arkham, help you make something of yourself, like a doctor or a lawyer," Judith replied.

"You're a Corey, what do you know about witch-things," Curtis grumbled.

"I know plenty: my great-grandfather several times over got pressed in Arkham in 1690," Judith argued. "Let's not judge kin for their idea of believing."

A buckboard wagon clattered past the windows. Zebulon, in the dooryard bringing in wood, hallooed, replied with a woman's grating squeak and a man's bass rumble. Judith, wiping her hands on her apron, went to the porch to join her husband in greeting their guests.

Moments later, the pair ushered in a pale woman in a shapeless brown stuff dress with white hair like a Halloween card witch, carrying a covered dish.

A stooped young man with a goatish face loped in, his rusty black suit tight over his broad shoulders and chest. Once he fully entered, he straightened up, his dense black hair brushing the beams above.

"My, Will, you've grown!" Zebulon cried, glancing to the dish the woman carried. "Must be from Lavinny's good cooking."

"Maybe it's the witchery she puts innit," Curtis pig-whispered.

"Kitchen witchery ain't my specialty. Callin' the seasons an' watchin' for them that watch beyond is."

Lavinny lifted the lid on the dish, uncovering a mess of baked acorn squash, still warm, drenched in butter and peppered with nutmeg and cloves. "Jest followed th' receipt in th' Ladies Home Journal to the letter. Wilbur kept an eye on th' stove like the good boy he is."

They added Lavvinny's dish to the spread, which Curtis and Ermangarde ferried from the kitchen to the front room.

When they had all but eaten their fill, Judith nodded to Ermengarde – allowed to share the table with the family since they had kin as guests. The girl went to the kitchen to fetch the pumpkin pie cooling on the windowsill.

She entered in time to see the pie rise from the sill and hover at eye level. Something moved behind it, like the pale reflection of a snake in a black glass mirror.

"Mrs. Judith! Something's taking the pie!"

Judith, the menfolk at her heels, rushed in. Whatever held the pie sucked it out of sight.

"Has to be a neighbor kid pulling a late Halloween prank," Zebulon said.

"Are you sure you weren't seeing things?" Judith asked.

"It better not have followed us. I told it to stay home," Will rumbled.

Lavinia stalked to the window, which started closing itself slowly. She pushed up the sash, calling, "Yog, you spit that out now! I promised I'd bring you a plate."

The empty pie tin appeared in mid-air, as if spat from an invisible gullet. It clattered to the kitchen floor, covered in a black, sticky substance.

"I didn't put any molasses in that pie..." Judith said.

THE WISHBONE
By Kim Plasket

Brisk chill in the air, hint of snow, a holiday wreath hung on the door. Looking through the window, the tree shone brightly.

Remnants of dinner on the table, walls and the floor. The whole scene was something out of a holiday comedy movie.

The part not funny were the bodies at the table, crimson blood pooling around their chairs; the smell of turkey mixed with the fresh scent of the blood and evergreen.

Leading from the bodies were footprints in blood, it seemed as if the killer walked around the table killing one person at a time. Carving into them as one carves a turkey. All knives are accounted for so the killer must have brought his own weapon; or found one.

The only thing out of place in the kitchen was the bloody wishbone on the counter...

BLACK FRIDAY
By Kyle Harrison

My family has a different holiday tradition than most. It involves standing in line for hours at stores, even in the freezing cold.

Anything to find the best steals. Dad saves up what little time off he has from work and grabs our Christmas presents. Mom grabs an empty cart and acts like she is at the speedway.

I'm the designated spotter, I search for what we need. I grab an advert off the shelf and scour the pages. We've come to learn how to map out the stores and predict where to go.

Our first stop is the boy's department. No one ever goes there except for new parents and school aged children. The dressing rooms are often ignored. That's where we hide what we need until the crowd starts to thin.

The secret you see isn't to rush and rush and grab all you can, that's just a waste of time and energy. Patience and planning are important.

Our method is full proof. Dad brings his hunting knife to cut off the price tags. Changing in the rooms takes time, but I know to keep quiet. The others not so much, and that makes dad a little manic.

Eventually it's time to leave, our new acquisitions in cart or in tow. The silent footsteps we make to the checkout counter are deafening in my heart. I imagine a million things can go wrong.

But no one notices. Everyone too busy to care. Grabbing coupons and stuffing their jackets with material things.

Those don't matter to us. All we care about is expanding our little family.

Yes, though we come into the store only as a trio, we never leave that way. A new brother or sister is all we ever were looking for.

This year we got two for the price of one, and that's just fine with me.

They'll learn their roles in our life soon enough.

They have no choice. Dad has made that clear.

Because there is no return policy in our household. What comes inside never leaves.

Appreciate what you have this holiday.

You never know, what matters most might not be around forever.

DEDICATION
By Jay Levy

Snow fell as Dad rounded the corner and rammed his crowbar through the zombie's head.

It stopped moving, dropped, and its eyes rolled down the pavement.

"Quickly," Dad motioned to follow. "That brick house with yellow siding. Slip around back to the garage door. There are Rots along the way. Weapons ready."

Mom had her axe.

I had my bat. It was small and aluminum, but it smashed a skull just fine.

Dad always took point and I always brought up the rear. We made sure to keep mom protected.

"You've had your Bar-Mitzvah," he'd said the first time. "You're a man."

"That just means I can read from the Torah," I'd shrugged in reply. "I don't think that's gonna happen anytime soon. We're lucky to find food, let alone a practicing community."

"Guard your mother," he'd sighed. "Be a man."

I've tried to ever since.

We dashed to the house down the street—a ranch style with a garage. We ran quickly, but the Rots spotted us. I knew they would; we were out in the open.

A decayed mailman lunged at Dad and he swung his crowbar, smashing it on the side of its head. It dropped and Dad clobbered again. Blood spattered all over the icy sidewalk. Mom chopped the middle zombie square in the skull and split its head in two.

My swing missed and I slipped on ice, tripping the dead jogger as I fell.

Before I called for help, Dad was there. He cracked the zombie's head and drove its body to the ground with his foot. It squirmed for a moment, but Dad jabbed the crowbar through its skull.

The jogger stopped moving.

I avoided Dad's eyes when he helped me up.

We got to the house and ducked around back, weapons ready, but it was quiet. No Rots back here. Good.

Mom tried the door to the garage.

"Locked," she whispered.

Dad slid his crowbar in the frame and popped the door open, breaking the lock. "Get inside!"

Dad shut the door and searched the frame, finding a key on top.

"Terra, stay here with Jordan," he said. "I'll try this key on the house. If it works, I'll clear it."

Mom nodded.

"Stay here," he said. "I'll be back."

We didn't hear him enter the house, or anything for several minutes. I wanted to investigate.

"Give him time," Mom said, reassuringly.

Silence followed. It seemed long. Too long.

"That's it, I'm going…"

A moment later, Dad came through the door. His shirt dripped with blood, but he smiled nonetheless.

Mom ran to him.

"Don't worry, "he said. "It's not mine. There were three, but I got 'em."

He led us into the house and we stood in the kitchen. For a house with Rots, it seemed really clean and tidy.

"Happy Hanukah." He laid a bloodied hand on my shoulder. "Tonight is the eighth night and I wanted us to have a nice place to celebrate."

"How'd you know it was Hanukah?" I asked.

"Two nights ago on patrol, I saw the menorah here," he pointed to the large window in front. "Remember, Hanukah means dedication. These people were dedicated." He looked right at me. "Faithful even in these distressful times."

"People?" My jaw dropped. "You mean... they were alive?"

Mom inhaled quickly and brought a hand to her chest.

I stepped backward, looking at him intently, and tried to see past the monster in his place.

"Don't worry," he smiled. "I said the mourner's Kaddish. Now, who wants to light the first candle?"

HAIL SANTA

by Aaron Morris

Howie and Rachel looked lovingly at Olivia as she watched the snow fall against the window. It was easy to be jaded and stressed around the holidays, but all they had to do was look at the joy on their little girl's face and all of the anxiety faded away.

Olivia had accomplished something big this year, too. She'd managed to write her letter to Santa on her own, a bittersweet moment for the both of them, but one they knew had been coming, since she could now write somewhat legibly on her own. It had also been a huge confidence boost for Olivia, who had been diagnosed with dyslexia recently.

They'd done a quick proofread together and Howie had even made a big show of putting a stamp on it and dropping it off at the post office.

It was getting late. Just as Howie was about to take Olivia up to bed to tuck her in for the night, the temperature in the house dropped, despite the happily roaring fire in the fireplace. Darkness seemed to be encroaching too, swallowing up the light from the fire. There was a knock at the door.

Howie approached the door with caution, but before he could even grab the handle, it creaked open on its own. There on the front step was a figure cloaked in black, with what appeared to be shadows billowing out behind it.

"C-Can I help you?"

"The child. She wrote to me. I came."

The figure reached out from its cloak, holding a present wrapped in black paper with red ribbon.

Olivia ran out from behind her father and hugged the figure.

"Santa! You came!"

"Yes Child. Although, I believe you've got my name wrong."

THE CHRISTMAS HUNT

By Nick Moore

We forgot. That is the primary pattern of human history. Our greatest fears, and the horrible lessons we learned from them, slip away.

It began on Christmas Eve. The first witnesses believed, against all belief, that they were seeing Santa Claus and his reindeer, flying across the sky. Only when the dark shapes drew closer did they realize that the bearded horror approaching them offered nothing but pain.

The sleigh was monstrous, black and twisted and evil. It was pulled across the heavens by a variety of huge beasts, and mixed among them poor souls who dared to stare too long at the promenade of the possessed.

People went insane at the sight of it. They tore each other apart, and the streets ran red with blood.

Worse still were the department store Santas, having traded for so long on the faded memory of the dread huntsman. They climbed buildings and trees, seeking the heights at which point they joined the haunted procession across the heavens, screaming in horror all the while.

People heard the horrible noises from outside and lifted their eyes to the heavens, going mad as their eyes met it. The curious were cut down quickly, failing to stay inside where they would be protected from it. Only those who remembered the old ways remained safe. They stayed indoors, keeping their blinds drawn and their doors locked.

The morning broke over a broken land. Scattered bodies, streets stained with blood, and piled among it all, giant piles of gifts.

For this is what we forgot, the Wild Hunt presages a great bounty, and those who survived the night woke up to a Christmas more opulent than they ever imagined. This new horrible world rewarded them for remembering the hunt, and for surviving it.

He paused. The children stared at him; their eyes wide with fear. The silence stretched until the older, his granddaughter, finally spoke, "When did that happen, Grandpa?" she whispered.

The old man smiled, "It hasn't my dear girl, it's a story for you to remember though. Never forget the old ways." His grandson responded with a nervous laugh, feigning bravery now that the fear had passed.

He kissed the two children on the head and ensured they were tucked in. "Remember the rules, no coming out of the room until morning!" He drew the old wooden blinds across the window, turning the small key with a tinkle until they locked. "Santa won't come if he thinks you're awake."

"We know Grandpa," the children responded in unison, dragging the "o" sound in annoyance.

He grinned, "goodnight then little ones."

He strode throughout the rest of the house, closing and locking the blinds. His keys jingled in his hand, a faint noise that sounded slightly like bells. From outside the noises of Christmas Eve trickled in. Carols and laughter and mirth filled his ears and his heart.

He finished locking the last window just as he heard the exclamation, "What is that Santa doing?"

The screams followed, along with howls that he knew came not from the ground, but from something soaring over the earth.

He paused a moment, considering opening the blinds and staring up at the sky until he joined the cavalcade.

Instead, he locked the door, and ate the cookies the children had left out as the screams continued. The morning would be bountiful.

NAUGHTY OR NICE

By Scott McGregor

Tonight, Natalie planned to enact her revenge on Santa Claus.

Since as long as she could remember, every Christmas Natalie awoke to find nothing but a fat lump of coal in her stocking. When she was five, she desired a Barbie, at six, a dollhouse, and at seven, she wanted nothing more than a Play-Doh machine. Instead, all her desires were replaced by a hunk of black disappointment. Nothing changed as the years continued.

There was only one person to blame for all her pain. One fat, beardy, holiday icon that mistreated her yearly.

Now, at thirty-seven-years old, Natalie stood in her kitchen, watched her batch of gingerbread cookies rise, and occasionally glanced at her fireplace. Her cookies, created from her grandmother's classic recipe, needed to reach perfection for her jolly guest.

"Mommy, I want to meet Santa!" Sofia enthused.

To say that Natalie's daughter loved Christmas was an understatement. The way she frolicked around in the apartment reminded Natalie of herself at a younger age during a simpler time. A time when Christmas actually meant something other than disparity. Sofia was too young to understand the truth about Santa Claus. She couldn't fathom the misfortunes of Christmas, unlike Natalie.

"Honey, I'm afraid that's not how it works. But I think if you've been nice, Santa might give you that toy unicorn you've been asking for." Natalie glanced at the clock, 10:02 PM. "Okay sweetheart, time for bed. Santa will be here soon."

Sofia ran to her bedroom in glee, and Natalie couldn't stray her eyes away from the fireplace.

She hummed Santa Claus is Coming to Town as she waited, specifically on the line he's going to find out who's naughty or nice. She figured, if the song was any indication, Santa put Natalie on the naughty list for reasons unbeknownst to her. Natalie had a list too, with only one name underlined. Instead of coal, Kris Kringle would receive a different kind of gift this year.

Soon, you'll get yours, Father Christmas.

The oven timer went off, and she removed her freshly baked cookies. The smell of gingerbread filled the kitchen, and the chocolate-chips glistened within the pastry. Many of the iconic ingredients in her grandmother's recipe included mint and extra sugar, but this year, Natalie slightly tweaked her grandmother's recipe. She added one special ingredient exclusive for Saint Nicholas; five tablespoons of rat poisoning.

She rested a dozen cookies atop a plate and walked over to her fireplace, humming the tune Santa Claus is Coming to Town. She planned to do exactly as the song requested, not crying or pouting, but watching out. Watching out to ensure Sofia didn't receive the treatment Natalie had for years at a time. "Let see how you like this, fat ass," she miffed, placing the plate next to the chimney.

It dawned on Natalie that she forgot to put up Sofia's stocking next to the fireplace, ready to fill it with gifts of her own once Santa kicked the bucket. She left the room to grab the bulky sock, and when she returned, she found Sofia by the chimney.

"Honey, what're you doing up?" Natalie asked. "I told you it's time for bed."

Sofia turned to face her mother and held a cookie with a large bite taken out. "I just want to meet Santa," she said as she chewed the baked delight.

By the time Sofia's mouth foamed, Natalie screamed, and she finally understood why Santa considered her naughty instead of nice.

CHE KRAMPUS CAME INSTEAD

By T.W. Grim

Santa didn't come to see us last night

The Krampus came instead

He came down the chimney with a burlap sack

And stole us all from our beds

Now, the Krampus is a horrible sight

A sight that cannot be unseen

He's short and squat and hairy and fat

A foul and devilish fiend

The Krampus lives in a dank old cave

Full of bats, pale toads and rats

The floor is littered with pajamas and bones

And the carpets are made out of cats

As Santa rides upon his sleigh

On a cold and crisp Christmas eve

The Krampus sits on a rotting mule

And he punishes all your misdeeds

He leaves no gifts behind in his wake

He feels no love in his heart

His teeth are sharp and his eyes are red

And his claws will tear you apart

Santa eats cookies and sugar-plum pie

A man eats meat, cheese and bread

But the Krampus feasts on naughty children

And uses their skins for his bed

And their souls he keeps all for himself

He keeps them locked up in a box

And what happens to them? Nobody knows

Maybe he wears them as socks!

Santa didn't come to see us last night

The Krampus came instead

To bite us and beat us, kick us and bleed us

And then he chopped off our heads!

WREN BOYS

By Vonnie Winslow Crist

"You need to hunt and murder a wren," said Sean as he buttoned his raggedy jacket.

His brothers, Will and Joe, stood behind him nodding masked faces.

"It's the only way we can get people to give us money," said Will as he pulled his torn sweatshirt's hood up so the string used to tie his mask in place was hidden.

"What?" Davy had been unsure about being a Wren Boy since his schoolmates proposed it after Christmas church service. "I'm not killing a bird."

"We need a dead wren to tie to a stick and decorate with ribbons," explained Will. "Sean, Joe, and I already collected ribbon from our Christmas presents and hung it on this mop handle."

He shook the green, beribboned pole he held. "All that's missing is the bird. So that's your contribution to our Wren Boys parade."

"Four kids is hardly a parade," replied Davy. He'd known from the get-go the O'Brien boys were trouble. Why he'd agree to participate in their money-making scheme he didn't know.

Yes you do, he told himself, you're an unpopular bookworm. You wanted Sean, Will, and Joe to like you.

Joe beating on a toy drum interrupted Davy's thoughts.

"The money people give us is for the wren's burial expenses." Sean wiped his nose with the back of his left glove. "Of course, we're keeping the money and tossing the bird's body into Asher's Woods."

"When I said I'd come, I thought we were just walking around the neighborhood dressed like beggars, singing songs, and getting punch and cookies. You know, like carolers." The thought of killing an animal, even a wren, made Davy's stomach knot up.

"Chicken?" asked Sean in a tone of voice that declared he believed Davy was lily-livered.

"No..." Davy tried to think of an excuse.

"He's a scaredy cat," mocked Will as he tried to scratch his cheek under his mask without taking it off.

"Not true," replied Davy. "I just didn't want us to get Bird Flu because we touched a wren. A fake bird from off my family's Christmas tree would be better. We can sprinkle red paint on it, so it looks like it was murdered."

Will and Joe nodded.

Davy knew they were the weaker of the trio. Sean would decide.

"Loser," scoffed Sean. "We'll kill our own wren, and keep all the money. You're officially uninvited to be a Wren Boy, so don't follow us into Asher's."

"Be careful," warned Davy as a chilly wind caused the wren pole's ribbons to flutter. "I heard there's a guardian spirit living in that woods. It might not like you killing a wren..."

"Weirdo," shouted Sean over his shoulder.

Still standing on his porch, Davy saw the shadow of a buzzard move across the snow in front of the O'Brien brothers as they marched to the beat of Joe's drum toward Asher's Woods.

He shivered.

That evening, Davy listened as the television newscaster reported: "The bodies of three local boys were discovered in Asher's Woods late today. Apparently attacked by animals, the authorities are awaiting the coroner's report before confirming the exact nature of their deaths.

"Anyone with information should..."

Davy didn't listen to the rest of the report. Instead, he looked out the frosted windowpane at the woods across the street. He half expected to see a guardian spirit with a singing wren perched on its shoulder and a wicked blade in its hand, looking back.

THE TENTH DAY
By Diane Arrelle

I thought he was kidding when he sat up in bed and said he was a demon.

That's what I get for having a one-night stand, I thought, another weirdo. "Now what?" I asked. "You going to drag me to hell?"

He shook his head and smiled. "Today's the tenth day of Christmas. "I'm giving you a present, he said and vanished.

His present arrived almost immediately.

Now, I've been evicted from my apartment, lost my job and those awful Lords-A- Leaping just won't leave.

"Well, at least I didn't have to deal with all those damned dirty birds," I sighed.

WHAT TO MY WANDERING EYES DID APPEAR

By Matthew A. St. Cyr

Ava laid in her bed, desperately trying to will herself to sleep. She heard Mommy and Daddy climb up the stairs and into bed long ago and she could now hear Daddy's soft snoring coming from their bedroom. Santa would be here any minute and Mommy said that he only came down the chimney when everyone was asleep.

She shut her eyes tight and thought of all the wonderful toys and goodies Santa would bring. She thought of her visit to Santa at the mall. She was very proud of herself for not freezing up as soon as she sat on Santa's lap this year and Mommy said that Santa told her he was proud of her too and was going to bring her something extra special. Ava's thoughts drifted like the snow outside and she fell asleep.

Brilliant red light flooded through her window just long enough to pull her from her slumber.

"Rudolph!" she quietly exclaimed.

Sounds drifted up the stairs from the living room. She could hear light footsteps and a strange rustling sound. Her eyes grew wide and her heart fluttered. Santa Claus had come! She knew that she should stay in bed and let the jolly old elf place the presents under the tree, but she just couldn't resist the opportunity to see him.

Quietly slipping out of bed and putting on her slippers, she snuck to the stairs as quietly as possible. She could see shadows moving in the glow of the Christmas tree lights on the far wall. She stopped at the top of the stairs and listened, hoping to hear Santa's laugh or at least a chuckle as he ate the cookies and milk that she left out for him. Instead she heard a series of clicking noises and something that reminded her of birds chirping.

She snuck down the first few steps and peered between the bannister columns. Four figures stood near the Christmas tree, their mottled grey skin glittering in the soft white lights.

Ava gasped and all four heads turned her direction. Large black eyes regarded her coldly. One of the figures extended a long finger, pointing at her and she again heard the click chirp. All four figures advanced towards her.

"You're not Santa." she whispered, her lip trembling.

The brilliant red light flooded the windows all through the house as the creatures closed the gap between them and the small girl. Two of them reached out and touched her arm, their cold, clammy skin seemed to paralyze her.

Mommy and Daddy were torn awake from their sleep by a short, shrill scream. As they opened their eyes, the brilliant red light faded, leaving the house in silent darkness.

The coming weeks were filled with investigations, interrogations and accusations.

Reporters flooded the neighborhood and the media storm that ensued became national headlines, the media dubbing her disappearance as a "Holiday Horror" and speculating on her whereabouts.

To this day Ava Moore's whereabouts are unknown.

A BRIGHT CHRISTMAS

by Cecelia Hopkins-Drewer

"Deck the walls with strands of paper," trilled the stereo.

The streamer twitched uneasily in the slight breeze from the open window. It was tired of being unpacked every year, stretched out for a few short weeks, then being packed in a box again.

"Tis the month to laugh and caper…"

The streamer managed to work an end loose. It tangled in the Christmas tree and brought the evergreen crashing down. Then it draped across a candle and rejoiced in the heat. Flames ran along the paper, taking hold of the curtains.

A wonderful display. Just wait until the family saw!

LITTLE VANDA'S LETTER TO SANTA

By Tricia Lowther

Dear Santa,

It's Vanda Williams here, from Abbey Lane, Whitby. I am still nine years old, even though I should be ten by now. I have tried my very best to be good this year. It isn't my fault, what I've become, so I hope you will still bring me presents.

I know I've done some things good little girls don't usually do, but my new Mama says that's it's just nature, so it wouldn't be fair to count them as naughty. I do try and stick to creatures that are already dying. Or that would be culled, (culled is like killed but different because it's allowed). Also, pests. Rats taste much nicer than I expected. And what happened to my stepsister, was kind of an accident. At least she's been happily reunited with her parents.

The present I would like most for Christmas is a kitten, (just to play with).

I would also like a beautiful crystal goblet, Vampire Children - the complete box set, and some turquoise satin for a new coffin lining (sooo bored of red - no offence). Oh, and I could probably do with a stake-proof vest too.

I'll leave milk and carrots out as usual. You don't have to worry about the reindeer, my new Mama and Papa have promised to leave them alone.

Lots of love,

V xxx

SPECIAL DELIVERY

By Akshay Patwardhan

Gary Durham found it lying on his porch in the evening of Christmas Eve. It was a small unmarked package which had been wrapped in tatters of brown paper grocery bags, whose pieces were hastily stuck together with crinkled, ancient masking tape.

Gary brought the box inside and ripped open the thick paper covering, tossing chocolate-brown fragments all over the carpet.

Inside the package, there was a steel tin covered in faint, but numerous scratches that had probably been engraved by a child.

He gently lifted the top off the tin and set it aside on the couch.

There were gingerbread men--at least six of them—all perfectly crisp, smiling with frosted eyes and lips. It must have been cousin Jenny who had sent these. Yes, she had always been fond of baking, and what time better was there besides Christmas? He'd be sure to call her in the morning to give his thanks.

Gary reached into the tin and plucked the gingerbread man closest to himself, and he inhaled the sweet fragrance of ginger and cinnamon before marveling at its perfectly symmetrical shape: there wasn't even one dot of frosting out of place. The humanoid delicacy grinned back at him as if to say "Hey there, I'd love it if you'd take a bite!".

"If you insist," Gary murmured with child-like delight and tugged at the gingerbread man's feet which snapped off, littering Gary's thighs with a smoky, brown dust. Gary chewed on a piece, and sighed with the light spice of cinnamon sizzling on his tongue and the creamy, sugary taste of fluffed bread tingling his taste buds. It was damn good, so he'd make sure not to eat all of it at once. Gary tossed the gingerbread man back into the tin, sealed it, and left it on the dining table.

Work had been less than convenient, and Gary was feeling surprisingly tired, so he took his shower, brushed and flossed, and slept soundly with the heater switched on.

It wasn't until half-past two that he was woken up to something cool and sharp grazing his feet. He glanced around the room in surprise, but there was no one there. He glanced at his feet, and then he began to scream. They were sitting on his shins--the gingerbread men--each holding a cleaver from his kitchen. The sugary dots on their faces had morphed into something malicious and jet-black, and he could have sworn that he'd heard one of them laugh.

Gary felt a brief tapping on his scalp, and he glanced upwards to see the gingerbread man--the one whose legs he'd eaten--grinning on his forehead. Then the pastry jumped into

Gary's throat, cutting off the man's shrill shrieks, and Gary could feel his gullet tighten and bleed around the gingerbread man's jagged feet. Gary reached inside his throat desperately, but the gingerbread man was lodged at an awkward angle. Gary uttered a pathetic rasp as the other gingerbread men began to saw off his feet--it was at the exact location that he'd snapped one of the men--and spurts of blood decorated his walls in a Christmas crimson.

Gary began to feel lightheaded, and there was a deep darkness setting in. Ignoring his leaking legs, he once-more reached inside his throat, and he grasped the head of the gingerbread man. He twisted his fingers with a violent jerk, hearing the satisfying snap of the gingerbread man's neck as his body finally went limp.

CANCELED CHRISTMAS

By C.L. Williams

I was there the day Christmas was canceled. Santa became less enthusiastic about Christmas. With each passing year, people cared more about receiving than giving. His naughty list also increased exponentially with each passing year.

All of it became far too much for him. I saw him enter a chimney with a sack of toys and come out with the same sack.

He and the reindeer started to fly off when I heard a gunshot. His reindeer fell, one by one. Santa saw that he survived the crash; and that's when he shot himself.

That's the final Christmas we ever had.

CHRISTMAS SPIDER

By Lisa Flanyak

Marley Gibbs reached into a box labeled 'Xmas' and pulled out several ornament bulbs. She placed each on different areas of the tree in front of her.

Daniel, aged ten, removed a few felt ornaments and placed them at the bottom of the tree.

Marley's husband, Randy, sat back in his recliner chair and buried his face in the sports section of a newspaper.

The Jimmy Stewart film, 'It's A Wonderful Life' played out on their big screen television.

"After this sappy soap opera, can we watch 'Jingle All the Way'?" Randy asked.

"Go ahead and watch it now or you could help us," responded Marley.

"Yeah Dad," chimed Daniel.

Randy folded up the newspaper and sat it in his lap.

"You two are doing just fine. Plus, don't forget, I'm the one who chopped the darn thing down."

"Bah humbug," responded Marley.

The timer on the stove sounded and Marley rushed into the kitchen.

"Cookies are done!" Daniel exclaimed.

Daniel played with the train underneath the tree. Above him, a spider emerged from within the tree and crawled out onto one of the bulbs. It slowly rappelled down via web to the floor.

As the spider touched down onto the floor, it caught Daniel's attention. He motioned towards it when, WHOMP! Randy reached out and smacked it with the newspaper. Daniel lurched back in shock.

"What was that?" Marley called out.

"Got a creepy crawler!" Randy responded back.

Randy looked at the flattened spider stuck to the paper. Daniel sat in disbelief.

"Spiders in your house at Christmastime are considered good luck. Mrs. Miller taught us that this week."

"Not for him it wasn't," Randy responded.

Randy got up and went into the kitchen and dropped the paper into the trash. He grabbed a warm cookie off the plate and devoured it in one bite.

"Come and get a cookie, Daniel. Bed right after. Santa will be here before you know it," said Marley.

Daniel went to the table and sat down to eat a cookie or two and drink hot cocoa.

At midnight, the grandfather clock chimed quietly. Marley and Daniel had gone to bed while Randy had fallen asleep in his chair. The tree was still lit.

As the clock did twelve chimes, the branches on the tree began to shake. A handful of spiders emerged from within the tree and all stopped on various ornaments. More movement of branches and more spiders emerged and took their positions. They all dropped to the floor and another round followed.

One area of the tree shook just a little more vigorous and out emerged the queen spider. She fell to the ground and joined the others who were already on the chair.

With the skill mother nature gave them, some spiders began to work together to spin a web around Randy's head. Randy stirred and attempted to swat at his face but did not make contact.

The queen spun webbing on his legs, while others worked on his arms.

As his air began to get cut off, Randy awoke; but it was too late. The entire front of his body was encased in a strong and sticky cocoon. He tried his arms to no avail. He moved forward and fell flat on his face.

The spiders crawled over to him and finished on his back.

Randy flailed about and tried to free his arms so that he could get some air. The spiders had done their job well and it was not long until he lost consciousness and was gone forever.

THE NAUGHTY/NICE PARADOX

By Tor Anders-Ulven

She'd been a good girl all year. Doing all her chores, playing nice in school, listening to her teachers and her parents. Perfect scores all around. There was no way she could have been any better.

This time around, Santa couldn't refuse her. He had to deliver. He just had to. It wasn't on any list. She couldn't say it out loud. It would get her into a world of trouble.

She'd done it before you see. Got her grounded for a week. So, she had to wish it inside. And she did. That's all she did. Whenever she closed her eyes, whenever she was in a room all alone, whenever she dreamt, the wish rang loud and clear.

I wish my baby brother wasn't my brother anymore.

He hated her. She hated him. He was only three, but she could see it in him. He didn't want her there. And their parents always took his side. It was so annoying. Whatever he did, no matter how mean he was, they always sided with him. Couldn't they see? See how mean and gross and selfish he was?

So she wished him gone. Every day, every night, for months.

And when she fell asleep on Christmas Eve, she had a feeling everything would be perfect. That she'd wake up to a whole new world. A better world. A perfect world. A world where she was an only child again.

Sweet dreams.

Wake up.

It was still dark when she woke up, and it took her eyes a few minutes to fashion shapes from the amorphous blur surrounding her. Everything looked the same. Except for the shadow in the corner. Except for the brightly shining eyes and that imposing ivory beard.

"'Tis Christmas Morning, child, " a dark voice called, "And we must converse."

"S...Santa?" she said, rubbing her eyes feverishly.

The shadow rose, the eyes glowed, and the beard rustled in the pitch-blackness.

"Yes," the voice said, "And no. It matters not, child, but we must discuss the paradox."

"W...What paradox?" she asked.

"Your brother," Santa said, "Specifically your wish to rid him from existence."

Santa edged closer to her. The shining eyes burned in the darkness. Glowing, eerie, floating orbs.

"The Naughty/Nice Paradox," he said, "The Algorithm cannot decide whether to reward or punish."

"I...I'm sorry," she murmured, "I didn't mean it. Not really. I take it back."

A horrible sound echoed through the room, "HO HO HO," Santa boomed.

"I'm afraid that's impossible. Already logged, you understand. I suppose I could kill your brother. Or you. Maybe even both. That would certainly clear everything right up."

She started crying hysterically. Sobbing and wailing uncontrollably. The ominous shadow edged ever closer.

"No!" she cried, "Please! Don't do it! I take it back! I take it back!"

Santa snapped his fingers, "I think I have a way. A perfect solution."

The shadow retreated. The shining eyes disappeared. The ivory beard vanished.

Sweet dreams.

Wake up.

It was Christmas Morning. And she was alive. She heard her brother giggling downstairs. It was just a dream. A horrible, horrible dream.

She skipped downstairs.

She didn't understand. Didn't understand when her parents yelled at her. When her brother cried. When they told her to get the hell out of their house. Didn't understand when the police arrived. Didn't understand when she looked in the mirror.

She's still around. The mad, old lady down by the tracks. She'll swear to you that she's just seven years old. Sit down with her. Hear her ramble.

Ramble on about the Naughty/Nice Paradox.

DR. FRANKEN'S SERVICE MONSTER

By Steve Oden

"This is my service creature."

White VR-helmet enclosing his head, the passenger stood in the hatch of Mars Express 217, a crowded in-system holiday flight already pushing the launch window for departure from Luna.

Impatient travelers queued behind him—or rather, behind the hulking gelatinous creature that filled the boarding platform. Its multiple appendages clutched carry-on bags, gifts wrapped in color-changing spectrum paper tied with musical ribbons and cages of small alien animals that resembled green elves.

Flight attendants tried not to stare when the monstrosity extruded hook-tipped tentacles and rubbery feelers to caress and soothe the man.

The ticket agent gulped. "Mr. Franken, your file contains no reference to a service animal."

The passenger released helmet clasps surgically implanted behind each ear and removed the sensory-assistance unit. The agent recoiled. Pits of inflamed scar tissue glistened where eyeballs had been. The man's face was gone.

"My name is Doctor Franken," he corrected her, "and this biological servitor has been cleared as a service companion by the agencies responsible for regulating planetary travel. Check the file's addendum, please."

Impatient travelers clotted the gate lounge. Shouts and curses could be heard.

"You're that Doctor Franken?" The agent was taken aback. Not only did she have a problem, it involved a wealthy scientist famous for engineering new life forms used in asteroid mining and the radiation belts.

She reviewed his passenger file.

"Your service animal must be properly ticketed," said the exasperated agent. "This thing will take up room. We have a full flight. People will lose their seats because of this!"

"Planetary handicapped laws state the precedence to be followed. I intend to board with my companion and enjoy the journey to Mars Colony," announced Franken.

A red-faced ticketholder in a Santa stocking cap shoved forward to scream, "If you let this man break the rules of commercial space travel, I will sue your company!"

The creature's multiple lidless eyes goggled. It sensed human emotions that might transform into physical threats. The servitor began to swell. Pores opened in its body and steam whistled out. Musical ribbons on the presents vibrated with an ominous tinkle.

Franken turned to the ticket agent, the ravaged face making her cringe. She now remembered the tragedy in which he had nearly lost his life. Many had died in the lab explosion.

Others were horribly changed by the alien DNA with which he experimented.

"Let me offer a proposition," he said. "For standby volunteers, I shall underwrite expenses for lodging, meals and entertainment until the next launch window, also providing an unlimited travel voucher to be used at their pleasure."

The angry man interrupted: "I won't allow it. Doctor Franken cannot legally be the guarantor of a benefit that violates international travel rules. That's bribery!"

"Under what conditions can the protocols be revised or waived?" the maimed scientist inquired.

The agent shook her head woefully. Reading from a digital handbook, she replied, "In the case of accident, illness or death of the ticketholder."

Gloating, the man wagged a finger under Franken's nose. The service creature bore down on the human threat after receiving a transmitted mental command. Miraculously, not a bag or box was dropped as it eviscerated and consumed him.

"I believe a ticket is available due to an accident," said the scientist.

Two volunteers had already stepped forward to accept his standby offer.

The monster belched and docilely followed its master up the ramp into the spacecraft, musical gift wrap playing "Holly Jolly Christmas." Waiting passengers cheered and clapped as the line began to move.

SANTA CLAUS IS COMING TO TOWN

By Melody Grace

Last Christmas Eve my daughter Annie decided she was going to stay up late to try and catch a glimpse of Santa. She was completely set on her task despite my warnings that Santa wouldn't come if she was awake; typical nine-year-old.

Around eight o'clock we sat down in our big comfy chair to read "A Charlie Brown Christmas," it was Annie's favorite since she was little. Halfway through the book I watched as her eyes got heavier and heavier, followed by a big yawn.

Her tiny body soon fell limp against my chest as a small snore escaped her lips; I loved those moments. While steadying her in my arms I attempted to get up when the chair gave a little creak.

Shit.

"Mommy, I'm so tired. Please tell Santa I'm sorry I couldn't stay awake to see him, he's going to be really sad. I promised." Annie mumbled before passing back out. I smiled and gave her a kiss on the forehead.

Once I laid her down in bed, she mumbled something else about Santa's letter before drool hit her pillow. I let out a small chuckle and then a thought hit me; we didn't write to Santa this year. We were too busy with all the hustle and bustle of the holiday that I completely dropped the ball. What letter was she referring to?

I looked down at her nightstand and reached for the drawer, trying not to make a sound.

When it was open a good two inches, I slowly placed my hand inside and felt around. It was empty except for a few crayons and some hair pins. I sighed and closed it; so much for a mother's intuition.

Quietly I turned on my heels and tip-toed toward the door. When I turned around to shut it behind me, a red envelope on her dresser caught my eye. Taking a few steps back inside I grabbed it and hastily made my way back out again.

Walking back to the living room I opened up the letter. Inside was a piece of paper that looked like it had been plucked from a trash can, smelled like it to. I flipped the folded paper up and my blood ran cold.

I see you when you're sleeping

I know when you're awake

Meet me outside on Christmas Eve

And I'll let you ride in my sleigh

- Santa

Shivers ran up my spine like tiny little spider legs, gently caressing my fears. I ran to the window overlooking our yard and that's when I saw him. Santa Claus. He stood about six feet tall, red suit and all, with impossibly long arms hanging at his sides. His face was sunk into itself with dark beady little eyeballs that locked onto your soul.

I inhaled sharply through my teeth while adrenaline coursed through my veins. He didn't even blink. A sinister smile spread wide, revealing rows of yellow teeth that looked like they smelled of death and despair. He outstretched his bony hand and shook a finger at me, then turned, and walked away.

I immediately called the police, but they took it as a prank. I was distraught. So, this whole year I've instilled the fear of strangers deep into my daughter. I even went as far as to crush her dreams of Santa by telling her he wasn't real; I'm a monster, I know.

Thinking we were in the clear, we began our yearly traditions; got a tree, hung some lights, the works. Everything was going great until the letter slipped through our door.

You better watch out

You better not cry

You better not pout

Tonight, your daughter will die

- Santa

FAMILY
By Eric Nirschel

Stanley Nowlan took a long drag from his cigarette, tilting his head back and sending a whirling blast of smoke up into a grey sky. Around him, the first tentative snowflakes had begun to fall, swirling and dipping like acrobats desperate to impress. Quality over quantity. Stan could relate.

He was on his third cigarette of the morning, which probably wasn't the best thing in the world for a man trying to quit, but it was what it was. His anxiety always amped up around the holidays, and Christmas was the final boss battle of the season. Holiday blues, holiday syndrome, Seasonal Affective Disorder...Stan always had that one. Some asshole in a turtleneck somewhere probably thought he was real goddamned clever for an acronym like 'S.A.D.' for seasonal depression.

"Stan, honey, can you come back in and help me set up the table? My parents will be here soon!

You don't want to disappoint the in-laws, now do you?"

Stan looked back over his should, offering a dull, reflexive nod.

"Ayuh, sure. I'll be in in a minute."

Stan looked down at the cigarette in his hand, the faint orange embers creeping closer to his shaking knuckles. He was sure that, if he could see himself, his face would be a sickly, sunken, pallid mask. How he managed to avoid screaming outright was beyond him, and he could feel the sweat beading on his forehead despite the cold. Inside, the sound of children laughing was grating on his nerves.

"Come play, daddy!" A giddy voice called.

"Ayuh." He replied robotically, "In a minute."

How many times had he said that, now? He wasn't entirely sure. He flicked the cigarette off the back porch into the snow, the embers hissing and dying in the cold. Fumbling, he reached for another, lit it, and brought it to his lips. Another long drag. He watched a snowflake spiral and pirouette like a figure skater out for the gold before it landed in the yard, vanishing in the sea of white.

"In a minute..." He muttered through a cloud of fresh smoke.

He was sure there were others out there like himself; people who just couldn't handle family gatherings. People for whom the prospect of sitting down to dinner with the wife and the kids and the in-laws would be terrifying. Dimly, though, he wondered how much like him they could really be. The screen door slid open behind him, and an icy chill snaked up his spine.

Long, arachnid fingers with far too many knuckles wrapped around his shoulder.

"Stanley, honey? Come inside."

Stanley Nowlan had never married, and he had no children.

DEATH BY TINSEL

By Kim Plasket

I never knew that tinsel, if wrapped tightly enough around itself, could cut.

Christmas Eve you told me was the last time we would be together. You found someone else but said you would give me one more night.

Little did you know I'd had enough of your crap when I grabbed the tinsel and informed you that you were going to die.

Why did you laugh? Your laughs stopped when I wrapped it around your neck. You tried to stop me but as usual, you failed.

Your ineffectual attempts were laughable. You stopped grabbing at the tinsel when it began ripping your flesh apart. I cared not that your blood was getting on my hands. In fact my dear, I relished the warmth of it as it dripped down my hands onto the floor.

You held to your word though; we had one last night.

CHE LASC COY
By Jay Levy

Monty stood outside the department store and fumed. He hated Black Friday, especially that it started Thanksgiving night.

"Hope there's no Christmas music in there," he nodded to the young woman behind him. "Am I right?"

"I like it," she timidly adjusted her glasses. "It's Christmas season. Yay."

Monty rolled his eyes at her weak cheer, looked at his watch, and shivered in the cold.

"Come on," he tapped his foot. "Open already."

He was here for one thing—and one thing only. This year's best-selling toy for his daughter, Grace—some only-available-in-stores doll with different styling wigs.

Monty hoped Grace wasn't getting interested in cosmetology. He'd taught her better than that. Hopefully, this was just a phase.

A couple of guys in red aprons unlocked the front sliding door and people shoved forward en masse. It became a bottle neck of deal seekers—with elbows and knees clearing the way.

Monty himself pushed a man to the floor on his way inside. Searching for the right isle, he ducked and weaved through the mob.

At last, he found the display and only a few dolls remained. Swearing loudly, he ran down the aisle. By the time he got there, only one remained.

Monty dove for the doll, but an old lady in a red bonnet snatched it first. She looked up at him through thick glasses and smiled.

"I need this for my grand-daughter, Leanne," she declared. "I'm sorry."

"I don't care," Monty grabbed the box. "Find another."

"Well, I never..." she protested.

Monty put a hand on the lady's forehead and pushed. She released her grip as she fell, and Monty turned, rushing to the register before she could rise.

He saved his laugher for the parking lot.

Monty parked in the back and didn't mind the extra walk, anything to stay away from these nuts. Days like today, people were lost in their own world—they hollered over spots and dented fenders out of anger.

A car suddenly backed out of a spot and Monty jumped. The guy in the car looked shocked, but then just smiled and waved.

"Moron..." Monty grumbled, but waved back anyway.

Once at his car, he tossed the bag in the back seat. The bag bounced, toppled, and fell over, spilling its contents to the floor.

Swearing, Monty kneeled to pick it up.

"I'll give you one chance," said a familiar, elderly voice.

Monty turned and rose. "You followed me to my car? Creepy, lady. Very creepy."

"Just let me buy it from you," she said. "You look like you can get another."

"Not a chance." He reached out to push her away again. "Now buzz off."

"My grand-daughter would love that toy." She grabbed his hand and twisted it.

"You crazy...," he started. But, she shoved him into the backseat before he could finish.

Her eyes burned fiery read as she revealed a gaping maw of needle-like teeth. Roaring, she lunged forward. The car shook in the tussle and the door slammed shut. Monty screamed

When she sank her fangs into his flesh, the back window filled with splattered blood.

As Monty drew his last breaths, she placed the blood-soaked bonnet back on her head, picked up the box, and hobbled away.

FIRST BITE
By Jay Levy

Tiny bells jingled when Santa brushed against the Christmas tree. He hunched over and laid gifts under the bottom boughs, all with a cookie shoved halfway into his mouth. As he rose to wipe sweat from his brow, he lamented his "old age" and wished for the strength of his youth.

"I've been at this a long time," he whispered to a bauble of himself dangling on the tree.

"Look, Mommy," said a little boy. "It's Santa. He's here!"

Santa turned, surprised. Normally, he was keen to hear even the slightest peep.

At the archway between family room and foyer stood a father, mother, son, and young daughter, each with red hair under pointed, crimson sleeping hats and baggy, earthen-hued sleeping gowns.

"You know," Santa patted his belly and laughed jovially. "Good boys and girls who sleep through the night get their presents in the morning."

Something about them seemed off--too old fashioned for this modern home. While this wasn't the first time Santa had been caught, there was something different this time, something that chilled him to the bone.

"I want to go first." The boy licked his lips, biting into a candy cane.

"Now, now, Kryan," the mother tsked. "You went first with the Easter bunny. It's Leanne's turn." She bent down and patted the small girl on the shoulder. "Go ahead Honey, it's ok."

The sleepy-eyed toddler took several smalls steps and tucked a doll—some sort Raggedy Ann, with a head of bright red hair – under one of her arms.

"Santa..." she said drowsily, and held out her free hand.

"Yes, dear." Santa's large heart pushed away his fear. "It's Santa Claus." He bent to one knee, smiled, and felt his cheeks flush behind his snow white beard.

When Leanne got close, she dropped the doll and lunged. She roared, revealing a gaping maw of pointed teeth. Knocking him back, she sank her teeth into Santa's flesh. He felt her pointed teeth chip against his molars as she punctured and ripped off his cheek.

Leanne looked at him with bright, fire-red eyes and blinked innocently before chomping off his other cheek. Blood stained Santa's beard to the tip as he screamed.

Rolling to his side, Santa knocked Leanne to the floor. He got to one knee and dove for the chimney, only to have Kryan smash a lamp over his head.

"Get him, Dad!" Kryan cheered when Santa fell to his knees.

A kick to the back drove Santa to the floor. They rolled him onto his back, loomed over him and smiled. Their teeth were long, sharp, and pointed, yet somehow fit the confines of their human jaws.

Santa trembled, but shock stiffened his muscles. Kryan held one of Santa's hands between long, skinny fingers. "Can I now?"

"We all can." The father said. "Your Christmas present has arrived, children. Let's eat!"

Santa wailed as the family descended on him, devouring his flesh like a pack of hungry wolves.

CHRISTMAS COMES EARLY

BY KYLE HARRISON

The calendar said it was another two weeks, it couldn't be wrong.

But the caroling outside spoke of much song.

I ran downstairs to see,

Eager to share in festivity.

I find my family meal already eaten.

The presents were all open,

The children had been beaten.

Someone had been here, taken all we had.

Someone left a note, telling us we were bad.

"You care only for gifts, trinkets and things.

This holiday I'll show you what true fear brings."

In a panic I looked to find those I love.

I prayed to god and heaven above.

I heard more screaming from the neighbors nearby.

Others who had been victims of this wicked Yuletide cry.

Krampus took what we never wanted to lose.

He showed us what it meant to choose.

We thought we needed gifts, toys and cash

But now our children are part of his stash.

Next holiday I'll be better, I promise, I swear.

Just bring them back, and I promise I'll care.

But my words land on deaf ears, my petitions a waste.

Because before the holidays are over, he knows how they'll

taste.

ALL THROUGH THE HOUSE

BY ERIC NIRSCHEL

The faint sound of snowflakes bursting like tiny white stars against the glass was barely audible over the sound of his own breathing. Timothy Flyte had gotten good at listening to the sound of his own breathing over the years; it was easier to focus on that than the sound of his parents arguing. There was a steady, comfortable rhythm in the sound. Some people counted sheep or listened to soothing ocean sounds to sleep, but Timothy found it easier to focus on the sound of his own breath.

He was doing it again, on this cold December night, but for a different reason. Outside, the snow was falling with almost practiced bravado, and in the living room, a glass of milk and a pair of comically oversized chocolate chip cookies had been left by the tree. His parents were out; trapped by the blizzard at an office Christmas party, and his room was now ever so faintly lit with the soft, fluorescent blue glow of the digital clock as it ticked over to midnight.

Timothy rolled over, his back to the door, and focused. It was difficult for him, now, though. His breath was more rapid, and his heart was fluttering in his chest. He was almost old enough to stop believing, but no child ever gives up the mysticism of youth without a little bit of a fight.

Above, on the roof, there came a thump, and Timothy's breath caught in his throat. In the darkness, outside the window, clumps of snow slid off and fell past the window, knocked free by big, jolly boots. Timothy couldn't bring himself to breathe again, and the sound of his own heartbeat filled his ears... until something interrupted. This time from the living room. It was a soft, pulpy sound, like the kind of noise meat might make when dropped on a counter.

Something wet moved, and the front door rattled, the door frame creaking with weak protest as something pressed against it.

A pause. Timothy hitched a shallow breath, pulling the covers up over his head.

A loud snap, like a muffled gunshot. Then another, and another. The door frame creaked, again, and now it sounded like a hand wringing a clump of celery stalks. The umbrella stand by the door fell over with a clatter, and Timothy didn't dare move. More snapping, more popping, more oozing and squelching. Then, rustling and the jingling of ornaments on the tree, followed by wet, gurgling chuckles.

It had to be an oversight only adults could make, Timothy told himself. No self-respecting child would design a house without asking 'How will Santa get in without a chimney?'

OH CHRISTMAS TREE

By N.M. Brown

It all started with the Christmas tree lots. Employees got sick one by one. They came down with a type of super pneumonia; resistant to anti biotics. Hospitals became full; turning some of the more able-bodied patients away at the door. Most died soon after.

Those with elderly loved ones and infants spread it to them instantaneously. Most of them succumbed to the same fatal result.

By the time the town of Brigantine figured it out, it had evolved to the forests and wooded areas. The trees had been slaughtered for years for mere decoration, and they'd had enough.

Now, it was humanity's time to pay. Poisonous spores gathered in their roots; seeping into their needles and releasing into the open air. Moisture amplified it's growth, raining down and infecting most of humanity with fatal toxins. Not a Christmas Tree could be seen form any window that year, and all the years after.

Merry Christmas.

GHE YULE CAG
By Alanna Robertson-Webb

It's all true.

Those stupid stories my Amma (grandmother) told me as a child, the ones that I didn't believe because I thought she was nuts, are fricking true. They shouldn't be, but they are.

I'm from Florida, but I'm visiting Amma in Iceland this year for Christmas. You would think I'd be used to weird things, considering what state I live in, but this experience changed my perception of everything.

Amma lives on the outskirts of the tiny town of Siglufjörður, and there's nothing within miles of her house except a dirt road and forest. Normally she would fly to Saint Augustine to see me, but she recently broke her hip. I decided to go there and surprise her, and after a nine-hour delay

I finally reached her doorstep late on Christmas afternoon.

When Amma saw me, she gave me a huge hug, and tears of happiness welled up in her eyes.

She couldn't get out of her bed, but she directed me around the tiny house until we had a delicious, traditional meal of humarsúpa soup and laufabrauð bread cooking.

While I was there, she spoke in Icelandic to refresh my terrible grasp of the language, and as night fell she began to get agitated about something. She kept glancing nervously out the window and muttering, "Jólakötturinn", but that wasn't translating well for me. I requested that she switch to English, but that only made me more confused.

"I am worried that Jólakötturinn, the Yule Cat, will come for you unless you are gifted clothes tonight. I am saddened that I have nothing prepared for you."

"Wait, what the heck is a Yule Cat?"

"You do not recall? I told you the stories as a child."

I shrugged, sheepishly reminding her that I had a terrible memory.

"Jólakötturinn is a malevolent spirit, a type of Grim Reaper, and every Christmas night he used to collect the souls of children who died from cold. Now that humans have better heat, he has taken it upon himself to collect the soul of anyone not gifted clothing, or anyone who's heat source fails on this night. He sees them as close enough to his original prey, and even adults are not safe now."

"Amma, while that's a pretty cool story it's a load of crap. I love you, but there's no giant cat who's going to kill me for not getting socks this year."

I scoffed, and that was when I heard a tree right outside of the house come crashing down.

The silence that followed was deafening, until it was shattered by a massive yowl. Amma looked at me, sadness etched on her face.

"It is too late."

CHRISTMAS EVE VISIT

By Alanna Robertson-Webb

Each year on Christmas Eve she would always comes to visit me. Normally she left me a little gift, such as cookies or my favorite flowers, but not this time. She was a day early, and when she entered the graveyard her steps were oddly slow. She was just skin and bone, and I barely recognized my lover.

She rested against my headstone, her breathing laboured as a single tear slipped down her gaunt cheek. After a time she bade me speak, though she knew that she could not hear me. I saw how red and swollen her eyes were, and it clawed at my heart. Her sad countenance finally broke me, and I spoke as the wind whistled over my carved teeth.

"Why does thou sit upon my headstone, and will my dead lips to speak? Why does thou weep upon my grave, and not let me sleep?"

She sighed, and with panic I watched as she went to lay her hand upon my likeness carved into the granite. I tried to warn her away, praying that she could somehow understand my ghostly scream.

"No! You know what the witch said: if the one who loved me touches me then cursed to die she shall be."

Her hand faltered, her fingertips just shy of my cheek, and it dropped to hang limply by her side. My heart shattered, and I wished to know what was so bad that she nearly signed her own death warrant. I wanted to know why the light in her blue eyes had dimmed, and why her skin was so waxen pale.

"Why has my fairest flower, that e'er I saw, withered to a stalk?"

I willed her to hear me, but I knew it was in vain. Tears were now streaming freely down her cheeks, and then she spoke. Her voice was so quiet that I had to strain to capture her words, which was not like her normal self.

"We shall meet soon, sweetheart, when the autumn leaves that fell from the trees are green again. A disease ravages me, and I have little time left."

She stood, and I felt my ties to the living world fade. I did not have the energy left to speak, not til the 'morrow, and I wished with all my soul that she would go find a doctor.

Just as I thought she was going to leave she reached out, her clammy hand grasping my granite one.

"At least you can take me now, my love, rather than I suffer through more pain-filled seasons."

Her eyes rolled back in her head, and as I faded out I saw her collapse to the frosted ground.

When the moon rose the next night she awaited me, and she looked like the healthy lass I had known in life. The villagers had taken her body away, and on Christmas Eve I kissed my love for the first time in a decade.

NO ELF ON THE SHELF

By Radar Deboard

Cory stumbled into his house, almost tripping over the doorframe in the process. By an absolute miracle he had managed to drive himself home without crashing into anything. He let out a hiccupped burp that was ripe with the smell of alcohol. Too tired to take off his shoes properly he instead kicked his foot forward letting the shoe fly off of it. He stumbled forward nearly falling on his face. He managed to grab hold of the fireplace mantel and regained his footing. He stood there with his head looking down at the ground with the feeling of bile rising up from his stomach.

He let out a loud retching sound as the dissolved plate of nachos he had several hours ago came rocketing out of his mouth. His body shook as he prepared himself for another wave of vomit. After a minute of waiting he decided that he was safe from anymore bile exiting his body.

He brought a shaky hand to his lips, wiping off the vomit that been left behind. His eyes scanned the mantel, studying the large amount of Christmas decorations that lay upon it. He noticed that the elf on the shelf that his wife adored seemed to be missing from its designated spot. Cory said with a smugness in his low voice, "She finally got rid of that thing."

Cory hated the whole Christmas season, but above all else, he hated the whole concept of an elf on a shelf. He always thought those things looked creepier than anything from a horror movie. He had been subjected to years of having to see one of them as a child. He could still remember that back when he was eight he could have sworn he saw the thing move. It's head had turned towards him and its smiled had turned to a frown. He tried to tell his parents about it, but of course they didn't believe him.

"Well at least it's gone", he mumbled to himself as he stumbled down the hallway. He creaked opened the bedroom door to see his wife sleeping soundly. She was on the far side of the bed with her back to the door. Cory fumbled forward in the dark trying to make his way to the bed. He finally grabbed hold of it and plopped himself down onto it. He was ready for a nice peaceful sleep as he started to doze off.

The elf waited for several minutes under the bed. The sounds of Cory's obnoxious snoring let the creature know that it was time to move. It crawled out from under the bed and made its way up onto the top of the mattress. It stared down at Cory as it brought the hammer over its head in preparation to strike. Cory had been very naughty this year, and it was time for him to receive his punishment.

SHORTCUT
by Nerisha Kemraj

Stacey turned, feeling eyes watching her.

No one there.

She walked briskly through the dank alley, uneasiness sending chills down her spine.

"Don't take the shortcut," her friend, Jill, warned her. "It's dangerous."

But already late, there was no way she was going to miss the Christmas-eve party. It was rumored to be the party of the year! Plus, Chris was going to be there. The shortcut would have to do.

Smiling to herself and momentarily forgetting her creepy surroundings, her thoughts roamed over to Chris. She knew he wouldn't resist her kinky Christmas outfit. Their last meeting definitely sparked chemistry, and now with the help of a little mistletoe, she'd have him right where she wanted. And she had her own special mix of eggnog, just for him.

A loud thud behind her, made her swing around to see a black figure approach her, arms outstretched. His face, covered in blood, contorted into an ugly grimace as he crawled towards her.

"Don't come near me!" she shrieked, regretting her decision to take the shortcut.

Her heart pounded as she clutched her heels, watching him as she tried to get away as fast as she could. Her earrings swung like a pendulum, counting down the seconds as she ran.

"No! Don't go there!" the man screamed.

Stacey rummaged through her purse in search of her pepper-spray, while the contents of her bag spilled out. She'd have plenty of time to regret that later. She had to get away to safety.

The house was only a few hundred meters away.

"Its not safe! There's some- " his warning was cut short as Stacey ran right into the killer's waiting knife. Lights flashed before her eyes as he twisted it into her gut.

"Ho, ho, ho. Merry Christmas, my little elf," he said, a throaty laugh echoed in the night as he placed her little elf hat onto his head.

He wrenched the blade from her body, wiping it onto his red, Santa coat, as she struggled to breathe, choking on her blood.

The flicker of the Christmas lights from the house in the distance was the last thing Stacey saw.

TWAS THE NIGHTMARE BEFORE CHRISTMAS

By Cory Stephens

'Twas the nightmare before Christmas, when all through the house

A creature was stirring, it was not a mouse;

The traps were all set by the chimney with care,

In hopes St. Nicholas would soon be caught there;

The children were hiding under their bed,

While visions of monsters danced in their heads;

And mamma with her knife, hid under her lap,

Waiting for the Santa as she pretended to nap,

When out on the lawn there arose a loud clatter,

I pulled on the trigger and saw a large splatter.

Away to the window I flew like a flash,

Tore open the shutters and saw a bloody gash.

The moon shined down on the blood-stained snow
Gave the lustre of murder on the reindeer below,
When, what to my wondering eyes should appear,
But a big red sleigh, and seven pissed off reindeer,

With an evil red driver, so lively and quick,
I knew in a moment it must be St. Nick.
More rapid than eagles his reindeer they came,
And he whistled, and shouted, and ordered them by name;

"ATTACK, DASHER! ATTACK, DANCER! ATTACK, PRANCER!
POOR VIXEN!
KILL HIM, COMET! KILL HIM, CUPID! KILL HIM, DONNER and
BLITZEN!"
To the top of the porch! I prayed I wouldn't fall,
Now Santa was coming, reindeers and all;

I slammed the door shut, the reindeer started to fly,
They had only one purpose, to see that I die,
So up to the house-top the reindeer they flew,
With the sleigh full of dead children, and St. Nicholas too.

And then, in an instant, I heard on the roof

The stomping and clawing of each hellion hoof.

As I drew the gun to my hand, and was turning around,

Down the chimney St. Nicholas came without making a sound

He was dressed all in fur, from his head to his foot,

And his clothes were all blood stained from the children he'd took;

A bundle of weapons he had flung on his back,

And he grabbed a knife and began to attack.

His eyes -- were empty! His smile -- was scary!

The look on his face, chilling and eerie!

His cruel little mouth was drawn up like a bow,

He stabbed me in the chest, I turned white as the snow;

The stump of the knife he held tight in his teeth,

And the blood dripped down and pooled at my feet;

He had a smile on his face and a big round belly,

That shook when he laughed at me like a bowlful of jelly.

He was chubby and plump, a fat evil elf,

And I laughed when I saw him, in spite of myself;

A wink of my eye and a twist of his head,

My wife had stabbed him leaving him dead;

He spoke not a word, oh how our plan did work,

His body was bloody; then gave one last jerk,

And laying dead on the floor, right where he fell,

My wife gave me a nod, she had sent Santa straight to Hell.

The reindeer sprang from his sleigh, and vanished with haste,

The children came out, they were finally safe. .

But I heard my wife exclaim, as she drove Santa out of sight,

HAPPY CHRISTMAS TO ALL, AND TO ALL A GOOD-NIGHT!

THE STOCKING STUFFER

By A.L. King

My family no longer celebrates Christmas. That would be like the few survivors of an airline crash flying together each year on the tragedy's anniversary just to exchange gifts in the air.

So, we avoid Christmas like the dickens. I don't know about the others, but even the best Thanksgiving dinner puts a sour taste in my mouth. Although they won't come out and say it, I think every holiday is ruined.

Or maybe we're just ruined for family altogether. My three siblings and I are in our forties, and none of us have spouses or children. Arnie was married for a minute, and that's barely an understatement. Divorce papers were signed after a little less than a month. Helen got knocked up once, but she decided not to keep it. April still gives me hope. She and her girlfriend have been together three years now. That's practically three decades in Amherst time. As for myself, I can barely imagine having a girlfriend, let alone a wife.

I suppose you'd feel the same way if your basic understanding of lasting love exploded in your face like a ticking Christmas gift that was a time bomb rather than a watch. That's a fitting analogy for what happened to us on the last Christmas Day we celebrated together. My family got burned. Scorched.

It was tradition for the eldest of the Amhersts to host the annual festivities. Although my grandparents on my father's side lived in Florida, a far cry from our Ohio home, we flew south near the end of each December to share dinner on Christmas Eve and a wealth of gifts on Christmas Morning. We usually arrived a few days before Christmas and left a few days after watching Dick Clark signal the New Year's ball drop. Our years blended together that way.

It was a lovely tradition, until...

I had noticed that the stocking with grandpa's name on it was wet. I thought maybe the liquid soaking the bottom of the cloth and dripping onto the floor by the fireplace was from a cracked bottle of cologne. My grandma was always gifting him those fanciful sprays, so I imagined she had unknowingly dropped a defective container into his pouch.

Had I further studied the wetness—the color and the smell, that is—I might have seen it for what it was. But I went to grandma instead.

"Something is dripping from grandpa's stocking."

"That's not surprising," she said with a slipping smile.

It was in that moment, when her teeth detached from her gums, that I finally understood she wore dentures. As if that wasn't jarring enough, her loose grin combined with wide and unblinking eyes to stir up suspicion. We hadn't seen the grand Amherst patriarch in a few days, not since grandma claimed he was bedridden with the flu. She said he was staying in their room because he didn't want to contaminate us.

"Is it a leaky bottle of cologne?" I asked of the wet stocking, hoping she would be her normal self again, with a normal answer.

"Oh, no," she said. At least that's what I think she said. Her false teeth had slipped even more, gumming up her gums and speech. She used her bony fingers to adjust them before continuing.

"That's not a bad guess, though. He stunk like a farm animal most of the time. His stocking is stuffed with his right foot, the only part I couldn't manage to use for dinner last night. He may have smelled bad, but he tasted great, don't you think?"

NO BADGERS FOR CHRISTMAS

By Diane Arrelle

"No live tree!" Mandy yelled at John. "They're dirty, they're fire hazards and they have animals living inside them. Do you want a badger jumping out Christmas morning and giving us rabies or something?"

John tried one more time. "But I thought—"

"No." Mandy interrupted, stamping her foot. "Now please go get my artificial tree."

John sighed. "Never should have taken a city girl to live in the woods," he muttered as he turned and left her in the living room. He trudged through the snow to the wooden garage behind their cabin. Exhaling puffs of crystallized air, John climbed the rickety ladder to reach the rafters and grabbed the bagged tree she'd brought with her when they married. Carefully climbing back down, he carried it to the house.

Once inside, he lit a romantic fire in the fireplace.

"I'm sorry," Mandy said bringing him a hot chocolate. "I'm just not used to living this way. Christmas to me means lights everywhere, music playing in every store and restaurant and the only animals are on leashes."

John smiled at his new wife, "I understand, you just got to get used to the great outdoors. In a couple of years, you'll be chopping down the Christmas tree."

She laughed, "I truly doubt that, but tomorrow, I'll try baking cookies for you."

John remembered her last attempt at baking, hid a shudder and forced a smile, "Sounds great." He turned his attention to the bagged tree and started to pull it out from the storage sack. "Damn, bag's torn, we'll need a new one after the holidays."

They decorated the pre-lit tree and drinking the now cold chocolate, sat on the sofa a few feet away. He put his arm around her and said, "Well, maybe you're right. The tree is perfect and I don't hear a badger anywhere."

As he gazed at the tree, and the dancing flames in the fireplace, he yawned then noticed Mandy snoring softly, her head on his shoulder. He watched the lights flicker and muttered, "I'm so tired I'm seeing spots." Then with another yawn he shut his eyes.

And woke to morning light.

He stretched and Mandy fell over. The spots before his eyes returned and he realized he was seeing hundreds of spiders crawling on the ornaments, hanging by threads from the ceiling, settling on his head, shirt and jeans. He looked over at Mandy, she was blue and dead, gift wrapped in fine, spider silk.

John jumped up and away, screaming, "Mandy! The spiders were everywhere biting his hands, his neck, his face. In a panic, John lit a candle and threw it. Hitting the carpet, the flames caught immediately and as the neatly wrapped presents under the tree burst into orange flames, he ran outside.

Watching the fire break through the roof of the log cabin, John felt hysterical laughter bubbling up his throat and blurted out, "Well honey, I think a badger would have been the safer choice after all."

The walls collapsed shooting sparks into the sky as his high-pitched laughter turned to gut wrenching sobs.

A CHRISTMAS TO DIE FOR

By Akshay Patwardhan

George Heyward awoke with a sweat-beaded forehead and cool, misty breath. The bedroom was dark and gloomy, filled with the wavering shadows of stuffed dinosaurs, plastic tractors, and "Splash Day Waterpark" participation trophies all enlarged to monstrous proportions in the faint moonlight creeping through blue silk curtains outside of which the December snowflakes were piling up on the windowsill in bunches of white mist.

It was the night of Christmas Eve, and that was when Santa Claus was supposed to show up all big-bellied and jolly with much-deserved presents for George. Perhaps that was why he had woken up in the middle of the night.

George heard a faint tapping, like that of knuckles rapping on a windshield, and he knew that it had come from the misty window. He peeked out a shimmering set of eyes, and he felt his legs quaking underneath the blanket. For a moment, there was nothing outside the window except for the unrelenting hail of snowflakes. Then a hand shot up seemingly out of nothingness, and he saw a white glove--flecked with something crimson and runny--press itself into a claw against the glass. It held a leather sack in its hand. George could feel a scream rising through his chest, but his throat had clamped shut with sheer terror.

Something red and pointy rose into view: a Santa hat with a white cotton ball attached to the tip like he'd seen in the morning cartoons, and then the pallid, wrinkled skin of a scraggly white-bearded face plastered itself on the window panes. It was the face of an old man--Santa Claus, George recognized instantly--but he looked...dead.

The man's eyes were directionless, milky orbs pointed two different directions. His once-pink lips were crusty and covered in horrid warts oozing a greenish-yellow pus. The man smiled at George with rotten, cavity-ridden molars that were dangling from the man's jaw like stringy puppets.

George began to scream.

George's bedroom door slammed open and his father Richard trudged inside rubbing his eyes. George glanced at his father for a mere moment and then returned his attention to the window, but the monstrous old man was nowhere to be seen.

"George, what's the matter?" Richard asked, glaring at the boy.

"Santa was outside my window, but he looked scary!" George wheezed as his heart began to beat steadily.

Richard shrugged his shoulders and muttered something as he glanced outside the window. "George, there's nothing there. I'm getting tired of your monster stories. "Monster Santa"? I mean, come on."

"Dad, I'm being serious!"

"Good night, George," Richard said firmly, slamming the door.

George shuddered underneath his blanket for seemingly an infinite amount of time, but sleep couldn't take over. There had been no trace of Santa since then, and George wished the old man would never come back. Then he heard glass shattering, followed by tortured screaming--his father's--which was abruptly cut off with a bloody gurgle.

George's heartbeat quickened as he heard footsteps approaching his bedroom, and he curled into a cocoon underneath his blanket. He heard the creak of the door, and he held his breath, his ears honed to perfection. George realized that his foot was sticking out slightly, and as he tried to curl it in, he felt something cold and bony grasp his ankle. He shrieked his lungs out, but there was no one to hear him.

He felt himself being pulled further and further until he was thrown into the leather sack, and he managed to hear one last thing before everything went dark.

"A little bite for the road," a voice rasped.

CRACKS

By Amber Keener

Cold snow crunched softly under Mary's boots as she walked along the path. Except for her own prints, the newly fallen snow blanketed the path undisturbed until she spotted a set of rabbit tracks leading off the trail and into the field. Curious, Mary followed the tracks into the field. As she followed, she thought of how Kyle, her six-year-old son, would have loved this if she had brought him. However, she had left the child with her mother in an attempt to gain a bit of time for herself.

Kyle this year had been particularly excited for Santa Clause, and spent much of his time talking about how he planned to catch Santa during Christmas Eve. From detail traps that he had drawn out on pieces of scrap paper, to creating his own hiding spot to watch for Santa all night.

Mary and his father laughed to themselves, amused and delighted at their son's creativity, until she caught him placing his father's sleeping medication into the cookie batter. Grabbing a wooden spoon, she swatted Kyle three times on the bottom with it before sending the wailing child up to his room. Her own mother, seeing her daughter's frustration suggested that she take a walk to clear her head.

Mary paused for a moment as she reflected on the incident. She hoped that Kyle's behavior had been caused by his excitement and not signs that he may have problems. No, she told herself firmly. Kyle was a good child. A perfect and polite little boy, her boy. Even if he did tend to go to the extreme sometimes. All children go through these phases, and like all children he would grow out of this. With renewed optimism Mary started to follow the tracks again only to stop after a few steps. The rabbit tracks had come to a sudden end with a set of feather imprints like wings of a large bird on either side of the rabbit's feet.

Poor thing, she thought to herself as she turned and began the trudge back home. Her husband greeted her as she walked through the door with a kiss to the cheek. Kyle, after she had left, had been given a stern talking to and had to promise that he would remain a good boy for the rest of the day, now sat happily in front of the television watching cartoons.

The rest of Christmas Eve went by pleasantly, and by nine Mary tucked Kyle into bed.

By eleven, after finishing up a few things, she finally crawled into bed. Slumber came easily pulling her into its dark embrace. She only woke briefly at the sound of a large thud hitting the roof before falling back to sleep.

Mary awoke to the sun just beginning to rise outside. Careful not to wake her husband, she climbed out of bed and put on a robe, and then headed downstairs for some fresh coffee.

When she passed Kyle's room, she found his bed empty. She let out a sigh. She wished that he would have slept just a little longer. No matter, she thought as she made her way downstairs.

When she reached the kitchen, Mary found the backdoor wide open and both Kyle's coat and boots missing. She could see a fresh set of child size footsteps outside in the snow. She quickly followed the tracks around to the front of the house before freezing into place as dreaded horror washed over her. Kyle's tracks had ended abruptly with a set of feather imprints surrounding his last footsteps.

WORK ON CHRISTMAS

By Mama Creep

It's Christmas evening and my daddy is going to work.

He is in his study, preparing to leave. Daddy is always gone when it's Christmas time.

This year it's no different. I don't mind because it's his jobby-job. I have a jobby-job too. But my jobby-job changes every year. Last year, I was assigned to design the cookies for Santa. This year, mommy told me I can hang stockings on the chimney because I'm a big boy.

So that's what I am doing today, hanging big socks on the chimney. I used a chair to reach the wall because I am not that tall yet. But daddy told me, that someday I'll be as tall as him. I stepped down from the chair and heard my daddy's deep voice as the door to his study opened.

Daddy came out smiling. I can see his fangs and his pointy tongue hanging from his mouth. He approached me and the house shook as his cloven hooves touched the floor. He raised me in the air kissing my brown fury cheeks. I giggled with excitement and stared at daddy. Daddy and I had the same horns but his are bigger.

He put me down and I gave him his sack. He thanked me and kissed mommy goodbye. I watched as daddy went out to the cold snowy night carrying his empty sack. It won't be empty once he comes back. I rushed to my bed excited for the next morning. Daddy told me he'll bring me a lot of friends to play with. I guess humans are naughtier this year.

GINGERBREAD BURN

By Katy Lohman

The house reeked of gingerbread, pine, cranberries, eggnog and fear. I met Leah heading downstairs, balancing the candle-box on her skinny preteen hip. "Status," I whisper-asked.

"Almost done, all sisters safe but Lynne. She won't go." Her voice was bitter. "You try. She listens to you." She fled.

Up to the Nursery. Pink, lace, castles, unicorns, glitter. The Tree with our yearly height measurements.

No time for memories. I found baby sis in the toybox, buried in toys, sucking her thumb like she was three. "I no go," she bellowed. "No like bad place!"

"Shhh, sweety." I hoped she'd never find this was the real bad place. "It's a gingerbread year; worst in the cycle. You just turned seven. I won't lose you to his madness."

"He won't hurt-" she began.

I took her to the Tree, showed my bloody year-seven measurement, showed her the scar on my thigh.

Showed her the other 7-year marks of our sisters.

She yielded; I carried her to the basement. Wending my way through the stacks of Mom's shopping obsessions, I found the secret door, and slipped through.

The second basement, an ancient brick maze with narrow-set halls. Even if he found the secret door, he'd never fit in this level. I set Lynne down; Lunette dashed out. "It's all in place. Except..." Her lower lip wobbled. "I couldn't get the Book."

I swore. If he found the Book, it was all for naught.

Turning, I worked my way back up, peeked out the door, and winced. He'd already set up the display.

Some would think us a family with true holiday spirit. The long hall, lined with tables of crystal; lit scented candles in candelabras, angels, bowls full of antique ornaments and Nativity Scene. Dozens of playing music boxes played clashing tunes amidst ornate gingerbread houses.

They'd be wrong. The display was a trap. Endless, breakable, invitations to 'play' with him.

Seven years old. Accidental fall. A shattered hundreds-year-old angel ornament. The rage. The horse whip. The costume bloodied for the first time.

No. No time for memories!

I made it to the kitchen with no mishap; it was oddly silent. Empty. The Book on its stand, under the hanging poinsettias. Closed, thankfully. He hadn't picked. We still had time; hide the Book, we'd be safe. His word. Clutching it tightly, I started back.

"L-l-l-lllloraiiiiiine," came, singy-songy, from the den.

No! It couldn't be!

"Lorraine Lorraine, it's time again," he sang, forcing the rhyme.

Better me than the babies. My abdomen cramping, I called out, in a cheery voice, "Coming, Sir!"

He wore the original suit and cap; his hair was like fluffy clouds. In one hand, the gingerbread maid costume; in the other, a present. Christmas lights everywhere made the room blindingly colorful. "Oh, it's time, dear girl. Wear these."

My foolish self had to ask, "Why me? You haven't even consulted the naughty-nice list."

"Everyone's nice this year." Taking the Book, he threw it in the fire. His cheeks flushed red, he laughed so his belly shook like a bowlful of jelly. He opened the box; the family diamond engagement ring.

"You wanted me to stay. Of course, I'd choose you to wed when you came of age."

He folded me close.

One last memory. Me, five years old, a forgotten sister to a new baby brother, looking up the chimney.

Gingerbread cookies and glasses of eggnog covered the entire coffee table. "I hate you, Daddy, and I hate Locke! I wish Santa Claus would come, make you all leave and stay forever and ever!"

NO MORE CHRISTMAS CAROLERS

By John Kujawski

The Christmas carolers only came by my house once and there was a good reason why. They picked the wrong night to bother me and I really let them have it. I don't know if they'll remember that particular Christmas, but I won't forget it.

I had put a lot of thought into moving to the secluded area in Missouri. The neighbors were pretty well spread out and there wasn't much going on. There were mostly trees and a church and that was about it. There was one big graveyard that wasn't far from the church, but I didn't hang around there much. I was a man living alone and that was for the best.

Christmas was said to be the perfect time of year to have the company of others. I didn't want it. For sure, I didn't require it on this particular Christmas evening. I think my animal instincts were even starting to get the best of me when I heard the carolers outside. I could smell the trouble right away and with it being one of those nights with a full moon I knew there was no place anyone could kind. I would see them in the light if I went outside.

Nonetheless, I ended up being the chosen resident that year and I could hear the singing going on outside. I was hungry and I knew there were plenty of hungry mouths out there. It wasn't Halloween but I knew they wanted to eat. They were singing but it all sounded terrible. I almost didn't want to open the front door. I could hear more and more of them walking towards my home. I wanted to claw their eyes out and I knew I could do it. It was just a matter of time.

While I was waiting for the changes in me to take place I managed to catch a glance of one of those singers. They were as pale as I expected them to be. There was one sickly figure out there that truly resembled death. He was belting the song out, too as if he wanted to be loudest one out there but I don't even remember what he was singing.

I know it was the effect of the full moon and my transformation took place before I knew it. I felt savage and angry and I knew I was ready to fight. I tore open the door and leapt out after the first caroler I saw. I knew they weren't there to make friends but they sure as hell were not going to kill me. I thrashed one of the male ones with my claws and destroyed them with everything I had.

It was a beautiful site to see my strength pay off. All of those damn zombies ran back towards the graveyard where they belonged. The one I had ripped apart was left out front for decoration. They never came back to bother me after that. I suppose it makes sense, though.

Those zombie Christmas carolers didn't know they were messing with a werewolf.

YOU BETTER WATCH OUT

By Alanna Robertson-Webb

He sees you when you're sleeping,

He knows when you're awake.

He knows if you've been bad or good...

So you better watch out,

Oh! You better watch out...

Growing up, I never realized that the classic Christmas song was a warning. Every kid in America eventually hears the jolly song, and most can sing along to the lyrics perfectly. It's supposed to be a reminder to be good for the year, or else you won't get presents, but that's not what it means to us.

To those of us in the tiny town of Little Browning, Montana the song is an annual signal, a reminder that death is coming.

Have you ever wondered why the population of our town is so small, only around 315 residents, or why most of us are mainly in our 20's?

It's because we have to be in good enough shape to fight off the thing that comes to kill us each Christmas.

We can't just abandon the town, though God knows we've tried. If all of us leave, then the creature takes its hatred out on the nearby pediatric hospital, and last time we evacuated it killed nearly a hundred people. The event was labeled as a tragic gas leak, and no one outside of the town believes what we go through. Our yearly terror has been called an elaborate hoax, and that's how the nation sees us.

What people don't get is that this is a very real threat, and we need help.

Our struggle has been going on since the days of my great, great grandparents, and we've lost countless townsfolk. The creature that stalks Little Browning was once a cobbler named Gerald, who was a simple man living a simple life. Then his wife cheated on him with the town's tailor, and in a fit of rage he murdered the adulterers while they were fornicating in the tailor's bed on Christmas Eve.

When his heart became twisted that day his body altered, morphing him into a nightmarish creature with fangs, claws and super speed that could fit down chimneys and rip families apart.

Since then the thing that was Gerald has stalked the forests surrounding Little Browning, and each Christmas he comes to cull the sinners from our population.

No one is safe, because every human lies or commits a sin at least once a year.

Every December 24th we manage to drive the creature back, but Gerald always kills a few of us. We perch on our snow-crusted rooftops like terrified crows, our shakily-held guns at the ready, and if you come to visit, you'd better watch out because he'll snatch you before you can blink.

GINGERBREAD BITES

By C.L. Williams

I'm taking my cookies out of the oven. The aroma is delicious, and I must let the smell enter my nostrils. While taking that sniff, before placing them on the counter, I feel something.

One of my gingerbread man cookies bites me before scurrying off like a rat with table crumbs. I drop the cookies from the pain of the bite. I begin to pick up the cookies but I'm noticing something peculiar, my arm looks like that of a gingerbread man.

I then see I am the same size as my cookies. I'm shrinking and becoming a gingerbread man.

THE SECOND NOEL

By N.M. Brown

We were careful; so diligent to make sure all candy and sweets were put away before bedtime. The Gingerbread house we made together the night before was placed in the highest cupboard in the house, well out of a five-year old's reach.

The usual clatter of our Daughter Noel's footsteps and exclamations about presents never came that Christmas morning. Instead, my wife Maureen and I were met with dead silence. A sinister aura permeated through the air.

Two green monster slippers twitched in different directions; a signal of our little girl's struggle with whatever had caused her to fall to the kitchen floor.

"Noel?"

No answer.

My wife ran over to her and crouched down on the floor.

"Bobby!" She wailed. "She's choking! Oh my god, her lips are turning blue."

I had her off the floor and well into the first steps of the Heimlich maneuver in less than twenty seconds. All the while, Maureen's sobbing hysterically in my ear.

"Bob, no! You're Not supposed to do it like that. She's too little; you're gonna hurt her ribs!"

In the adrenaline of the situation I find myself shouting back. My hands are shaking so badly that I can barely keep them grasped together under her tiny frame. I'd say my heart was beating faster than my breath could keep up with, if I couldn't feel it shattering more every second that Noel didn't take a breath.

"I'm trying to save our daughter's life! Ribs won't matter if I don't clear this airway in the next thirty seconds. God knows how long she's been out here like this!"

Maureen fumbles through her purse and the contents of the clusterfuck that is our kitchen counter, searching for her phone to call 911.

"Lift her up by the feet and pound her back Bob!" She demands.

The moment I go to respond, a sharp, jagged shard of something flies into my left eye. My right eye watches as it falls to my lap and rolls to the very floor I picked Noel up off of not moments ago; a fucking peppermint. Our little girl almost lost her life over a goddamned peppermint. We had used them to decorate the roof; Santa's shingles Noel called them. One must have rolled off when we were putting it away last night.

Noel's face goes through a barrage of colors until it returns to its usual pink state. She's coughing quite a bit. Maureen and I are both crying at this point; clutching our daughter to our chests like she'd float away if we ever let go.

"Jesus Christ sweetheart, you really scared us. Can you breathe okay?"

Our little darling nodded her head.

"Are you sure?" Maureen asked. Pulling her in for an even tighter hug before giving her a chance to answer. "I love you Noel."

She pulls away from us. Her face looks the same as our little girl's always has, but her eyes are oddly different. There's a subtle change that I can't place. As she opens her tiny mouth to speak, her irises turn black. The voice that follows comes out in a deep, menacing rumble.

"Noel isn't here anymore."

A STITCH IN TIME FOR CHRISTMAS

by Alyson Faye

The Angel Gabriel was crying her eyes out, whilst Joseph fought over her with one of the Shepherds. Mary, who never had a good word for anyone, was moaning to Melchior, and baby Jesus was being kicked around as a football by several angels using the crib as goal.

It was the usual denouement to the Oakley Amateur Dramatics Post-Nativity Party.

'There's no respect,' Melanie whispered to a drunken shepherd, 'this is supposed to be the season of good will.'

She left the pub in disgust, her head busy with plans for the festive season. At home Melanie brought out her trade kit - her needles and thread. She sewed several dolls from cloth scraps. She dripped a few drops of murky belladonna tea and frogs' blood onto their faces with a tiny pipette, before retiring to her bed; sober and at peace.

Christmas Eve dawned the next morning in Oakley, and 'Mary', also the pub's landlady, woke up, stretched and tried to yawn; her fist-pounding fetched her husband up the stairs, where, to his horror, he discovered his wife with her lips bloody, and sewn together with perfect little stitches in silver thread and her wrists tied up in tinsel.

'Joseph', also the village butcher, stumbled out of his front door, screaming, 'The devil's been in the night!' His hands tinkled merrily when he shook them because of the ten pretty silver bells neatly stitched to his digits.

'No more throwing your right hook about for you, Joe,' laughed his neighbour. 'It's a pacifist Christmas for you.'

In various junior angels' homes, screams ricocheted, as bedclothes were thrown back to reveal toes stitched into pajamas - flesh to fabric.

The macabre discoveries were happening all round the village for each Nativity cast member had been, overnight, stitched up, wrapped up and decked out like Christmas gifts.

A fleet of ambulances descended on Oakley and carted the patients off to hospital. The medical staff commented on the fine detail of the stitch work and even took photographs on their iPhones to share on social media.

The images started trending on twitter with hash tags such as #creativeChristmasembroidery #Santaselvesatwork.

The atmosphere in The Oakley Arms that evening was however subdued. For a start only half the regulars were present and there was much discussion as to whom the 'Christmas Embroiderer' might be.

Melanie perched alone, in the nook by the fire, with a glass of mulled wine reading her book. Halloween was usually her preferred time of year for working, but she was happy to be flexible and include Christmas especially as the results were so bewitching.

CHEN ONE FOGGY CHRISTMAS EVE

By Matthew A. St. Cyr

Having sold the last Christmas tree on the lot, it was time to close up shop. Bing Crosby wished for a White Christmas through the loudspeaker as Andy pushed the broom, clearing the majority of the pine needles towards the dumpster at the side of the trailer he used as an office.

After picking up the needles, he went in the office and sat down at the desk to run final numbers for the season.

Sipping on a mug of brandied eggnog, he turned off the loudspeaker and the outside flood lights. He shifted around his Christmas playlist and found that after three weeks of selling

Christmas trees for twelve hours a day, he didn't feel like listening to Christmas music anymore.

"Bah humbug." He said out loud and laughed.

Andy turned on the small portable radio he kept in the office and settled on a classic rock station. Bob Dylan was singing Lay, Lady, Lay. Sure he could have just as easily pulled up classic rock on a streaming app, but he still loved listening to live radio. It made him feel connected to the world, especially when he was out here after hours. His Christmas tree lot was a converted farm stand that stood alone out on Route 119 just outside of Huxbury.

After about forty-five minutes or so, he had crunched the last of the numbers and was pleased to find that he was firmly in the black.

"It's a damn Christmas miracle!" he said and refilled his mug with more eggnog.

He drank a toast to himself and shut off the desk lamp, leaving him in the soft glow of the string of christmas lights that circled the interior ceiling trim. Grabbing his coat and hat, he flicked the switch killing the rest of the lights and exited, locking the door behind him.

Fumbling with his car keys, he realized that last eggnog may have been one too many. A rustling and snapping sound from the woods behind the trailer gave him pause. The moon was high in the night sky, casting a silvery-blue light over everything. Another rustle and Andy could make out a dark form coming through the brush.

Finally the dark shape stepped into the light and Andy smiled. It was another Christmas miracle! A reindeer stood no more than twenty feet away from him, chewing on what looked like a branch.

The smile quickly faded however as the creature caught sight of him and began to charge towards him. Something was terribly wrong with the animal. He realized that he could see bare ribs sticking out from its side. It's eyes were a solid white and tattered flesh hung from it's face.

It dropped the object from its mouth, which Andy could now see was a severed human arm. He dropped his keys in the snow, desperately searching and now horribly sober. The last thing that Andy Durmand smelled was the fetid breath of the undead creature bearing down on him.

CHE PERFECC GIFC

By Nicole Henning

Christmas time is the hardest time of year for me; all the gift giving and happy faces.

This year there's one person I can think of when I imagine the perfect gift, her name is Kathryn. She's the image of perfection, her smile can brighten the darkest day. Her voice sounds how I imagine Christians think Heaven feels. I know, a messed-up comparison but I can't even articulate how perfect she is. So of course, I'm standing outside the back door of the restaurant she waitresses at when she's done with her shift.

The look in her enchanting brown eyes when I put the chloroform rag over her mouth and nose was magical. They almost twinkled before they shut, and she went limp in my arms. I've imagined this hundreds of times in the past year. I first saw her last December, so this was an anniversary for us. I carried her to my car and got her back to the family cottage before she could wake up. I had timed the drive impeccably, of course, this was for Christmas, so everything had to go according to plan.

I could smell the loaf I had in the bread maker cooking and the crock pot was bubbling with yule tide soup. I had to drag her into the bedroom to get her ready for dinner. I was careful not to touch her anywhere unwarranted. After all, from what I had seen, and that was a lot, she was pure of heart and body. Like I said she as perfect in every way. I got her into one of the dresses and tied into the wheelchair before she woke up. Thankfully I had remembered to put a gag between her pouty lips before she came to.

She woke up slowly, her head lolling to one side and then the other as she tried to orient herself. We had kept the cabin sparsely decorated so all she saw were the logs that made up the cabin's walls. Once she was fully awake, she jerked and tried to pull at her bindings. Of course, they didn't come undone. This wasn't my first rodeo; I knew how to keep someone tied up.

Everything had to be perfect, or it wouldn't be a Merry Christmas.

I wheeled her into the living room and parked her so that her back was to the large fireplace that occupied the majority of the wall. She struggled to break free while I padded to the kitchen to check on the food. Somehow, she was able to get those pretty lips around the gag and used her tongue to push it down and pleaded "Please. You don't have to do this."

Coming out of the kitchen, I smiled a wide grin and smoothed down the front of my dress excitement beating in my breast. I looked at the shadows on the walls and saw them stretch and move. I murmured the ancient words and almost fainted with joy as the shadows converged on Kathryn's panicked form. She shrieked once before going completely silent.

Once I was sure it was done, I unbound her and helped her stand up. She wrapped her arms around me and kissed me lovingly on the lips. My true loves voice came from those sweet lips, "Merry Christmas my love." I kissed her back passionately and held her hands. I had picked the perfect vessel to bring my love back to me, she truly was the perfect gift.

IT'S SO COLD

By Al-hazred7

A cloud of breath flowed between my teeth and out of my mouth. I turned my eyes towards the ceiling, watching it ascend, and smiled. As I did so, I felt my lips crack and a single drop of blood fell on my white shirt.

"It's so cold in here" I thought to myself.

I remembered what Christmas was like in my home country, fake snow decorating the palm trees, temperature never descending below 20 °C and people walking down the street with t-shirts and flip flops.

I always complained that I never got to know what real Christmas felt like. I wanted to have the kind of Christmas that we saw on western movies with hot chocolates, warm sweaters, real snow...

- "It's so damn cold in here"

This time I said it out loud, letting my voice bang against the metallic walls surrounding me.

It's such a shame I didn't get to see the snow. I had checked my smartphone before we started moving and I knew that, by this time, it must have been snowing outside. I wished we had a window so that I could have seen it for the first time. I wished we would make stops so that I could touch it. But that wasn't going to be my fate and I was starting to come to terms with that fact.

This was the first time I felt what real cold was. I looked down at my fingers, they were starting to turn blue now. Funny, I thought to myself, I never knew that cold could feel this warm. It was as if my fingertips were burning.

I felt my chest getting heavier and heavier. As the hours passed by, it was getting harder to pump that frozen air inside my damned lungs. I suspected it had something to do with the tiny figures looking at us from above.

I don't know how long they had been there, but I only started to notice them when the cold had really started settling in. Those hateful little creatures with their sharp features, thin limbs and freaky blueish skin, clinging from the corners at the top of our cubicle. I abhorred them.

At the beginning they were just there, facing the walls in complete silence. But then after a few hours they began whispering, turning their heads 90° towards each other. I could see their aquiline noses, minuscule rows of green needle like teeth and shiny melted copper eyes. They reminded me of 5 cent coins.

That's when I began to throw my breath vapor upwards, at least that way I wouldn't have to see them. I could still hear them whisper though, with their broken fragmented voices. They sounded like the sound of ice breaking under one's boot.

- "They are never getting out of here"

- "I'm having the tiny one first"

- "Be patient, soon"

That's when I began talking to myself, I figured that at least that way I wouldn't be forced to hear their horrific little voices.

But deep down, I know they are right, we are not going to get to our destination. It is getting harder and harder to breathe, and my eyelids feel as if they were made from lead. I'm falling asleep.

Picking up the remains of my willpower and using the little battery that my phone had left I wrote one last text to my mother:

I'm sorry Mom. My path to abroad doesn't succeed. Mom and Dad, I love you so much! I'm dying because I can't breathe.

WHAT I SAW UNDER THE CHRISTMAS TREE

By K.M. Bennett

I thought my husband left me one Hell of a Christmas gift today.

I thought he did it because he wanted me to know where we stand. He's been waffling for months about whether to go to couples counseling. Neither one of us was sure whether it was worth trying any more. There was so little to make us hold on to each other after our kids left the house. And then she had entered the picture.

But neither of us let go. It was like we were both waiting for the other one to deliver the killing blow to our marriage, even if it would be a mercy killing at that point. I didn't know what to do. But I guess you could say a miracle happened, as horrible as it is—now everything's as crystal clear as the image on an LCD screen.

He left the Christmas present on the security cam, where he knew I'd find it. There was a red bow around the base of the little camera and attached was a small note that said. It's Over. Blood slammed my ear drums and the tendons in my neck went stiff and taught like bow strings. My hands trembled as I opened the app on my phone that would show the security footage.

There they both were, horizontal under the twinkling Christmas tree. One of the boxes in bright red paper had been crushed under their bodies as they rolled. He was above her, and he was really giving it to her.

In and out, in and out.

I knew that the things he did to her—he would never do to me. In fact, I thought with a pang, it seemed he was showing off for the camera. He moved with a ferocity and stamina that I didn't even know he had.

And her? She just laid there. It was sort of pathetic.

When I took my eyes away from the screen, they filled with tears. He emerged from the hallway and stood, waiting for me to say something. His eyes were as cold and hard as the frosted windowpanes in our living room. Mistletoe brushed his graying hair as he stepped through the doorway.

"Is it really over?" I rasped.

That was when he dropped the knife to the floor. It was slick and red as the holly berries that dotted the wreath over our door.

"Now we don't need counseling," he said. "She's gone."

I picked up the knife and considered what I'd seen.

"Wow! You really shouldn't have," I said, smiling like I hadn't in years.

"Well," he said, eyes bright with cheer, "You better watch out."

I froze as he wiped a tear from my cheek. My throat clenched and the smile on my face went slack.

"You better not cry..." he sang.

A whimper came from the back of my throat unbidden. I brandished the knife.

"I'm telling you why," he said, twisting my wrist. The knife fell.

UNDER THE MISTLETOE
By Cecelia Hopkins-Drewer

The office Christmas party used to be fun. However, in these politically correct times the spirit of camaraderie was mightily dampened. A drunken misdemeanor could lead to dismissal; and a mismanaged office romance might result in a court case! Kelsie sometimes wondered why the company even bothered serving alcohol.

This year the food was nice, and the inter-departmental greetings were pleasant enough. The wad of notes in her official Christmas card was a welcome bonus, but after that, the speeches began to drag. Sitting around, listening to her immediate supervisor's political commentary, and not daring to express her own opinion was simply boring.

Kelsie stood up, made a polite excuse about the ladies' room, and discreetly left her assigned table. Someone had hung mistletoe above a dark alcove around a twist in the corridor. 'How inappropriate!' Kelsie mused with a chuckle. 'Kissing a workmate at a function like this would be an invitation to disaster.'

The upstairs boss didn't seem worried, as he was standing directly under the bough, his posture broadcasting a casual vibe. Kelsie was unable to pass her employer unacknowledged. She stopped politely. "Mr. Jones, sir."

"How are you Kelsie?" Brandon Jones' devilishly compelling eyes locked with hers.

Kelsie felt her mouth go dry. She had always nursed an embarrassing infatuation towards him. "Very well, thank you sir."

"Are you having a good time Kelsie?"

"Yes sir!"

"I don't believe you." Brandon Jones tone was wicked. "Admit it, you are bored."

"If you say so sir..."

"Come here Kelsie, we will see if we can liven the evening up a little."

Temptation sparked. Although Kelsie suspected what might be going to happen, she stepped beneath the greenery. Strong arms encircled her. She gasped. Brandon

Jones was ageless, devilishly handsome and incredibly rich. Kelsie lifted her mouth for his burning kiss.

"Would you like to be my girlfriend Kelsie?"

Kelsie could hardly believe her ears. "I don't know sir – you are my boss."

Brandon took Kelsie by the hand and led her through a hidden door into a sumptuous apartment. Kelsie was dazed by the honour of his attention and the fiery lust his caresses had roused, but she could not avoid noticing the portraits. They all appeared to be of one man – Brandon himself, although the costumes implied they had been painted in different centuries.

"Are these all you sir?" Kelsie gasped.

"Call me Brandon, and yes!"

"How old are you sir?"

"Now or when I died?" Brandon appeared to hesitate and momentarily become vulnerable. "To tell the truth – the answer is the same – around twenty-five."

"I don't understand." Kelsie was confused. "I must have misheard."

But Kelsie knew that she hadn't been mistaken. Brandon had said that he was dead. If he were dead though, how was he here with her that night, able to touch and hold her? How did he also continue to run a multinational company?

"I have the soul of a dragon." Brandon laid a burning hand upon her shoulder. "So naïve Kelsie. Who did you think you were to interest me?" Sharp teeth protruded from his jawbone to penetrate the side of her throat.

No fairy tale, this kiss with the dark prince of the business conglomerate would be Kelsie's last. Her workmates were too dull and inebriated to notice when she did not return from her trip to the powder room. With the arrival of the New Year, her supervisor was forced to promote one of the girls from the casual pool to Kelsie's position, and by then, the trail was as cold as Brandon Jones was hot.

SANTA CLAUS
By Kim Plasket

Every year Santa came to the small town. The singers would start their songs; voices raised in harmony.

This year it's the same thing, only something is missing. Their songs seem to lack soul.

Their pale faces stare off in the distance, eyes glazed over as if bored with songs. Santa sits on his throne, no longer the jolly old elf. He looks more like a skeleton dressed after its been dead for centuries.

They keep singing, but the notes are wrong. The snow is falling, but the cold is not felt.

It is so hard for zombies to celebrate the holidays.

THE BAD ELF
By Rosè Black

There is a creature who loves this time of the year.

His grin stretches from ear to ear.

He doesn't love this season because the merriment becomes considerable.

He loves it because it is when people make themselves vulnerable.

His ears are as pointy as his teeth.

He loves to hang his prey like a Christmas wreath.

Being a perfectionist is his only flaw.

This makes him one of the most miserable people of all.

The only color in his eyes is a dark blue.

Even from a distance you will know him by his pale hue.

Like a cat he loves to play with his food.

You don't want to know what happens to his victims when he is in a bad mood.

His light frame makes him exceptionably nimble.
Escaping him is futile.

I am sure you have heard the saying of how he likes to nip at your nose.
It is never the only thing that he bites matter how much his victims oppose.

Avoid this creature at any cost.
His name is Jack Frost.

GOOD NEIGHBORS

By Wynne F. Winters

Carol crossed the street, a plate of fresh-baked cookies in her mittened hands. Up and down the avenue, lights twinkled from house eaves, reflecting the warmth within. But the house Carol approached was dark—Mrs. Woodsworth, well into her eighties, was in no shape to hang lights and didn't have any children or grandchildren to do so for her.

Or to shovel her walkway, as Carol soon found. She slowed down, picking her way carefully through the powdery snow. On the way, she passed a snowman with twig arms and pebble features, no doubt erected by neighborhood kids during the school holiday. *I hope they asked permission*, Carol thought, though she doubted it. No one seemed to think of asking poor Mrs. Woodsworth about anything these days.

At last Carol reached the front porch, pausing on the steps to stomp snow off her boots. A tired, brittle wreath hung from the door, crackling as the wind blew through its dry frame. Though it was well into evening, the porch light was still off—not at all like Mrs. Woodsworth, who was fastidious about turning on her light and locking her door well before the sun set.

Ignoring an itch of unease, Carol rang the doorbell. Though she waited several minutes, there was no movement or sound from inside the house.

Concerned, Carol rang the bell several more times. Could the elderly lady have suffered a fall? A heart attack?

"Mrs. Woodsworth? Mrs. Woodsworth! Betty!"

Still no response. In desperation, Carol pounded on the door, only for it to swing slowly inward under her hand.

Lying in the foyer, a pool of darkness soaked into the carpet around her, was Mrs. Woodsworth.

The rest of the evening was a blur of sirens and flashing lights. Carol did her best to answer the police's questions as nosy neighbors crowded beyond the crime scene tape. Even when the ruckus ended and Carol was allowed to go home, the event stayed with her, the image of bloody Mrs. Woodsworth tattooed inside her eyelids.

After lying in bed for several hours unable to sleep, Carol finally gave up and headed to the kitchen to make herself some hot cocoa.

In the early morning hours, she sat with her mug, staring at the empty house across the road, still cordoned off with yellow tape. As she stared, that anxious itch returned, telling her something was off, though her tired mind couldn't quite put the pieces together.

It wasn't until a car drove past, kicking up fresh powder, that she finally realized what was wrong:

The snowman was now on *her* side of the street, its shiny pebble eyes looking right into her window.

YOU DAMN ZOMBIES!

By Anthony Giordano

Black Friday. 5:30 a.m. sharp. Bismarck Grove Mall.

Ambient music kicked in. Bing Crosby crooned from beyond the grave. Security gates of 128 stores rose; clattering in cacophonous unison.

The mass of bodies assembled before Randall's Toy Emporium tried to enter as one; creating an aggravated, impatient bottleneck.

Derek Webb shouldered his way through the stumbling, bickering, undisciplined crowd. There. Right there. Hanging from the rack, third down, fourth from the left. Kamaitachi, the black-clad ninja, rarest character in the Series 3 line of Covert Ops action figures. Moist fingers, beaded with sweat, grasped the priceless find.

He surveyed the crowd. They'd taken notice. They'd torn through racks of secondary and tertiary figures in the line; the lesser heroes and nameless evil minions.

Kamaitachi was the hottest figure of this Christmas season; with prices on the online markets climbing into the hundreds of dollars.

But Webb had it now. And he'd be God-damned if these brainless trend-followers would get it from him.

They were pointing; lowing like distressed cattle. They began closing in on him; a mob predicated upon envious greed.

Webb's egress was halted by a weight dragging on his right side. A woman had flung herself forward, grabbing his wrist and reaching for the figure in his left hand. He yanked his left arm back to distance the figure from her flailing swipes, only to have another desperate lemming attach himself to his left elbow.

A cold sweat formed on Webb's brow. The hell with this. "You damn zombies!" he screamed at the closing mob. What right did they have to steal his find? He had memorized the UPC code on the toy rack; mapped the most expedient route to Aisle 5, where the Covert Ops figures were.

Touched base with the supplier to verify that each store would get at least one Kamaitachi figure.

Randall's was a low-end venue. They were getting exactly one. And it was going to be his.

These brain-dead consumers just shuffled wherever they damned well pleased; expecting their endless hungers to be sated; shuffling and groaning until they got their way. Just a bunch of damn zombies. Mindless, soulless.

"Off of me, you damn zombie!" Webb shouted at the female assailant. He twisted his right hand, pressed it into her face. The zombie snarled; bit deep.

Shit. Webb panicked. I'm infected now.

The walker on his left elbow was growling, twisting. The crowd was closing. He could feel them; smell them. Eyes devoid of intelligence; gaping, groaning mouths. Humanity reduced to a mindless, malicious force of nature.

I'm done for. They're gonna steamroll right over me. Tear me to pieces. Take my Kamaitachi.

It's not fair, he argued to himself. I did my work; my research. All you zombies do is take, take, take.

Webb snapped back to attention. Every zombie movie he'd ever watched had prepared him for this very moment.

He kicked away the female zombie; shook off the elbow-grabber.

With practiced ease, Webb drew the concealed Glock 43 from its back holster and assumed a power isosceles stance. With fluidity born of years of practice, he dispatched his previous assailants with precision headshots; the satisfying, squelching exit wounds spraying waves of blood and brain matter onto stuffed animals and dress-up dolls.

Webb was a portrait of focus. All background noise was tuned out. Gone were the blood- drenched Christmas decorations; the screams of terrified consumers, the Christmas music, still blaring happily above the carnage. Derek Webb kept his pistol trained on the encroaching zombie horde; and then, taking a deep breath, he began thinning their numbers.

BAGS OF COAL
By Kyle Harrison

"You need to behave, or Santa will only bring you coal." my mother always used to tell me as a kid. She often sounded like a pastor berating his parishioners, claiming that good deeds would get them into Heaven.

I grew up a skeptic. My father an alcoholic and my siblings' bullies. Teasing me for my weight they often stole what gifts I got anyway. Why should I care about whether I got coal? I often imagined grabbing a chunk of the stuff and slinging it toward their skulls. That would solve my problems, kill two birds with one stone.

Eventually I insisted on the coal. My desire to be free from them was the only Christmas miracle I ever wanted.

But no matter how bad I was, the gifts kept coming. Mom didn't understand. I reasoned she was just as bad as the rest. The only solution was to get rid of the whole lot. I think I planned it all year, gathering stones and rocks to bash their heads in.

Wintertime came and I followed dad to cut the tree. It was a family tradition. This time though I came home alone. A bloody black stone in my hand.

My older brothers were next, they put up little fight sleeping in their beds.

Last but not least was mother. How I hated her so. The holidays would be blessed only with her gone. I shoved the rocks down her throat, I watched her tongue bulge and her blood vessels snap.

Then I went down to the living room, casting their bodies into the yuletide flame.

My small boyish frame was mesmerized by the flames, impishly dancing across their paralyzed bodies. I liked to think that mom could still feel the fire.

Soon there was nothing left but ash and bits of flesh that had blackened like rocks. I picked them up, a token of holiday cheer.

I made my own coal and I would treasure it.

Then I left, singing tunes of Merry and joy. I walked away as my home burned to the ground.

Finally, I came across a neighbor, their family happy and thankful for the miracles I never saw.

As I glared across the snow and watched them open presents gleefully, I thought of how unfair it was. Why should my suffering be isolated?

I had more than enough to go around.

GO SANGA, FROM CHARLIE
By Tor-Anders Ulven

Her friends spent days, weeks even, on their list to Santa. Vivid descriptions, colors, models, shapes, every little detail seemed to matter. They wanted everything to be perfect. Nothing left to chance. Christmas, to them, was an endless pile of new toys. Things. Objects.

Not her though. She'd sent her list months ago. It only had one item on it. Everyone told her it was impossible, but she believed. Santa could do anything, right? He was magical? So why couldn't he just do this one little thing for her?

She sat in bed and stared at the letter. She'd made a bunch of them. Passed them around to every fake Santa she could find. At the mall, on street corners, even that strange one that stumbled around Main Street with the stinky breath.

To Santa

From Charlie

She hoped Santa would know who she was. She didn't like Charlene very much. It felt so old fashioned and boring. Charlie was playful and cheery. But she didn't feel playful and cheery anymore. But Santa could fix that. Santa could fix everything.

Falling asleep wasn't easy. All those thoughts just spinning around in her head, her body all tense and jittery. She kinda wanted to stay awake, but she knew it would be cheating. You're supposed to sleep, and let Santa do his job. She'd left plenty of milk and cookies, though.

Can't have a hungry, grumpy Santa running around.

It was well past midnight when she finally drifted off to sleep. She dreamt of blood and screams and pain; a dream that had been on repeat for months. Yet, there was something different. A tiny fragment of hope. A split second of peace and quiet. A fleeting sensation of happiness.

She jolted awake in the pitch-blackness of her room. What was that sound? Was it in her dream? Was it real? It had to be night still. Hours until dawn. But she just couldn't help herself. It could be him. It could be Santa.

She carefully made her way down the stairs, all the while worrying that the noise would wake someone up. She almost fell over several times, the full force of her body slamming into the wall as she struggled to regain her balance. But when she finally made her way down, she was alone. Not a soul in sight.

But the cookies were gone. The milk too.

He'd been there! It had to be him! She stumbled excitedly to the kitchen counter, examining the cookie crumbs gleefully. She couldn't think straight. A crippling mixture of anxiety and doubt and anticipation overcame her as she eyed the stocking hanging by the fireplace. It didn't look empty.

She was shaking like a leaf as she slowly took the stocking down. It was heavy. But just the right kind of heavy. A smile stretched from ear to ear as she peered into it.

"Charlie?" her father suddenly stood in the doorway, "What are you doing up?"

"I'm sorry daddy, I just couldn't help myself," she lowered her head apologetically, "But look! Look what Santa brought me!"

It took her father a few seconds to register what she was holding in her hands. What she was cradling so tightly. Then came the scream; a high-pitched hysterical wail.

Charlie didn't understand. Sure, it smelled really bad, and it had all the wrong colors, but it was hers. No doubt about it. Santa did it. The one thing she wanted, and he delivered.

To Santa

From Charlie

All I want for Christmas is my leg back

ITS COAL BLACK EYES

By Aaron Morris

Charlie crouched behind the railing of the porch, scanning the yard for any sign of it. The thing that had taken his friends was still out there somewhere, but Charlie knew that as long as he wasn't touching snow, he should theoretically be safe. But how long could he remain on the porch, before he needed to eat, or worse, use the bathroom?

It was supposed to just have been an exciting afternoon, taking his friends to explore an old abandoned house Charlie had always been told to stay away from. They'd even been confronted by a raving old man as they opened the front door. Something about "leaving it be" and "its coal black eyes". Being teenagers, they'd ignored his warnings.

"We should have listened to that crazy old man", Charlie thought. "Should have just left that old hat in the attic. Must have been some kind of weird magic in it."

After about an hour with no sign of the horror in the snow, Charlie finally felt like it might be safe to attempt escape. Preparing to bolt as soon as his feet his snow, he leapt down the stairs and began sprinting to the far end of the sprawling property.

Charlie was halfway across the yard and feeling like this was going to work when he hit the rock. His foot smacked into it with full force and there was an immediate pain that let him know that it was at least fractured, if not outright broken. He got up and tested it. It would support his weight, but there was no running in his immediate future.

Charlie fought to bite back the panic clawing at his brain as he limped across the yard when he saw it. An old top hat carried on a sharp winter wind that fluttered down onto the snow in front of him, and he knew immediately that it was over. The snow on the ground underneath the hat shuddered before him, as it began to rise, forming the hideous white creature that had eaten his friends.

It opened its mouth to speak, its a voice like an icy knife that cut through Charlie's head, as it spat out one halting phrase.

"Look….at….Frosty…..Go."

The last thing Charlie was aware of was its eyes. Those terrible coal black eyes.

SUPPLY AND DEMAND

by Trevor Newton

Customers snaked from the counter, out the door and into the street. The elderly woman—first in line—smiled and nodded thanks as I dropped a few coins into her hand.

Carefully, I wrapped her ornament with three cotton cloths before placing it into a brown bag with our store logo prominently displayed on the side. I handed it to her with equal grace. She smiled, showing off many missing gaps within her ivory mouth.

I took a deep breath as she walked away. I hated this part.

"Everyone!" I shouted. "Everyone, If I could have your attention, please, I have an announcement!"

A blanket of silence fell over the customers. They stared at me with vicious but fearful expressions, waiting for me to break the absence of sound.

"I regret to inform you that we've just sold the last ornament!" I shouted

"You did what?"

"What the hell is he talking about? That can't be true!"

"Dear God!"

A young man, no older than fifteen, stepped out of line and tossed a soda bottle in my direction with all his might. I ducked. The glass shattered behind me, ricocheting off the wall and into my hair. I quickly stomped my foot against the floorboards; the secret signal to my parents that the customers were beginning to get angry. But they had to know. The shouting was so loud.

"Please!" I began shouting again. "We'll have more soon! Just be patient!"

"You better, you piece of shit!"

"Yeah!"

My heart thudding against my breastplate, I opened the cellar door and nearly tumbled to the bottom. I could hear my mother shouting in pain before I came around the corner; hoarse and riddled with despair. "Dad!" I called. "They're getting violent!"

Mom was laying on the table, her distended stomach kicking and pulsing with movement. Her knees were bent, her legs spread. Dad was face to face with her crotch while my older sister stood next to her. "Push, Momma, push!" she hollered.

Ornaments fell and busted on impact against the concrete floor.

"Get a bucket!" Dad instructed.

RIGEL, THE WRATHFUL REINDEER

By Anthony Giordano

The days after The Great Ride did not shine brightly for Rudolph.

Santa commended him. The Chosen Eight cheered him. But Rudolph did not live with them. He still lived in the common stables, with the other aspirants. He felt their ire, their bitterness, their envy. Felt it in stabbing antlers, jabbing hooves.

His body was battered by violence, his confidence shattered by mockery.

As the New Year dawned, Rudolph's nose emitted the faintest glow, barely illuminating the broken, quivering creature that wept in its stall.

Word travels, as it is wont to do. Word reached the ears of Rigel, the son of Stout – former Chosen and also father of Rudolph - and a common reindeer.

Rigel seethed, his nostrils flared, exhaled puffs of rage. He bellowed in primal fury, made his way to the Workshop.

Rigel was a massive specimen, a half-ton of solid muscle. He could have easily bested the other aspirants, but his common birth precluded his participation.

He cared not. He bore no love for these anemic, inbred fools. He burst into the stable, his impetus exploded the doors to splinters. Most aspirants cowered, pissed themselves. One bold youngblood, a bull named Ribbons, took a defensive stance. Rigel lowered his head, charged, and carved Ribbons into his namesake.

Rigel spared none. He did not stop until the only other living thing in the stable was the sobbing wreck of his half-brother.

He stepped out; the frozen northern winds buffeted his blood-soaked frame. He spied smoke piping from the chimney of the Great Hall. Heard the sounds of laughter, industry.

Rigel's work was not done. He set off at a brisk trot.

Santa felt something was amiss, but could not put a finger on it. The myriad assembly lines were working at optimal efficiency, the cookies and milk were fresh, and Mrs. Claus looked fine as she sashayed past in a high-cut, white-ruffled red skirt.

Post-Christmas toy production was running smoothly, efficiently. So then, what was bothering him?

Santa jumped, startled by a pair of ear-splitting shrieks. The screams had come from the elven sentries outside. Nothing should have caused them to scream like that.

A mighty hoof kicked the door in, knocked it clean off of its hinges. Santa saw one sentry; laid flat, head fully caved in, blood soaking the snow. The other sentry was on his knees, squealing as he scooped at steaming, falling innards, tried in vain to return them to his opened bowels.

In two effortless bounds, Rigel had Santa pinned to the wall. Santa's stomach lurched at the heady odor of Rigel's breath; the stink of reindeer blood, and the sickeningly-sweet tang of elven guts. Ice-blue eyes pierced his soul; conveyed unbridled hate.

The antlers which held him were massive; honed to piercing points, coated in brutal steel tips. Santa's eyes traced along the length of the antlers, saw words scrimshawed along the length of them. Declarations made in the Old Tongue, soaked in the blood of the fallen.

FAMILY. HONOR. DUTY.

VENGEANCE.

Santa stammered. "L-look, Rigel. I-I-I didn't do anything to him..."

"No, Fat Man." Rigel's throaty croak revealed the verbal limits of his half-breed nature. "But you allowed it to happen."

Santa watched in terror as the mass of muscle lunged forth; pushed wicked antlers into his corpulence. His screams echoed through the Great Hall; were heard for miles.

Santa Claus is no god, but he is still a celestial entity. His work mandates a corporeal presence, but his nature grants immortality.

Rigel knew he couldn't kill Santa Claus. But Rigel knew he could hurt him.

And hurt him he did.

CHE EVIL BENEACH CHE SNOW

By Tina Piney

There was once an Evil that roamed the earth, so fierce... so foul, that it could not be destroyed.

Generations of ancient people died in conflict with it, their blood lapping on it in waves, like the sea on the shore. Through trial and error, the ancients finally found a way to contain the Evil.

The people observed that it followed the sun and stayed in the places where the summer never faded. On the coldest days it never appeared. Where stones and blades could not touch it, the cold burned like a flame. A plan was hatched.

When a bitter day finally arrived, the people were ready. Ice, dragged from far and packed in straw, was brought to the Evil where it slept. It was surrounded and forced to move, in fear of the icy touch on its hide.

North they pushed it, night and day. Relief soldiers and stashes of ice were placed strategically along the route until finally it was backed up into a place it could not flee. A high, steep slope of black stone formed a semi-circle at its back. The humans pushed their ice slabs and closed the circle. The north was so cold its body was failing, and the Evil bellowed in pain. The sound echoed and set loose a torrent of ice and snow from the cliff top above.

The Evil was sealed in, unable to move - the cold had trapped it thoroughly. Though it was alive, the menace it was had perished. The people headed back home and within a few generations, the Evil was forgotten.

Life carried on much the same for centuries. Innovations advanced the people, but nothing would have prepared them for the beast that was the industrial revolution. In just a few short years everything began to change. Certainly not the least of which was the change in weather.

When measured against the life span of a human being the change seemed sluggish, but for the trapped Evil, the years went exceedingly quick as the earth began to warm. At first the ice covering it quit accumulating, and then started to decrease. The pain of the ice's touch still burned it, but the hope of revenge warmed its ancient heart and made it beat faster.

It was the mildest Christmas Eve on record. Where furnaces usually pumped a steady stream of heat, windows were open to let in the gentle breeze. The Evil managed to shake itself loose. Ice shards flew and the surrounding hills shook with the echo of its roar. The setting sun behind it cast the shadow of its enormous form on the village in the valley below. It set its merciless eye on the small collection of buildings and, oblivious to the remaining snow that still stung its hairy feet, stomped off to get its revenge.

Its huge green eyes reflected the horror in the faces of the people who tried in vain to scamper out of its way. The blood ran like thick veins in the streets. It danced in them to warm its feet as it started a fire that burned the little town into oblivion.

As it settled in close to the fire to drive the last frost out of its bones, the sun had completely disappeared, and the moon was out. At first light it would set out, back into the world. This Christmas would be warm and green with growth... and red with blood.

NICKLAUS'S GOAT MONSTER
by R. C. Mulhare

From its lair among the spruces and fir cloaking the slopes of the Alpine peaks, crept Krynvpk, the eight hundred-tenth spawn of the Black Goat of the Forest, Mother of a Thousand Young. As one of her younger spawn, their mother had indulged their unusual curiosity, letting them wander and indulge their appetite. For a time, Krynvpk tarried under the spruce trees, eating the odd hunter or woodcutter.

Once in a while, a child or two wandered into the deeper woods, into Krynvpk's clawed tendrils. So savory, these small humans, Krynvpk crept closer to the edges of the forest, the better to find more prey to devour.

In the depths of winter, they reached the edge of the snow-covered village, now well-lit with candles on the windowsills and lanterns at the doors. Bonfires burned at the corners of the town and beside the roads and paths that lead through the village.

Strange lilting sounds like bird songs rose on the cold night wind. Outside a house and beside a well, stood a donkey hitched to a red sleigh laden with bags and baskets. Too easy, but Krynvpk could not resist. They struck the beast with one horn before lashing out their claws. The donkey let out a startled heehaw before Krynvpk engulfed it.

A robust, brown-skinned human male in a long red robe trimmed in black fur appeared, an empty sack over one shoulder. Krynvpk backed away, intending to scramble back to the woods. But the human lunged at them, throwing the sack over Krynvpk's horns. The creature tried to buck, but the human spoke over them in the Elder Tongue, words that bound Krynvpk's feet to the snowy ground. They felt a length of chain with cold iron links wind about the roots of their claws.

"Clawed One, I have seen you lurking in the woods. I know you have had a hand or a claw in devouring the villagers that vanished in the forest."

"How… know?" The human words fit poorly in Krynvpk's mouth.

"I am Nicklaus, the guardian of children. I reward the good and leave the bad to the fate they choose by leaving the path despite the warnings. But even a guardian will take exception in some cases. You crossed a line of your own. I heard my donkey cry. I found you where he stood. That beast helped me with my rounds, bringing food and clothing and cheer to the needy. It did no wrong." Even through the bindings and the cold iron, Krynvpk could read Nicklaus's spirit, his anger and frustration, at the delay caused through losing his donkey, at this predator that took the beast.

"Shuuh... suuh... sorry," Krynvpk slurred.

Nicklaus removed the sack. "Fair enough, but you must make amends. You can help me pull the sled. You can even help me punish some of the bad."

"To...eat?" Krynvpk asked.

"No. By spanking with a broom," Nicklaus said, picking up a broom from beside the well and brandishing it.

Krynvpk reached out, taking the broom in its claws and waving it. "Is... simple. Can... spank."

Even still, for the especially naughty ones, who made Nicklaus's heart ache, the ones who harmed other children, the older humans, animals, they deserved a special visit. One of the baskets holding the gifts would suffice. Krynvpk could spirit them into the woods, to consume them in peace.

The villagers would never miss them.

THE STOCKING RAIDER

By Robert Allen Lupton

Danny tiptoed downstairs after midnight. It was Christmas. He went straight to the fireplace like he'd done every night this week. He took two pieces of candy from each stocking. He added six pieces to his own stocking and put the other six in his pajama pocket.

He took a cookie from the tray left for Santa and stood near the fireplace while he ate it. His sister, Margaret, had been insufferable all week. He shoved his hand into Margaret's unicorn and rainbow covered stocking and grabbed a fistful of candy.

His hand wouldn't come out of the stocking. He quietly fought to free himself. He remembered a story about a little boy caught in a cookie jar and he dropped the candy, but Margaret's stocking held him captive. He tried to unhook the stocking from the mantel, but he couldn't.

He'd stood on his toes to reach into the stocking and he had to maintain that position. It hurt. He wanted to cry, but he didn't want to wake his parents or his siblings. He shifted from one foot to the other. He tried to slowly slip his hand free. It didn't work. He tried to jerk his hand out quickly. He clenched and unclenched his fist, but the stocking trapped him like a mouse caught stealing cheese.

Suddenly, the fireplace vibrated, and Santa Claus rolled into the living room floor. Santa stood up, shook his head at Danny, and signaled the boy to be quiet. Santa took several packages from his bag and placed them under the tree. "Danny, you're on my bad boy list. Twelve years old and robbing stockings, for shame. You're coming with me."

He grabbed Danny's pajama collar, touched the side of his nose, and the stocking released the boy. Santa stuffed him in the toy bag.

It seemed like he was only in the bag for a couple seconds, but when Danny tumbled out, he was in a different place. It was cold. An elf sat at a desk in front of a sign that said, "Santa's Workshop."

The elf said, "Danny Mapplethorpe, you've been a bad boy. You stole eighty-six pieces of candy from Christmas stockings this year. Eighty-six pieces means eighty-six years in Santa's Workshop making toys. You'll make trucks and trains at bench TT28409."

The elf rang a bell and another elf opened the door. "Hello, Danny. I'm your foreman. I'll get you an elf suit and take you to your desk."

Danny grumbled. "I thought elves made the toys."

"We did, but we negotiated a new contract in 1975. Now elves work as supervisors. Try on this red and green hat."

'You can't make me work. I want to go home."

"And so you shall. In eighty-six years, Santa will use his magic to return you home on the same Christmas Morning that you left. As for working, that's entirely up to you, but any day you don't work doesn't count toward your eighty-six years. Here's your workbench. The toy designs are in the drawer. Parts will appear when you need them. Your quota is fifteen units an hour. If you don't meet your quota, you don't eat. Merry Christmas."

Danny refused to work for three days. He was bored and hungry, very hungry. He picked up a toy truck and attached the wheels. While he was painting the truck, a plate of fried chicken appeared on his desk. He reached for the plate and asked out loud. "Is there pie for dessert?"

A HOME FOR CHRISTMAS

By Mama Creep

Christmas this year is going to be different. Instead of working through the Holidays, I've decided to spend it with a family. I've never had a family.

I never knew my mother and father, and I had been bounced from one foster home to another. It was a difficult childhood but I got my bearings and was lucky enough to land a job in a construction company. They offered rooms and free food in exchange for a job and a meager salary. It wasn't at all great but it's way better than being homeless. Eventually, I started doing odd jobs in my spare time just to save money.

My diligence at my day job paid off though-- two years later I got promoted and had people working under my supervision. However, I still know something is missing in my life—I still wanted a family. That's when I decided to go out to the world and sell myself to the world of love. It wasn't quite as fruitful as I'd hoped. I slept with a few women but none of them wanted to commit to a relationship, that was until I saw my first love again-- Jade. She was working in a flower shop around somewhere near my workplace; we lost touch over the years but there she was, attending to customers with a familiar and still captivating smile. She then turned in my direction and when our eyes met, I felt the warm fuzzy feeling in my heart that's just right for this December winter. I thought I found my home.

I quickly went over to greet her and I could tell by her reaction that she was delighted to see me. She flinched and took a step back, eyes wide open. I inquired about roses and made an excuse that I would be giving them to my mother before milking out every bit of info I could get from her.

Her voice was shaking as she answered my questions, but I guess she was just excited to see me. I extended my hand to shake hers; but she resisted. She was playing hard to get again. I always loved that about her.

Days after that lovely encounter I began observing her from afar, just like in high school.

As Christmas approached, I made my way to her home to surprise her, making sure to be as early as possible. It was easy to pick the lock on her door. When I got in, I stopped and took a deep breath, taking in the scent of my will-be new home. I grabbed a nearby picture of her from a drawer and admired her face. I then quickly made my way to her closet and hid there. I heard her open the door while giggling, followed by a man's voice.

I took out my phone and looked at her profile. Jade, 25 years old, in a relationship. I smirked and whispered, *"not for long"*.

SO, WHERE IS IT?

By Michael Borge

"Dad, here come the Carolers again!"

The one thing I don't like about this time of year, is weirdos coming around and singing songs from when Jesus was conceived.

"Honey, run into the house, I'll follow you in," I said to my daughter.

One thing I love about my kid, is that she takes after her old man.

Those bastards are quick; they caught up to me right at the door. One of them grabbed me by the shoulder as I was entering the house.

"Hi, Sir would you mind if we sang you a few carols this evening?"

"No, now fuck off," I said like the loud and proud father that I was.

This guy was persistent however and kept singing. Seriously... why can't I decorate my house in peace?

"Now, now... where is your Christmas spirit? We merely want to bring joy to your night," The caroler inquired.

"To be frank, you're annoying me. Now please, I don't have any figgy pudding for your bullshit," The man grabbed my arm and squeezed, to the point where it was hurting.

He had this grin from ear to ear and looked into my eyes with pleasure.

"Oh, I'm afraid we something else kind sir," he snarled at me. My kid was watching the whole thing and started approaching my handgun on the counter; smart girl.

"Watch out Dad!" she yelled as she fired one off. She missed the caroler, barely. It was enough though to spark something amongst the tree huggers. It wasn't just the guy who had the hots for me, the whole group seemed thirsty. The shot from Maggie was enough to bounce the guy's grip off me as I dashed inside the house and locked the place down.

"Dad, what is going on with those people?" she said. "I don't know kid; but it looks like they want to eat us," I explained. "You mean like zombies, zombie carolers?" she asked. "I know it sounds stupid, but it looks like that's the case here," I said.

"Hey, you know what? Let's run over to Phil next door. I bet he has plenty of guns for this situation," I said.

The kid nodded as she followed me out of the house through the back door. As we were leaving, we could see the carolers swarming the inside of the house through the windows. We made it through to Phil's house and barged in.

"Phil always lets me in; no matter what," I boasted.

The kid rolled her eyes and followed me in. I kept calling for Phil as we entered the house, to no avail.

"We can't wait on Phil; we have to find something. Aw, look... he got me a shotgun for Christmas," I told her, bittersweetly.

As soon as I grabbed, it one of them smashed through the window and threw something at us. It was Phil's head.

The caroler is a fast one. He latches onto me. As I drop the gun, Maggie picks it up quickly. The caroler had a tight grip on me; like he wanted her to shoot me as well. She's crying and shaking as she stared at me with the gun. "Baby, you got to fire at some point otherwise more people are gonna get hurt," I instructed.

She nodded as she took aim. I closed my eyes as a blast rang into the night.

THE DISAPPEARANCE OF THE BRIGANTINE CHILDREN

By N.M. Brown

December 25th, 2018 was the worst day our town had seen since its founding. People call it the Christmas of the Lost. My heart yearns to shatter just writing about it.

Hundreds of parents laid out gifts under their Christmas Trees the night before. Each parent woke up to an identical scene as when they went to sleep. Cookies and milk were untouched, stockings bulged with undisturbed treats, and gifts rested in their places under the Christmas trees; cold from the lack of children's joy. My wife Nina and I were no exception.

I remember us tiptoeing past our son's bedroom as we carried his gifts from Santa down the hall. Nina was tipsy on eggnog and I had a bit of a holiday buzz going myself. We giggled and shushed each other as we stumbled through the house. It's one of my best memories, because it's the last time we ever laughed together. Hell, I can't even remember if we've laughed at all since then.

Ronnie was sleeping in his bed as he always was. I know this because my wife and I bickered about her going in there to give him a goodnight kiss. Looking back now, I thank God that she won that battle. It brings me something close to a hint of solace to know that some of his last moments in this house were spent under his mother's love.

We set up his tricycle; placing the largest yellow bow atop the handlebars that we could find. Nina's mother's tradition dictated that we place an orange at the bottom of his stocking; but the rest was filled with little toys and candy. I groaned as she handed me the full plate of cookies.

"Ugh, why do we always make so many again?" I joked.

"Because it's fun! I don't know about you but when Ronnie and I are making them, a small part of me actually believes they'll be eaten by Father Christmas." She blushed as she placed an amber strand of hair behind her dainty ear.

The thick peanut butter cups atop the cookies were killing me that year. I remember choking on my own saliva;

turned into a biting syrup by sugar. We got it done though, leaving exactly one cookie uneaten for Ronnie to sneak in the morning. The milk however, was all mine.

We awoke to the sounds of sirens and the sun shining through our windows. Nina's bedside clock read 9:18 AM. As much as I tried to fight it, a cold chill enveloped each cell in my body. We knew something was wrong. It's not normal for Ronnie to sleep in past 7 o'clock, but especially not on Christmas.

Nina took off running to his room on instinct, fearing that he'd left the house and gotten hit by a car or injured. I held my breath, praying to hear his sleepy little voice. But so far, my wife's calls had gone unanswered.

"Chris! Ronnie's not here." She yelled down the hall.

"What do you mean he's not here? You haven't even checked the living room."

"CHRIS, I'm telling you our baby's not fucking here!" She choked out through sobs. Her footsteps boomed through the house and I hear the front door slam shut as she left.

My breaths started coming in faster and larger puffs as I tried to process the quickly unfolding situation. The robe I wore the night before was disgusting on my skin. Nothing felt right. It's like in that moment, I already knew that the joy in my life was over. I just couldn't accept it.

Thousands of scenarios invaded my rationality from the corners I'd done so well at keeping them hidden in. Each fear I've ever had as a parent that was always out of reach for someone like me was now all too tangible.

When I opened my front door, I was met with an overwhelming number of sobs and wails. Dozens of people on our street were outside of their homes. Most of them were crying hysterically, some wore blank expressions of shock. Others demanded to search every person's home on the block who didn't have children.

I held my wife as she tumbled to the ground. An officer had told her every child in the county had gone missing Christmas Eve night. My brain fought with itself as to how I should feel. On one hand, hundreds of children kidnapped at the same time would be hard to house and even harder to hide. On the other hand though, the irrational part of my mind told me that something unnatural had happened altogether, and none of us would ever see our children again.

As the months went on and the seasons changed, most of the parents in town had reached the same heart rendering conclusion; until this morning.

Nina and I are still married, though we sleep in separate bedrooms now. She got on this kick right away about trying for another baby; which I was... am fully against.

First off, I felt that if we had another child we would be replacing Ronnie. Even worse, we'd be accepting the fact that he was never coming back. We didn't know that. I always held out heartbreaking hope that they'd find him; find all of the missing kids.

Secondly, if something in this town was taking children, I certainly didn't want to give them a new target.

Nina's screams woke me from a heavily medicated sleep.

"Chris, it's Ronnie! He's home!"

The covers are thrown in a corner of the room as I spring out of my now cold bed. Each step closer to my son fills my heart with a happiness I feared I no longer possessed. The long lost and dearly missed sound of his voice stops me cold. Whoever is talking to Nina is not our little boy. His voice sounds low and detached; like it's being run through a voice synthesizer.

My stomach heaves when I finally bring myself to finish taking the steps to his bedroom. A mutilated, mangled body lay in the bed that was once meant for our son. Don't get me wrong, he is alive and healthy. He just came back...wrong.

His face is a mingle of features that seem random at best. It was as if Picasso had genetically designed a human being and brought them to life. One leg is shorter than the other by six inches. His left arm is thinner and four shades lighter than his right. The left eye placed haphazardly on his face is one of the only qualities that proves to me its really him. The eye on the right looks like it belongs to someone else entirely.

Once again, the street is thick with police officers, but fire rescue is here this time too. Parents are holding disfigured children as they're laid on stretchers. Each one yelling about how they're fine and don't need treatment. I caught eyes with the little girl who lived across the street from us and I recognized one of them as my son's.

Whatever happened, it's as if each child was put into a machine, had their DNA all mixed and randomized, then spit back out. The children walk, talk, eat and play like they always have. It's almost impossible to tell whose is whose anymore.

This Christmas, I'm hearing whispers of a reckoning of sorts. The town leaders and religious figures have labeled these children, some of them their own, as abominations. I've heard there will be a massive event to return the children to the melting pot from which they came.

I'm writing this as a warning and for proof for Ronnie down the line to know that his Dad and Mom love him, and never regret a single thing about who he is. We're taking him the Hell out of here. By the time they notice a child's missing, we will be long gone. Surely there's somewhere in the World that will greet him with acceptance and love. We're just happy to have him back.

Though, I can't help but wonder what surprises Nina and I will wake up to this Christmas Day morning.

ALL THE CREATURES WERE STIRRING

by Michelle River

Looking back, I should have known something wasn't right, but at the time it never occurred to me to wonder where the trees had come from, or who put them there. I was just doing what everyone else in town was doing. Buying a Christmas tree, or should I say picking up a free Christmas tree. Jerry's Used Car Lot had been abandoned for little over a year now, ever since the economy in our little farming community crumbled. You see, when there isn't enough money to put the same food on your table that you grow yourself, there sure isn't enough to spend on a used car. So Jerry packed it in, along with a few other local businesses, and got out as fast as they could. Lucky buggers.

So when, seemingly overnight, Jerry's abandoned lot of crumbling asphalt and oil stains became a bustling little

Christmas tree market with free trees, adorned with what looked like handmade pinecone elves, and a "tree care package", we all just thanked our lucky stars and grabbed a tree. Now, some may have complained the sap was a little bit red and smelled of old pennies, and the spruce needles seemed unusually sharp, but it was with a smile on their face as they loaded it into their rusting old ford and skedaddled home.

I unloaded the tree carefully, mindful of the delicate looking figures and sharp needles, placed it right in front of our picture window in the living room and stood back. I must admit, it looked mighty fine sitting right there. I remember the first thing Jenny said when we walked into this house over thirty years ago, that window was the perfect Christmas tree window, and darn it if she wasn't right. For the last thirty years, we placed our tree right there and watched our boy Jimmy opening gifts year in and year out. This would be the first year it would be just me on Christmas morning. You see Jimmy and his new wife and baby are up north spending Christmas with her family, and my Jenny passed this summer. The cancer took her quickly, which is a blessing they tell me, but I can't see how it is yet. She was always the one that took care of the Christmas tree, got up every morning and made it a sugar-water mixture with a shot of whiskey, filled it every day. Said it made the tree green and strong, even left me her recipe on a card before she died, the silly woman.

So just like my Jenny did for all those years I fed the tree, day in and day out, the same recipe down to the type of whiskey, only with much different results. Within a week the thing was dead, the sharp pin-like needles had browned and littered the floor like glass shards. Even the dam elf ornaments had shriveled into dried-out husks and fallen from the tree, their little faces somehow frozen in agony. I tossed the whole lot right on the bonfire that night and poured myself a thumb of whiskey and apologized to the tree for letting it die, as the wood pop and screamed within the flames. I could almost see Jenny now, shaking her head from across the fire. She would have had a good laugh at me killing that tree so quickly.

I was tidying up the room the next morning, getting ready for a treeless Christmas when I noticed the box mark "Important Care Instructions", that I had carelessly tossed in the corner and forgotten. Now I have never been one for instruction for anything let along a tree, but I opened the box curious to see what tricks or secrets could have saved the tree from its fate in my fire pit.

Inside was a letter marked "Rules", a plastic bucket marked "Food" and a large ladle. I opened the envelope and began reading.

Rule #1: *Place tree in a window which features direct sunlight.*

Rule #2: *Do not place the tree near an open flame*

Rule #3: *Do NOT remove Wooden Elf Decorations.*

Rule #4: *Feed the tree with the provided "Food" marked container ONLY. Do not add sugar or water. The food has been engineered to provide the tree with all the sustenance it needs.*

Rule #5: *You must feed the tree after dusk. Do NOT feed the tree while the sun is out.*

Intrigued, I opened the bucket marked "Food", a vile sour smell wafted towards me, it reminded me of the time I found the bloated corpse of dead skunk inside an old freezer four summers ago. Inside the bucket was a tar-like substance, almost black in colour with a sheen like an oil slick in the rain. I immediately closed the lid and put the container straight into the trash. Looks like the tree was always going to end up on the fire.

Three days later on Christmas morning, I was awoken by screams. It didn't sound like the normal "Christmas cheer" shouts of joy. For a moment I lay there listening intently, wondering if it was all just a dream. But another scream pierced the air, shaking me to my core. It was close, it sounded like it was coming from the Gray's house next door. I quickly grabbed my shotgun from under the bed and ran next door.

I don't know what I was expecting to find, a thief stealing gifts, a drunk vagrant passed out on their couch? But what I did find was something I can never forget. The sight of it is burned in my memory. I found Mrs. Gray first, her body torn to shreds at the bottom of the steps, her head twisted at an ungodly angle from the fall.

I could hear the boys screaming from in their rooms, the loud sounds of footsteps and furniture being tossed around echoed through the hall. I bolted up the stairs, taking them two at a time, finding Mr. Gray just outside his bedroom door, his body ripped to shreds much like Mrs. Gray's.

Whatever this was, it wasn't just an intruder.

Shotgun and poised outside their door, I shouted out to the boys, "Tommy. Jacob. I am coming in."

With a swift kick, the door flew open. Tommy and Jacob had taken refuge on their beds, below them a swarm of pinecone elves with daggers and claws were attacking. The same elves from the Christmas trees, but at least double in size, they must have kept growing after the trees were brought in the house.

They turned towards me, eyes filled with pure black hatred and mouths of sharp pointed teeth. I quickly fired, an explosion of wooden limbs went flying, black ooze splattered the bed, as I fired again, hoping to at least scatter then while I grabbed the boys. I ran to the bed, kicking the injured and disoriented elves on the way and grabbed the boys, one in each arm and ran out of the room.

"Close your eyes, boys don't look. Please don't look." I said as we made our way down the stairs and out the door, their tiny arms holding on to me for dear life. We had almost made it to my front door before we say them. Thousands of elves began piling out of the neighbouring houses, headed towards us. Their screams of war piercing the air.

With no time to think I jumped into my truck, thankful I always leave the keys in the visor and fled. My plan was to head to the nearest police station, but we have been on the road for hours now trying to find a place that hasn't been touched by the free trees. But everywhere we go we find a "Free Tree Lot" and a town filled with Christmas screams.

(Π)EE(ΠIƆ SAΠƆA

BY Charlotte O'Farrell

It didn't seem long ago that I was visiting little Jason's parents when they were children, dropping presents into their stockings on Christmas Eve night. But here I was, looking down at the sleeping boy, dreaming away like an angel.

I held the year's most popular toy in my hands: a remote-control car that could go up walls and across ceilings.

The bells on my coat jingled as I got closer to his bed. Suddenly, he jolted awake.

Jason didn't cry out. His face lit up with the joy of a thousand Christmas mornings.

"Santa!" he cried. I put a gloved finger to my lips.

"Shhh. You don't want to wake your little sister."

"Oh – sorry Santa."

I grinned.

"No problem, my boy. You've been very good this year. You've tried hard at school. You haven't been too nasty to your sister – although you could work on that one next year, if you please. And you always do the dishes when your parents ask you to."

He nodded so hard I thought his head might topple off.

"Yes, yes Santa! I've been good – I promise."

I pulled out the toy car from behind my back. His eyes widened.

"Thank you!" he cried.

He held out his hands hungrily. He looked surprised when I pulled it away.

"Not yet. You have to give me something first."

"Anything!"

I leaned in close.

"Would you give me... your soul?"

He lowered his arms. Did seven-year-olds even know what souls were?

"Go on," I coaxed, grinning. "You want to make Santa happy, don't you? Say you'll give me your soul."

"Erm – okay, sure."

And that was it. The magic from his words worked instantly. He fell down backwards on his pillows, asleep.

He would forget his promise. The magic would replace the memory of me with dreamless sleep. He would grow up, learn that Santa "isn't real", and in time he'd pass on my legend to his children. The magic would make him think he'd bought his kids the presents they found in their sacks at Christmas. I'd visit them in turn on their seventh Christmas Eve night, hot presents of the year in my hands, and take their souls too.

He'd remember one day, though: on his deathbed, eighty years from now. I'd reappear on that day to claim my prize. I wouldn't look like a jolly bearded guy then – he'd see me in my true form. I often thought the shock would've killed my victims, if they hadn't already died!

Then I'd take him to the North Pole to make and wrap toys, a job without any respite. I'd release his soul eventually – I'm kind that way – but only once he'd made the toys that entrapped one hundred others in the same way.

"Merry Christmas, Jason," I whispered to the sleeping boy, placing the car in the sack by his bed.

SACKED

By Akshay Patwardhan

Buddy the elf glanced across the whirring conveyor belt full of Christmas toys and wrapping paper at the elderly elf named Alfie. Alfie was old--the oldest that Buddy had ever seen in the workshop. The fat man in the red suit--Santa Claus.

Buddy felt sickened to say his name--would usually bring in a fresh worker every time an elf showed the first signs of aging.

Alfie was essentially a living treasure. He was ninety-seven days old--elves have surprisingly short life spans, and their hair begins to whiten by their mid-sixties. Alfie's pupils were pallid and milky, covering almost the entirety of his iris.

It was a damn miracle that he could even see what was a foot in front of him. Alfie's fingers were arthritic and awkwardly bent, and his breathing had become an engine-like rasp since just ten days ago. But Alfie was a determined fellow, Buddy could see. He was determined to avoid the grisly fate that his co-workers had met for as long as he could.

Buddy glanced at the indoor balcony from where the fat man was watching the workers waste their lives away, being forced to make toy-after-toy for those damn ungrateful brats on Christmas Eve. The fat man was leaning over the railing with his fluffy white mittens and pointy red hat, grinning through his overgrown, snow-like beard at the desperate workers. Buddy felt vomit rising up his throat, but he clamped his mouth shut.

Buddy suddenly heard Alfie's deep grunt as the old elf fumbled with an action figure's loose arm, but then there was a sickening crack as his hips gave out. Alfie shrieked and glanced up at the fat man who was smiling at him. Buddy stared in horror as Alfie tried to lift himself up with his bent fingers, but the pain was simply too enormous for such an elderly elf.

Buddy heard a faint tapping as the jolly, fat man skipped down the stairs and grasped Alfie's shivering, calloused hand. The old elf was lifted over the fat man's shoulders with a wheezing shriek, and the duo strolled over to a steel padlocked window, Buddy's heart sinking into oblivion. He'd seen this happen dozens of times throughout his short life, but every time, something inside of him broke.

Outside the window was the reindeer pen, and all the other elves--young and old—were holding their breath with apprehension as Alfie futilely beat the fat man's back with closed fists and stared at his co- workers with a desperate expression that could only mean "help me".

Buddy could hear the reindeer snarling and yelping as Alfie was edged out the window, and he could hear Alfie shrieking as he saw the monsters prowling in the darkness. The worst of them was Rudolph--the fat man's favorite pet--whose nose was always soaked with the blood and viscera of the old elves. Buddy winced as he heard the pain-filled screams and the riled-up howls of the beasts.

Suddenly, the screaming was cut short, and the fat man emerged from the window and grinned at the workers.

The fat man went through a sandalwood door and returned with a twenty-something elf. He brought her to where Alfie had been working, and Buddy noticed her naive, unknowing face.

"Buddy, this is Penny. Show her the ropes," the bearded man said cheerily and strolled back upstairs, observing them.

"Welcome to Santa's workshop," Buddy said with a strained, twitching smile which faded as the fat man momentarily glanced away. "There's no way out," he whispered.

THE CHRISTMAS KILLER

By Kim Plasket

You stand at the window, the Christmas tree behind you. It's twinkling lights hide the fact there is a killer on the loose. The blood-stained snow showed the path he travels isn't a straight path. He seems to be traveling all over the town. You wait, to try to figure when he will strike next. Part of you wants to follow him, you wonder why he takes such a winding path; while part of you wants to hide from him.

The Christmas killer doesn't care who stands in his way, he will be more than happy to take out a whole town. He wanders, killing randomly.

This has been going on for days now, most folks have taken to hiding in their homes. It started in the center of town; he blew up half the block. He knew once that happened there would be some who would try to leave town, he wanted the ones left to be scared. You knew this was why his path seemed random; so nobody knew just where he was going to strike next.

Some would ask you why you stayed since you knew he would not stop until everyone was dead or somehow, he died.

You knew others tried to kill him shortly before they died. The bloody trail, the tinsel, and ornaments he left in his wake proved he was almost impossible to kill. Nobody knows just what he looks like; he is a shadow in the night.

He is named The Christmas Killer simply because he goes from town to town on Christmas Eve and starts to kill. By the time Christmas Day rolls around, half the town is dead while the other half's left terrified.

You hear a scream from right down the street. You stare at the door, just wanting him to come in.

You will be the one who ends his spree.

After the scream there is not a noise, you wonder if he is standing right outside the door. Wishing you had a weapon you walk to the door, as you pass the hall you hear a noise.

Turning around you see him standing there; blood dripping from his face. Tinsel sticks in his hair as he grins at you.

You take a step towards him; he seems to take a step back. You see the look on his face. He seems almost afraid;

as if you know something he doesn't. You wonder why he looks scared when you're the one who is terrified.

He was grinning but the grin's faded. You approach him, wondering why he hasn't struck yet. You know he's not done killing, but for some reason...something about you stops him in his tracks.

The hall's dark, the only thing down the hall is the mirror. You stop to realize the reason you lived while others died. You smile, knowing this night is far from over.

Walking away, you leave a trail of tinsel as you continue your bloody killing spree.

THE SNOWDOME

By Cecelia Hopkins-Drewer

On Christmas Eve I was given a glass dome filled with water. Inside were little figures, kneeling shepherds, sheep, mother, father and babe in manger.

When I shook the dome, fragments of glitter rose to the surface and floated down, settling gently upon the nativity. It was magic. Fascinated, I looked closer, and the figurines looked back at me. Their mouths opened in frozen screams; limbs stretched in unproductive movement.

The snowdome was my favorite toy; until one day I woke up and looked at the world from the inside. Trapped in glass forever, with tinsel falling on my head.

WHEN KRAMPUS COMES

By C.L. Williams

This Christmas, I know I've been good

I have done all the good that I could

Then come the sleigh bells ringing that fateful night

Instead of joy, I am now drenched with fright

I hear the footsteps, that is not Santa up there

It's something else to give me a scare

I soon realize it is Santa's nemesis

It's Krampus, the Santa Claus antithesis

I've not been as good as I had hoped

When I saw the Christmas demon, I choked

I know he is here to condemn my soul

After all I've done, it has taken its toll

CHRISTMAS DINNER ON THE TABLE

By Diane Arrelle

Georgi pulled down his fur hat and wandered the woods searching for something, anything, to bring home for Christmas Dinner. Looking for animal tracks, he suspected they'd already eaten every living creature in Nebraska. Hell, in the entire North.

Shivering in the subzero cold, Georgi grasped his jacket tighter and started toward town. He was thinking about the Christmas roast. At least the townspeople wouldn't turn to his family. He and Nina had supplied little Marie for the summer barbeque. Poor Nina, still crying about their little girl.

As he left the woods, the frozen breath caught in his throat. Silver spaceships occupied the entire field around town. He ran to the people crowding around the ships.

"What's happening?" he gasped, winded, the icy air burning his lungs.

"We are saved!" the mayor shouted. "Our new friends from across the galaxy learned of our perpetual winter and brought us food."

Georgi popped a proffered crystal into his mouth only to spit the vile tasting thing out. His mouth burned and blisters covered his tongue.

The "food" they'd brought obviously wasn't edible to humans.

Everyone cried out as one, "We're doomed!"

But then Georgi smiled, and shouted over the wails. "This is no way to behave.

We must invite our new friends to dinner."

A moment of silence, then cheers of agreement.

That night, Christmas Eve, the townspeople had the best tasting roasts they'd had in years and there were probably enough left over to freeze for next Christmas as well.

COAL FOR CHRISTMAS

By Stephanie Levy

Victoria had not been a good girl this year. She'd fought, let her grades drop, and lied.

But every time she passed Santa at the mall, she begged to see him. Each time, her parents sighed, but took her anyway.

"Have you been a good girl this year?" Santa always asked. She'd plead her case, knowing she hadn't been. And at the very important question, "What do you want for Christmas?" she would only ask for one thing.

"Santa, I want a kitten."

This was no surprise to her parents. Victoria asked for one every time they passed the pet store. She loved the black kittens with the sharp, little baby teeth and needle-like claws. But the answer was always no, and she'd scream, needing to be dragged away from the store.

Initially, her parents proposed the kitten as a reward--for better grades and no more calls from the principal.

Excitedly, Victoria promised, but always broke her vow by the end of the week.

On Christmas morning, Victoria eagerly opened her presents. Threats of getting nothing had clearly been empty, as there were boxes and bags wrapped in holiday paper and bows. Her parents sat sleepily on the couch, drank coffee, and nodded to campy Christmas songs as Victoria dumped her stocking's contents--a toothbrush, bubblegum flavored tooth-paste, mint flavored floss, and other practical things.

Nothing to brag about.

Even the gifts, with deceptive wrapping, were packages of socks, underwear, and clothes.

"That outfit is for tonight's dinner at grandma's," her mother said, smiling.

After a whirlwind of unwrapping, Victoria came to one conclusion. Santa was a fraud! Just when she was about to throw a tantrum, a shiny red box with a bright green bow caught her attention from behind the tree. In the midst of cleaning up the living room, her parents weren't watching.

"A kitten!" Victoria shrieked when she opened the box. She lifted a small, fuzzy, black kitten with a bell around its neck and tree lights reflecting in its big green eyes. "His name is Coal."

Her parents jumped and looked at each other with confusion.

For the rest of the day, Victoria was a perfect girl. She behaved, remembered her manners at Christmas dinner, and even played well with her cousins. Her mom and dad drove home that night happy it had been such a peaceful holiday.

Being carried up to bed, Victoria groggily asked for Coal, but the kitten was already waiting on her bed. Her dad tucked her in, kissed her forehead, and left her room. Victoria dozed, twirling her fingers in the kitten's fur.

"Why did you buy her a cat?" her father asked in bed a short while later.

"What do you mean?" her mother sat up. "I figured you got it."

"No. She didn't deserve it."

Rolling to her side, Victoria held Coal close to her chest. He was so warm and snuggly. A few moments later, something also rubbed against her back. She turned and, by the light of her unicorn night-light, saw another pair of green eyes.

"Another kitten?" she asked, sleepily.

Kittens suddenly appeared around her room. Their paws became smoky tendrils and enwrapped her. She tried to scream but was muffled and removed--disappearing with the kittens into the darkness of the void.

Santa knew who was naughty or nice, after all.

YUKI

By Amber Keener

It always snows when she arrives. That's how I know that's she's coming. Yuki with her long silky raven hair that shines a midnight blue in the light, skin pale as ivory, and icy blue shaped almond eyes. I met her five years ago on Christmas day when I decided to head up to my hunting cabin in the mountains. I lived only an hour away, and despite my wife's protest, I left to go hunt deer for the day with the plan to return just in time for Christmas dinner.

The first flakes of snow began to fall as I skinned my prize, a well sized doe, before Yuki came walking out of the wood. Whatever misgivings I had about the situation fell away as she spoke to me. I do not recall what we talked about then, I just remembered that we had talked long into the night, and that when she finally had to leave that I felt a great sorrow wash over me.

My wife, furious that I had come home after midnight, didn't speak to me for days, and even after spending several weeks making amends, I still risked the ire of my family by making the hour drive up to the cabin on

Christmas day in the hopes that I might see Yuki. As the snow began to fall, I felt joy at seeing Yuki walk out of the woods toward me. This time I had brought my smoker with me, and together we set about skinning and cooking the buck that I had shot earlier that morning. It had been and remained in the following years to come the best Christmas ever. However, when Yuki left, I knew until I saw her again it would be agonizing.

Over the next two years my relationship with my family began to fall apart. Even though I devoted every day to them, they took it as an insult that I left them every Christmas to hunt and see Yuki. The hunting had become worse as well, making it harder to find game each year. Yuki enjoyed game that had been freshly killed, so last year when I had only managed to catch a few wild hares, she mentioned that she may not return the following year.

My heart sunk in fear at losing her. I needed to see her again no matter the cost. I told her as much and begged that she give me a chance to prove that I could do better. She nodded her head and disappeared into the dark night. This last year a dark cloud as hung over my head as I contemplated my task. If I could not hunt something of worth, then Yuki would never come back.

The agony of it tortured me, driving away any thoughts of hope and happiness, until this morning when my wife, my dear wife, gave me the best of Christmas gifts. She announced that her and our children would be joining me at the cabin this Christmas. My anger lasted for a moment before turning into joy. The answer to keeping Yuki had never shown brighter. We all climbed into my truck and made our way to the cabin.

With the last light of the day fading in the western sky I now wait. My wife and children our in the cabin, I made sure that they were properly prepared for Yuki's arrival. As the first flakes of snow begin to fall, I smile. It always snows when she comes.

UNDER THE MOON

By Gabriella Balcom

Jill blinked awake as light shined in her eyes from the sliver of moon above her in the sky. She rolled onto her stomach but felt something pressing into her, and shifted to her side. When she still felt whatever-it-was poking her hip, she changed position again. With Christmas only three weeks away, she'd decided to go camping, taking advantage of the mild temperatures before the next cold front.

Finally comfortable, Jill dozed off.

Something icy touched the middle of her back, and she shrieked. Sitting up in her sleeping bag, she looked around wildly. Clouds obscured the moon, but she could see well enough to know nothing was nearby. Brain fuzzy, she yawned widely and assumed she'd been dreaming. She didn't know why, but something felt wrong. Off.

Then it hit her. She'd gone to sleep in her tent but saw it a few feet away, right where she'd set it up.

A faint scraping noise behind her grabbed her attention.

Santa sat a few feet away in traditional Christmas attire, scratching his large belly. But the resemblance to the joyful Saint Nick ended there.

His face wasn't jolly, but a twisted, leering parody with glowing-black eyes, and skin that looked like raw hamburger meat.

Breath catching in her throat, Jill's heart pounded. This had to be a dream. She pinched her leg, but Scary Santa was still there. His beard moved, and she grimaced, realizing white worms hung from his chin, twisting in all directions.

The nightmare Santa wheezed, its mouth curving into a horrifying grin.

Jill scrambled to her feet, planning to dash to her car, but lost her balance as the ground beneath her moved. Glancing down, she froze, not believing her eyes.

Bones littered the ground. Some moved, inching their way toward others, connecting into feet, legs...

A complete skeleton soon stood close to her.

Jill turned to run, but discovered other skeletons had formed behind her, barring her way. One pointed a bony finger, tipped with a long black fingernail, at her. Before she

261

could react, it slashed her arm with the nail, tearing off a strip of her skin and bringing tears to her eyes. The skeleton raised the piece to his mouth, licking it before devouring it whole.

Another lunged forward and yanked a clump of hair from her head, making her cry out in pain. She gingerly touched the spot, whimpering when her fingers came away red. The skeleton tossed the clump to Santa, who sucked on the bloodied ends.

Chest tightening, Jill felt sheer panic racing through her, and struggled to think of a way out.

Her breath came faster and faster; she was panting within seconds.

She yelled for help when Santa stood, shuffling closer, and the skeletons advanced. Jill wailed as they roughly snatched hair from her head. Her wails turned into hysterical screams when they tore skin from her arms, then chunks of flesh.

Soon, all that remained of Jill were drops of blood and an empty tent.

ƉECEIVIŊǴ ǴREETIŊǴS

By Thomas Baker

Barry woke up drenched in a cold sweat. He was in a complete state of bewilderment. The last thing he remembered was sitting at the dining room table in his house, enjoying a post-Christmas Eve dinner bottle of wine while his wife Christy loaded the dishwasher in the kitchen.

The two of them had spent a great day together for once. They put their differences and bickering aside for the holidays, it seemed. Barry even took to helping dig the hole outside for the new fish pond scheduled for installation in the Spring. Now he lay here, blinking his eyes several times, trying to gather himself. Barry could not move much, he felt caged in, like someone had tucked him in too tight under the covers. His vision began to adjust to the colored lights that dangled in his face, he realized they were Christmas lights.

It was upon investigating them further and tugging at them he realized someone locked him inside some small space. Barry was pushing up against the top of the enclosure when he spotted the red envelope taped above his head, with his name written on it. It was his wife's handwriting.

He pulled it down and opened it, using a strand of the battery powered, multicolored Christmas lights to see it a little more clearly. He pulled a fancy looking Christmas card out; it was white with glittery, silver snowflakes all over it and read *"Happiest Of the Holiday Season To You!"* But instead of the word *"You"* someone had scratched it out with a black sharpie and instead said *"Me"*.

When Barry opened the card, something fell out onto his face. He gathered it up and in the rainbow glow of the lights he saw three photos of himself, in his car, with his mistress Rita. They were photos of the two of them in some very precarious positions. Anxiety and panic started to set in as his breathing quickened.

Barry's hands trembled as he held the card back up. On the right-hand side of the card was the generic holiday greetings.

On the left side, again in his wife's handwriting it read, *"You dug this hole yourself! Merry Christmas and Happy Rotting In Hell, Love Christy."*

MORE THAN ONE KIND OF FRUITCAKE

By Aurora Lewis

I opened the front door and Mrs. Myers shouted Merry Christmas and hand me her disgusting fruitcake that she gave us every year. I put in extra rum and a little something special this year she told me. My parents would have preferred the bottle of rum. On the entry-way table were festively wrapped plates of fudge, I grabbed one for Mrs. Myers who appeared giddier than usual, perhaps she took a few sips of that rum? Opening her gift, she greedily shoved a piece of fudge into her mouth, mumbling "My diabetes, you know." As she walked back home. I placed the fruitcake on top of the box of clothes my mother planned to take to the Mission tomorrow.

The next morning as my father was lifting the box, saw the fruitcake and chuckled," I hope someone enjoys Millie's fruitcake."

"She said it has extra rum this time and something special." I told him, rolling my eyes.

"There isn't enough rum to make me eat that crap." My father continued, laughing.

"You two cut it out, it's the thought and someone down at the Mission will enjoy it." My mother scolded.

When we arrived at the Mission, an odd, little man covered in dirt was sitting on the curb. He smelled like a dead rat.

"Got any Christmas eats, there?" The man asked my father who was carrying our box.

My father looked at the fruitcake and back to the man. "Would you like a fruitcake?"

"You bet your bottom!" He said excitedly while looking at my mother.

My family and I went inside and delivered our box of clothes. When we came out the old man was nowhere to be seen, but the wrapping from the fruitcake was on the curb. My little sister picked it up and tossed it in the trash can near the Mission steps. As we were making our way back home, there was a sudden thud on the roof of our car. My father pulled over; the old man leaped down in front of us. My father got out and asked him what the hell was going on?

"Name's Mitch, Mitch Myers." The smelly old guy said in a low menacing voice.

"Why in the hell were you on top of our car?" My father shouted.

"Are you related to Millie?' My mother's shaky voice asked from her car window.

"You bet your bottom, I've got a little something for you and your hubby."

Before my father could say anything, the old geezer was holding Millie's fruitcake and was shoving it down my father's throat. My mother, sister and I started screaming, the old guy started laughing like a lunatic. My father fell to his knees clutching at his chest spitting out chunks of fruitcake. Mitch started walking towards my mother's car window and he still seemed to have a lot of that fruitcake left. My mother quickly rolled up her window. Mitch let out a howling laugh and was suddenly gone along with the fruitcake.

My mother, my sister, and I helped my father back to the car and my mother drove us home.

When she got there, she went directly to Millie's and banged on her door.

"What's the matter, Edith?" She asked my mother.

"Is your brother some kind of nut case?" My mother screamed.

"What brother?" Millie asked, confused.

Your brother Mitch, I think he's some kind of deranged madman!" My mother said, still screaming.

"My brother Mitch, what are you talking about? Mitch has been dead for over 10 years."

CHE KALIADY ANGEL

By Drew Starling

The sound came from the bathroom. Plastic and metal clanking on the tile floor. Probably Juan trying to pee and missing the bowl. Dumb kid. I got up to go check it out. Not like I was sleeping anyway. It was Christmas Eve after all.

No one in the bathroom at first glance, but all kinds of crap from the cabinets littered the ground. Something scuttled behind the door of the large armoire next to the tub. I yanked it open, and Juan was inside, curled up on the bottom shelf.

His face was vacant, like he'd just seen a ghost. The boy wouldn't speak. He just wanted to hide. I reached to scoop him up, but he winced and recoiled. Black marks stretched across his forearm, a handprint as if someone had dipped their hand in ash and wrapped their fingers around my kid brother's wrist. Juan motioned me to come closer. I leaned in. He spoke. The faintest of whispers.

"There's an angel downstairs."

His words sent a shiver through my body. This black mark on his arm terrified me. Nightmares are one thing, mysterious handprints are another. I pulled him out of the armoire and washed his arm. Thankfully, the stuff came right off. Whatever it was.

On the way back to my room, my eye caught the soft, rainbow-colored glow of our Christmas tree from downstairs. Angel? What's he talking about? I had to find out.

The temperature plummeted as I descended the stairs, as if the heat hadn't been on in hours. It occurred to me that Juan could have been talking about this Christmas angel our mother brought back from Belarus last summer. The "angel" was heinous. It had a pale-white face, red eyes, and black wings wrapped around its body. Mom explained that in Belarus they celebrate Kaliady, a tradition that mixes elements of old pagan culture. Christmas was darker there. A little more rooted in lore, and a little less rooted in capitalism.

A foreign energy stopped me dead in my tracks when I reached the living room. I noticed the Kaliady angel on top of the Christmas tree was gone, but in the corner of the room stood a tall figure wearing a long black robe. Red eyes glowed from underneath its hood. The angel had changed form. I don't know how or why; I just knew. I felt parlayed.

I tried to scream but nothing came out. The angel made no sound and made no movement. It just stood there. We both just stood there. The only movement in the room was my breath as it hit the freezing cold air.

After what seemed like hours, the angel's eyes stopped glowing. It emitted a low, croaking sound, like a tree branch bending in the wind, and it lifted its arms to pull back its hood. It revealed a featureless, white orb of a head. The mouthless head hissed at me in a an utterly alien voice.

"Join ussss."

It moved towards me and reached out a bony white hand, its palm covered in black ash.

Something rose up inside of me and I regained control of my motor functions. I lunged for the light switch on the wall. When the lights came on, the robed figure was gone, and mom's Kaliady angel fell to the ground where the figure once stood.

I stared at the inanimate object. It seemed to stare back at me. I picked it up and threw it into the fireplace. It hissed as I watched it turn burn to ash.

DOWN THROUGH THE CHIMNEY

By Radar DeBoard

He grabbed onto the side of the chimney and climbed up onto the top of it. He placed a hand on both sides of it and slowly lowered his feet into the dark beneath him. He picked up the sac beside him and let it fall down into the unlit fireplace. He took a deep breath and then placed his hands against the inside brick walls and slowly lowered himself. It was a slow process as he moved each limb only a few inches at a time. About halfway down he could feel his legs start to get tired. He carefully picked up the pace and climbed down several feet in little over a minute.

When there was only a few feet from the entrance of the fireplace he dropped down the rest of the way. His feet landed with a thud that was partially muffled by the large amount of soot that rested in the fireplace. He carefully pushed aside the fireplace cover in front of him.

Crouching down he moved out into the living room before him. He turned and grabbed the sac that he had brought with him. An audible gasp from behind him made him spin around. There, standing beside a large, illuminated Christmas tree stood a little boy.

He took a small step forward towards the boy, putting his finger over his lips to tell the boy to be quiet. The boy said in a whisper, "I knew you were real!" The man gave a small chuckle as he saw the pure excitement on the child's face. He opened his sac and rummaged through it. "I can't wait to tell mommy and daddy that you were here", the boy whispered in an enthusiastic tone. He finally found what he was looking for and pulled the large knife from the bag.

This is going to be too easy, he thought as he moved towards the unsuspecting boy.

HAINT
NICHOLAS
By W.H. Gilbert

Any new scabs coming into town by way of the rail heard the stories. Around this time of year when the families and fortunate adorned their beloved homes with lights and every storefront wore tinsel and wreaths, they turned their backs to the homeless. They didn't like the reminder that life can be cruel to the unlucky ones who chased their dreams and failed and refused to compromise.

So word spread from bummouth to bumear that if you find yourself on the road or rail headed into the town in the valley, charity would not be given nor found. But there were many, too many, who did not heed the word and wound up in what was known as the "Bumtrap" around Christmas time, and there they withered in the cold and the snow.

There were no soup kitchens or shelters in the town, a deterrent folk thought might turn undesirables away, but by the time they discovered this truth it was too late. Often they became snowed in, in the valley. And the only place they could bed down for a rest was the park under the eaves of the cedar grove.

But there were other stories told by the light of roadside fires about the town. They were stories about a man who watched over the cast out, the unwashed, the stepped and looked over.

He was a man all covered in soot but for rosy cheeks and nose, who rode the nighttime winter winds as one my ride the rails. He whipped about the tops of trees and on the night of Christmas Eve would deliver to the weary homeless the greatest gift of all. Mercy.

He covered them with soft blankets of snow, blowing into their mouths the winds from all corners of the earth, they were carried away to something else, the Great Second Chance. The people with roofs, and those without, knew him by the name of "Haint Nicholas", and at first mention, anyone unfamiliar would chuckle at the name. It was just a colloquialism, most thought. It was, they said, just a story for children. But the truth remained that the little town in the valley was overrun every early winter with teems of the homeless, and yet every Christmas Day there were none to be found. It came to be an unspoken thing even amongst the police. It was just something that happened. Every year.

And it was on the one hundredth Christmas Eve in the town's history that a young boy wondered how many of the homeless men and women had died and disappeared in his hometown in the valley. It had to be over a hundred. It seemed there were at least a new hundred every year. And after a hundred years, who knew? He was bad at math. Perhaps thousands?

But the boy wondered aloud as he wandered through the park and came to the cedar grove. It was empty, not a soul in sight, and when his eyes landed on the scorched message carved in earth at the grove's center, the boy ran home without a sound. He went to bed without dinner. His parents worried but said nothing. They would ask him if he was still worried in the morning. He laid awake all night, watching the wind blow the trees outside his window. He listened to the night sounds and fretted, hoping the whistle through the chimney was only the wind and nothing more. He could not shake the message from the cedar grove from his mind.

It had read: *We'll have homes for Christmas*

IS THAT YOU SHADOW CLAUSE?

By Tina Piney

Black as death from head to foot,

I thought it was from the chimney soot,

Slinking 'round my tree...

Is that you Santa Clause?

I saw the children start to pout,

When they couldn't make his features out,

Stinking of brimstone...

Is that you Santa Clause?

Hey! What's that in your bag there?

Glowing eyes return my stare,

Thinking, "time to flee" ...

Is that you Santa Clause?

Something here is very wrong,

From the sack comes an evil throng,

Blinking lights reveal...

Is that you Santa Clause?

Oh no! I'm afraid it's much worse,

The result of some horrid curse,

Drinking in our screams...

That's not Santa Clause!

It's only his cruel shadow there,

Spreading searing pain and despair,

Hide your Children...

It's Shadow Clause!

THE STRAY

By Dean King

"Is the tape running? Okay. This interview pertains to case number VC3487

—December 25, 2019, 10:32 a.m. Vilas County Sheriff's Department. I'm detective Paul Meyer, and present with me is Gunnar M. Christiansen, dob September 21, 1981.

"Mr. Christiansen, I know this is a difficult time for you, but please do your best to explain what happened on your farm this morning."

"Okay, I, ah . . . "

"It's okay, Gunnar. Take your time. Would you like some water?"

"No. It, ah . . . it looked like an ordinary gray cat. Dori, my thirteen-year-old daughter found it hiding in the barn when we went out to do chores last evening. Dori's always good about helping out. We never have to get after her to do her chores, but my eleven-year-old son, David, well, it was always a struggle to get him to pitch in and help. It gets old, you know?

So I decided to take it easy on him since it was Christmas Eve and so cold and windy outside.

Dori and I could handle it, so I let David skip his chores.

"Anyway, Dori begged me to let her take the cat inside to get it warm and feed it. I said she could, and she cuddled and played with it all evening. When it was time for bed, she put it in a box next to the woodstove, and that was where the cat was when my wife and I went to bed around ten o'clock. We didn't hear a thing all night and then this morning I- "

"Mr. Christiansen, I know this is hard for you. I'm going to shut off the tape for a moment and let you compose yourself. It's 10:38 a.m."

"Are you ready to continue, Gunnar? Yes? Okay, resuming the interview with Gunnar Christiansen at10:45 a.m. Go ahead, please."

"Ahhh, so this morning, my wife and I got up extra early to get the morning chores done, and Erika wanted to make hot cocoa and get the house warm before waking the kids to open gifts. We didn't look in on them; we just assumed everything was . . . um, we just thought everything was okay, you know? As soon as I opened the door and stepped out into the snow I knew it wasn't. I found David, and, ah, . . . there was blood everywhere. I ran over to him, and he was—"

"Please try to go on, Gunnar."

"It was that damned cat! It lured David outside. Dear God, my poor boy was lying there in the snow, half-eaten, and it's my fault! Don't you see? If I had just made him do his chores, it would have been some other child and not David. This is all my fault."

"I don't understand, Gunnar. How could this be your fault? Your son wandered outside in the night, and a wild animal attacked him. It's rare here in Northern Wisconsin, but cougar attacks do happen."

"It wasn't a damned cougar! It was Jólakötturinn. It was the Yule Cat, just like in the story told to my grandfather when he was a little boy in Iceland. Jólakötturinn goes after lazy children. He left Dori alone because she did her chores, but I let David stay in and play his video games instead of making him do his work.

"Gunnar, those cat tracks we found in the snow were massive. A house cat doesn't make tracks like that."

"You don't understand. Jólakötturinn isn't a house cat. He only pretends to be."

SISTERLY LOVE
By Kevin J. Kennedy

I bought her a sexy little Mrs. Claus outfit from the lingerie store. I thought she'd love it.

"Who would wear something like this?" she asked, holding it out and looking at me as if I was stupid.

Your sister for one, I thought to myself, picturing the evening before when I fucked her sister in the matching costume I'd bought her.

In the end, I just left. I could never bring myself to knock her off. We had been in love.

Her sister wouldn't have it though.

"I'll kill the bitch myself" she said, storming out into the snow.

AN OWNER OF A WISH
By J.T. Hayashi

My brother was always twisted.

At age three he ripped wings off insects. By age five he'd graduated to torturing stray cats. He tormented his classmates by age eight, and unfortunately our Mom loved him too much for her own good--never disciplined him. As a result, by age thirteen he was *quite* a pain.

I'd come home from school to find my bedroom lock broken and stuff in shambles. Hazardous objects often found their way into Dad's walking path--especially near the stairs. Mom would wake up with a lock of hair missing sometimes. Mom silenced my protests with excuses for him. Thing is, he hated us all. Openly.

Ever since he was old enough to speak, every Christmas he'd ask Santa to kill us. Later on he reconsidered and decided, "I want them to suffer a fate WORSE than death!" He used his charms to convince Mom to buy him occult books.

I told him to stop messing with that crap. He sneered, spat at me in response, then turned back to his archaic texts and dark dreams.

Unfortunately, he was determined, and continued researching and practicing. Around that time, I started seeing shadowy figures in the corner of my eye. Strange whispers kept me awake some nights. He directed a homicidal glare towards my father while muttering foreign tongues under his breath. Nonetheless I brushed it off as devil-worshipping nonsense.

That is, until the Christmas following his thirteenth birthday, when he went and did *it*.

Whatever magic he'd managed to cast, whatever nightmare he'd summoned, it subjected us to utter hell. Just Mom and I. Between his sadistic laughter and his I-told-you-sos he admitted Dad had been the sacrifice for "it". All I recall is rousing on a cold floor, feeling heavy.

Now Mom and I are imprisoned in a basement, burdened by numerous limbs. A bell rings somewhere, faint and afar. Then the "elves" come for us. They're grey masses with teeth and deep green scraps on their heads and torsos, not easily distinguishable from each other. Rows of canines rip into my mother and I, cruelly tearing away at our flesh. Agony couldn't begin to describe the feeling.

After they scramble away and the sounds of machinery start up again, our bodies, naught more than bones, gradually regrow the lost flesh. It burns like acid and fire. Mom whimpers quietly as we suffer, but takes it in stride.

The last time we saw my brother, he appeared atop the basement steps alongside a large, bulbous goblin. Its skin was grey-green, cloaked in crimson tatters. Grey tufts erupted from its chin, and atop its head sat a red scrap of cloth. My brother looked down on us and laughed at our misery. The accompanying creature belted a raspy, grating "laugh", its large stomach bobbing up and down.

Finally, my brother turned and hugged the figure, giggling. "Thank you, Santa!" he cried.

He shot us one last smirk and departed with the dark master, gifting us a sorrowful future.

THE HITCHHIKER

By Tor Anders-Ulven

You're not supposed to pick up hitchhikers. Everybody knows this. There's really no telling who you invite into the car with you. An escaped lunatic? A serial killer? An escaped lunatic serial killer? Some maniacal pyramid-scheme salesman? You just can't tell by first appearances alone. So, with that in mind, I suppose the obvious question would be: why did I do it then? Why did I pick him up?

It was the holidays. It's different. And it was cold. And there was snow. I was just being a good Samaritan. Possessed by the Holy Spirit of Christmas.

I spotted him far away in the distance, which gave me a good minute to think about it. He had this strange, jarring walk, like an escaped lunatic, and as he turned to the road to stick out his thumb I got some real serial killer vibes from his weirdly maniacal face. But still I stopped.

Pulled right over to him.

"Need a ride?" I asked once I'd managed to roll down the window. It was kind of stuck because of the cold, which made the whole gesture very awkward.

"I do indeed," he said, "I'm freezing my fingers off out here."

I sort of leaned over and opened the door for him, which again was a peculiar gesture considering the door had a handle on the outside too. He smiled and climbed in, huffing and puffing dramatically on his strangely exposed fingers.

"Quite the weather out there," he said, "I'm truly grateful for your assistance."

"Don't mention it," I said, "So, where are you heading?"

"Oh, just up the road," he smiled, "It ain't that far at all."

That was a fucking weird thing to say. The whole guy was fucking weird. He wasn't dressed for the winter at all. Ragged jeans, sneakers, a thin, scruffy hoodie. It was like he welcomed hypothermia. The only thing that insolated him from the freezing cold was his wild greying beard.

"How about you?" he asked, "Heading home to the old family for the holidays?"

"Hardly," I said, "Visiting a friend. Family isn't really my thing."

We were sort of in the middle of nowhere. Miles between houses. Picking up hitchhikers here was stupid as fuck and I knew it. But I just couldn't help myself. It was like it was meant to be.

"Rosie," I suddenly said, "My name's Rosie by the way."

"Oh, I'm Adam," he said, "Nice to meet you."

We'd passed a few houses at this point, and I was desperately trying to ascertain if he recognized where we were. It was snowing pretty heavily, and the exits became increasingly harder to spot, and I had this creeping feeling he didn't know where he was going at all.

"There," he suddenly said, pointing to what could look like an abandoned farm just up ahead,

"That's the place."

There were no lights to be seen anywhere as I carefully pulled up the driveway, and I couldn't help but to notice the sinister, deranged smile manifesting on my passenger's lips.

Never pick up hitchhikers, my mother always told me. Sound advice. Just not meant for me.

The hitchhikers smile suddenly vanished when Hank's lumbering figure wandered into the headlights of the car. I parked the car by the barn and rolled down the window.

"Rosie!" Hank said, "What a pleasant surprise! You brought a friend?"

I smiled and turned my gaze to the increasingly confused hitchhiker, "Not exactly," I said. "I brought us Christmas dinner."

NOT THE SURPRISE THEY EXPECTED

By R.C. Mulhare

They appeared unannounced among the other kitschy gifts on the seasonal shelves in stores across the globe: a nostalgic throwback "The Pet Rock", the gag gift that made a hit in the 1970s. People laughed at them, but bought them anyway, for the heckuvit. Perfect pet, no muss, no fuss, right? They turned up under trees, beside menorahs, in holiday gift displays in homes across several continents. Friends and family members chuckled, unsuspecting, though the more observant noted how the rocks had oddly uniform shapes.

No one gave them much mind, not till late in the night, when people lay sleeping off the Christmas festivities, when the boxes started to rustle and rattle, emitting soft snaps and crackles, when tendrils sprouted from the contents, slithering out to introduce themselves to the family.

A pet that fed itself and cleaned up afterwards, though it had a strangely fast reproductive cycle, splitting into two every time it finished eating. Aside from that, a perfect addition to the family, right? Even if it caused some screams that didn't sound delighted while the newcomer made some subtractions from said families....

Somewhere in the center of Chaos, the shaper and sire of these gifts gibbered in glee: it hadn't taken much to usurp the latest of Earth's would-be masters. Their own greed had proven the perfect lever to topple them...

I'VE GOT SOMETHING FOR YOU

By Lorenzo Crescentini

Translation By Amanda Blee

The boy's sleepy eyes opened wide, brimming with happiness. "Santa Claus!" he shrieked before clasping both hands over his mouth. "Santa Claus!" he gasped.

The old Psi smiled.

There were no chimneys in the house, so he'd had to climb in through the window. He was way too old for this.

He swung his sack down onto the ground and glanced around, then stuck his hand in the pocket of his red suit and felt around, pulling out a sheet of paper. 'Celeta Wuan?" he read.

"That's my mom", the boy whispered. "She's asleep."

The old man looked at him tenderly, then nodded. "I see. And what's your name, little man?"

"Biro. Biro Wuan."

The old man thrust his gloved hand into another pocket and pulled out a quill pen. He wrote a note on a piece of paper, the child watching the fluttering feathers, fascinated. He put the pen back in his pocket and looked around, taking in the cheap furniture, the cracked plaster on the walls, the sad, grey tiles on the floor.

'All we have are our dreams,' he thought.

They were in the living room that, judging by the cot where he'd surprised Biro, also doubled as the kid's bedroom. His heart ached when he saw the sad, little Christmas tree in the corner.

"I don't see many toys around," he said softly.

Biro frowned for a moment. "No." he replied. "Mom doesn't have enough money for toys. I had a yellow truck, but it got broke."

His face lit up again, his sadness dissolving like a cloud in the sun. "Did you bring me a present?"

The old man smiled and nodded.

There was a door to the right of the tree. He concentrated, probing the room which lay behind it. A woman was sleeping. Celeta Wuan. He entered her dreams, dreams as agitated as a stormy sea. An undercurrent of fear, exhaustion, anguish. Humiliation for what she sometimes had to endure to put food on the table for her son, her hatred of the man who had used her, deceiving her with promises of a better life before disappearing from one day to the next.

The Psi withdrew from her head and looked back at the child.

"You're a Psionic, aren't you?" Biro asked. "That's how you found me."

"People express their desires through their thoughts," explained the old man, kneeling. "Once upon a time they wrote letters, but, deep down, is what we write really what we want? No, not always. Our thoughts, on the other hand, are what our hearts really desire, even if, at times, we don't realise it. When a thought remains strong and constant for a long time, then I hear it and come and make it come true. Or, I try to, anyway."

The child's eyes were bright with a joy that he hadn't felt for a long, long time.

"I've got something for you," announced Santa Claus, opening his sack.

The old man clambered back onto the roof. His sled waited for him silently. He cleaned his boots and then climbed in and started the engine.

Before taking off, he pulled a list and a pen from his pocket. He ran down the list until he came to Celeta Wuan:

"I wish he'd never been born." And he ticked if off.

CHRISTMAS ELF
By Dan McKeithan

Jerome and Cindy searched the row of coloring books at the supermarket. They both wanted to find that special holiday one. They each wanted to one-up the other. It was always a competition with them. Their mom, Lucy, waited patiently. She knew how important it was for them to find just the right one.

Cindy made her choice first. A coloring book with Santa Claus on the cover. Not to be outdone, Jerome found the same one. Lucy knew they would be fighting before they got home over who would color the best picture.

Lucy paid and they walked to their car. A gnarled older lady sauntered over to them. She smiled at the kids, showing one silver tooth. Lucy immediately thought of the old crone in Snow

White with the poisoned apple. But that's crazy.

"Nice kiddies," the lady said.

Lucy smiled and nodded, holding the kids a little closer.

The lady reached into her handbag and pulled out a coloring book. It had Christmas elves on the front. She held it out to them.

"Who wants this?" she asked.

Cindy grabbed it from the lady's hand. "Me."

Lucy took it from her and turned to give it back. But the old lady was gone.

Jerome cried. "I want one. What about me?"

Lucy tugged them both to the car. "We can share it," she said. "I'll color one with you both."

Lucy sat down at the kitchen table of their small trailer. She'd ripped out a picture of a large burly elf with what looked like sharp teeth—in a coloring book for children at Christmas no less—to color with Jerome. Cindy picked a small elf the size of a mushroom. It wore a pointy hat and had a wicked grin.

Both kids grabbed for the same colored pencil—light green. Of course, they both needed at the same time at that very moment. Before she could react, Jerome hit Cindy in the arm and took the pencil.

Cindy played it up the best she could. That girl would make a great actress someday. She cried and rubbed her arm as if it had been hit with a hammer.

"Jerome, go to your room this instance," Lucy yelled.

"But, Mom—"

"Now, no back talk."

Jerome bowed his head and went to his bedroom. He gave Cindy a nasty glance as he entered his room.

Cindy—not to waste a moment—took the green and colored her elf's uniform.

Jerome screamed from his room.

Lucy and Cindy ran to the room. A giant elf with a light green uniform was dragging

Jerome from his room and out the window.

Lucy froze.

Cindy ran to the coloring book and drew large black marks across the elf's face and a red line on his neck.

The elf stopped and dropped Jerome to the floor. His face went dark and his neck bled from a gash on it. He hopped out the window and ran off into the woods.

Lucy grabbed her kids. They took the coloring book and lit it on fire. No more arguing about anything anymore.

CHE GIFC
By Al-hazred7

5 th of January 1846,

Rebordechao, Galicia, Spain.

Dear Baltasar,

This year I've been on my best behaviour.

Mother says that, out of her 12 children, I've been the most polite. I haven't talked back to my parents, I've kept quiet when not addressed to and I've always been fast to comply with any of grandma's requests. I haven't missed a single mass nor failed to complete any of my daily tasks, not ONCE! I've even covered Francisco when he fell asleep and forgot to take the goats back to the corral.

As you can see, I've been a really, really good boy this year. There's a single thing that I would like to ask from you this year, and I ask for it with all of my heart.

Someone took Mariela when we were playing with the snow in the woods on the first morning of the year. It all happened really fast and none of us could do anything to prevent it. Mother has been crying ever since, 5 days and 5 nights she hasn't slept. Father is going crazy, he spends his *full days outside looking for my sister and comes back only when the sun sets down again. He has lost two toes because of the cold.*

Please Baltasar, mother says that you wise kings know it all and see it all, you must know where Mariela is. My only wish this year is for you to bring her back to us sound and safe.

Our new neighbour is writing this letter for me and says he'll have it sent to the Orient for you to read before tomorrow, may his soul be blessed too. -Carlos

The next morning, Romasanta passed by the house of his 12-year-old neighbour wanting to check whether his gift had been granted. He found an unlocked door and a whole family sporting a puzzled expression, staring at the little boys' shoes.

Inside of them lied two objects, the first being a tiny paper note and the second being an orange intricately decorated bar of soap. They handed him the letter, as Carlos's family was illiterate, and he read it out loud.

"Dear Carlos,

Here's what you wished for, take good care of her.

Best wishes, Baltasar."

A CHRISTMAS TO DIE FOR

By Akshay Patwardhan

George Heyward awoke with a sweat-beaded forehead and cool, misty breath. The bedroom was dark and gloomy, filled with the wavering shadows of stuffed dinosaurs, plastic tractors, and "Splash Day Waterpark" participation trophies all enlarged to monstrous proportions in the faint moonlight creeping through blue silk curtains outside of which the December snowflakes were piling up on the windowsill in bunches of white mist.

It was the night of Christmas Eve, and that was when Santa Claus was supposed to show up all big-bellied and jolly with much-deserved presents for George. Perhaps that was why he had woken up in the middle of the night.

George heard a faint tapping, like that of knuckles rapping on a windshield, and he knew that it had come from the misty window. He peeked out a shimmering set of eyes, and he felt his legs quaking underneath the blanket. For a moment, there was nothing outside the window except for the unrelenting hail of snowflakes. Then a hand shot up seemingly out of nothingness, and he saw a white glove-- flecked with something crimson and runny--press itself into a claw against the glass. It held a leather sack in its hand. George could feel a scream rising through his chest, but his throat had clamped shut with sheer terror.

Something red and pointy rose into view: a Santa hat with a white cotton ball attached to the tip like he'd seen in the morning cartoons, and then the pallid, wrinkled skin of a scraggly white-bearded face plastered itself on the windowpanes. It was the face of an old man--Santa Claus, George recognized instantly--but he looked...dead.

The man's eyes were directionless, milky orbs pointed two different directions. His once-pink lips were crusty and covered in horrid warts oozing a greenish-yellow pus. The man smiled at George with rotten, cavity-ridden molars that were dangling from the man's jaw like stringy puppets. George began to scream.

George's bedroom door slammed open and his father Richard trudged inside rubbing his eyes. George glanced at his father for a mere moment and then returned his attention to the window, but the monstrous old man was nowhere to be seen.

"George, what's the matter?" Richard asked, glaring at the boy.

"Santa was outside my window, but he looked scary!" George wheezed as his heart began to beat steadily.

Richard shrugged his shoulders and muttered something as he glanced outside the window. "George, there's nothing there. I'm getting tired of your monster stories. "Monster Santa"? I mean, come on."

"Dad, I'm being serious!"

"Good night, George," Richard said firmly, slamming the door.

George shuddered underneath his blanket for seemingly an infinite amount of time, but sleep couldn't take over. There had been no trace of Santa since then, and George wished the old man would never come back. Then he heard glass shattering, followed by tortured screaming-- his father's--which was abruptly cut off with a bloody gurgle.

George's heartbeat quickened as he heard footsteps approaching his bedroom, and he curled into a cocoon underneath his blanket. He heard the creak of the door, and he held his breath, his ears honed to perfection. George realized that his foot was sticking out slightly, and as he tried to curl it in, he felt something cold and bony grasp his ankle.

He shrieked his lungs out, but there was no one to hear him. He felt himself being pulled further and further until he was thrown into the leather sack, and he managed to hear one last thing before everything went dark.

"A little bite for the road," a voice rasped.

HE KNOWS WHEN YOU'RE AWAKE

By James Dorr

He woke in the dark, his head throbbing with pain. He had no recollection of how he got here, or even who he was. But as he thought this, some memory came back. He'd been struck from behind, by some heavy object, while running from something. . . .

So the memory loss would be temporary -- he now had the thought that something like this might have happened before. Perhaps more than once. An attempt to escape -- he still had no memory of exactly what from. But, again, having failed.

Or was that just déjà vu -- and, for that matter, how did he know that phrase? Something, too, that he'd wondered before? But that thought led in circles. It would be better to concentrate on the here and now.

It was dark, and confined, wherever he was. He tried to stretch his arms and legs, but he seemed to be tied into some kind of bag. He felt rough cloth around him, but also, as he tried to move, that the bag itself was in some kind of close space. The trunk of a car? He felt himself occasionally jouncing, being rocked from side to side.

So then he was in motion -- being taken to some destination? With that another thought came to him, that he himself was small in stature. He didn't take much room. And more memories seemed to come as well -- he knew now, somehow, that with every new memory, every reminder of what or where he was, another cluster of knowledge would come back. He felt now as if whatever vehicle he was in was going downhill.

Or maybe descending for a landing?

And now his fingers and whole hands hurt, along with his head, as if he'd been working for hours on end at some kind of close labor, with no chance for rest. And with cuts and splinters -- woodworking? Sewing? And told to work faster, on some kind of deadline! Until his body could no longer stand it --

With that he felt a thump!, followed by a swishing sound, as of runners on snow, and his name came back to him! Windhover? No, Windblossom! -- just as huge, mittened hands opened his sack and dragged him out, bodily. Holding him up before a gigantic roseate face with a tangled white beard and a bulbous nose.

The laughter was deafening. "Ho! Ho! Ho!" The figure's belly shook under its fur- trimmed, red pinstriped snowsuit.

"So, Windblossom," it roared, "you keep trying, don't you?" Behind the figure's bulk, Windblossom saw the long barracks-like sheds and the barber-striped post that marked the North Pole. Familiar . . . and hated. As the voice went on: "When will you elves learn that you're nothing but slaves, condemned to toil in my toy works forever so that the Earth's children will have their Christmas?"

THE TOOTH
By Jay Levy

"You've lost all your baby teeth, right?" Dr. Matthews raised an eyebrow.

"You tell me." Kevin shrugged. "You're the dentist. Why?"

"That broken eyetooth has to come out." The dentist brought up the x-rays and shrugged.

"But, you have another tooth underneath. That's rare. It might mean no artificial replacement after all."

Dr. Matthews numbed Kevin's mouth and pulled the tooth. It felt like a pressure point he didn't know he had, being finally freed.

"If it is a baby tooth," Dr. Matthews held it up in the pliers, "it's a big one."

Bringing in Kevin's mother, Dr. Matthews explained the recovery requirements and medication. "Let's give it a week or two. That other tooth should be growing in nicely by then, but if not, we'll discuss a replacement."

As the dentist showed the two out, he handed each a candy cane. "Have a Merry Christmas."

"And, a profitable new year," Kevin's mom grumbled when they got to the car. "Giving out candy at a dentist office is like an insurance policy for repeat business."

"I don't know," Kevin shrugged. "I think it's nice."

Kevin didn't need the pills; he wasn't in any pain. His dad and sister made a fuss when they decorated the Christmas tree that evening. But once Kevin convinced them he was, indeed, fine, the tone changed to holiday cheer.

The shock of his new grin, however, was more than his high school classmates could handle. Already the calm-natured outsider, the missing tooth gave most everyone something to poke fun at and laugh.

Attention isn't always a bad thing, though. Mary cornered him in the hall and asked him to the Christmas dance.

"Sure," Kevin stammered. "But, you sure you want to go with me?"

"There's something about you. now. I couldn't see it before." She touched his shoulder and smiled. "See you then."

Even though he normally hid the missing tooth, Kevin smiled the rest of the day.

"Mary—wow," Kevin said aloud. He'd just showered and the steam-clouded mirror distorted his reflection. "Go dude."

Kevin wiped the condensation with his hand and saw the tooth had grown.

It had gone from missing to snaggletooth as he showered. And still, it grew.

In front of his eyes, the tooth elongated and Kevin panicked. He meant to scream, but his body went numb with pain.

His other bottom eyetooth split and fell out— and right away, another also grew in its place.

Kevin fell to the floor, paralyzed by pain. He gazed at the linoleum pattern beneath and felt his teeth grow like red-hot pokers on his jawline. The world around him faded.

When Kevin awoke and got up, he came face-to-face with an unfamiliar reflection in the mirror.

Both bottom canine teeth protruded from his mouth like a sabretooth tiger. His eyes shimmered yellow in the dim light in a face surrounded by dark, coarse hair. Now oily and red, his skin was hot to the touch.

Kevin didn't see Kevin anymore. He was a beast and he needed to feed.

Sniffing, he caught the scent of human all around.

He licked his lips, smiled, and stepped into the hallway of Kevin's home. Following the scent, he went downstairs to meet Kevin's family.

Their shock was brief.

CHARITY DRIVE
by Trevor Newton

I rang the bell up and down outside the Independent Grocery, sending a madman's jingle echoing across the busy parking lot. Shoppers glared at me as they exited the store; some silently expressing remorse and pity while others appeared smug.

One lady, yacking on her cellphone, even tossed a wad of trash into the donation bucket by my side. I had half a mind to cram it down her throat.

An elderly man with deep interlacing wrinkles slowly shuffled from the warm interior of the store into the cold, snowy night.

"Care to donate any change, sir?" I asked

He appeared mildly startled by the sound of my voice, nearly dropping his ice-cream scoop and tub of Neapolitan. I smiled and he returned the gesture; the first cordial acknowledgement I'd received from anyone.

"What's the cause?" he asked, approaching me.

"It's a non-profit," I responded, "for underprivileged children suffering from blindness. For every eight dollars donated, a child receives an educational book in braille."

He frowned as he got closer, peering into the red and green bucket which contained no money—only a crumpled snack wrapper and soda bottle.

"It's a shame; the level of selfishness the holidays can hold," he said. "They'll buy their family and friends items they'll never use while their fellow humans ache for even the most basic needs." He fiddled the round scoop in his hand, staring at it briefly before returning a hardened gaze into my eyes.

I exhaled, suddenly realizing I'd been holding my breath. "That's true."

He placed his hand on my shoulder, digging his thumb deep into fleshiness.

Mere inches away from my face, he said, "I shall give them sight."

Before I could respond he was walking away with a distinct purpose in his step.

As he disappeared into the blizzard, I saw him drop the tub of ice cream.

A few bystanders overheard the man's spiel and, apparently overtaken with guilt, decided to toss a few coins and singles into the bucket. I smiled and thanked them profusely, taking the time to answer any of their questions about the organization.

By the time I saw the old man strolling back across the parking lot in my direction, the moon was directly over my head and the copious amount of sudden interest had died down.

In his right hand, he still held the ice-cream scoop, now dripping red splotches against the fresh coating of alabaster snow. With his free hand he fished a dampened brown bag from his coat and tossed it into the bucket, producing a moist thud.

His smile returned as he looked back into my eyes.

"Afterall, sight truly is the greatest gift one could give."

TAKING THE REINS

by Ariana Ferrante

"Julie, Julie, I think there's a reindeer on the roof!"

Julie cracked open her eyes, gaze settling on the image of her brother standing at her bedside. She groaned, lifting her head off of the pillow and brushing her sleep-snarled hair out of her face. She turned her attention to the digital clock on her nightstand, tired eyes registering the bright red numbers. *11:07.*

"Michael," she grumbled, "it's not even Christmas yet. Go back to bed."

"But there's a reindeer!" the boy insisted, grabbing her hand and giving it the strongest tug his 8-year-old arms could muster. "Maybe it got loose from Santa's sleigh!"

Julie huffed, sitting up. "If I come to see the reindeer with you will you go to bed right after?" she asked.

Her little brother nodded, head a blur as it moved. "I will, I will!"

Julie climbed out of bed, wiping the sand out of her eyes and slipping her bare feet into her nearby slippers. After throwing on the heaviest jacket they had, Julie and her brother ascended the stairs leading up to the house's widow's walk.

Julie pushed the door open, the cold, snow-filled air striking her face at full force. Michael ran out ahead of her, up the smaller flight of stairs leading up to the fenced-off area on the roof.

"I knew it!" he squealed, his little voice nearly inaudible over the winter whirlwind. "I knew it, I knew it, I told you!"

Julie ascended the stairs after him, eyes widening as she laid eyes on it.

It was a reindeer, there was no question about it. It was giant, dwarfing Michael in size even on all fours, cloven hooves scraping against the snow-covered roof of their home. It wore a harness studded with bells, and a pair of reins rested on its back. Its beady black eyes fell over Julie's stupefied frame, and the beast let out a huff of air from its flaring nostrils, breath fogging in the cold.

Michael approached the reindeer, hands gripping and rubbing the animal's fur.

"Michael, guh-get away from it," Julie begged, teeth chattering in the cold. "That's a wild animal!"

"No, it's Santa's!" Michael protested, still running his hands along the animal's side. "I bet, if we bring it back to him, he'll give us so many pres-"

The reins, once resting on the beast's back, reared up like cobras before lunging at Julie's brother. The now impossibly long leather straps wrapped around both of the boy's wrists, then around his chest, before pulling him tight against the reindeer's flank.

Michael screamed in fear, his cries for help mingled with the beast's heavy grunts. With a clattering of hooves against wood and jingling bells the reindeer ran. It jumped off the roof, airborne and ascending, the reins restraining Michael keeping him in place. The horrified child dangled by his hands as the animal carried him further and further into the sky.

"Michael!" Julie shrieked, running to the edge of the widow's walk and reaching for her sibling's leg, fingers brushing the sole of his shoe before the boy flew out of reach.

"Julie!" Michael wailed, and then was gone, the rapidly shrinking silhouette of the boy and beast further obscured by the flurry of snowflakes filling the air.

Within moments, Julie was alone, eyes wide and unblinking. The only sign that her brother and the reindeer had been there not minutes before were the marks of their feet in the snow, quickly covered by falling flakes.

CHRISTMAS MORNING

by Matt Hoffman

Remnants from yesterday's snow poured off the awning. Josephine followed the drips with her eyes as they exploded on the pavement. Her mother walked down the steps, sleepy- eyed, smiling.

"You're up already, Josie?"

"Yeppers!"

"How about we open up some presents before Daddy gets home?"

"Yay! Yes, please!"

Mommy walked towards the tree, grabbing one of the bigger presents.

"How about this one, baby?"

Josie grabbed the present from her mommy's hands, practically begging to open it. It was heavy in her delicate hands. She clawed at the wrapping paper, ripping it open in a matter of seconds.

As she slowly opened the box, a fetid smell came across her nostrils. Beady eyes stared back at her, sunken into a deflating skull. Josephine's deafening scream echoed throughout the barren house.

"Sweetie, what's wrong?" her mother asked. "Don't you want to play with your new baby sister?"

LIST OF GRIEVANCES

By N.M. Brown

The line for the grocery store Santa line was impossibly long; weaving in and out of the aisles like the frayed ends of Audrey's hair. She reminded herself that even though her daughter Lillie was three and likely wouldn't remember, it was an investment for her future. It meant a lot to Audrey as a mother to have these memories with Lillie. She would only be little once.

Audrey's husband, Kevan had been working two jobs to ensure the best Christmas possible for their family. That's what she told herself at least. In reality... the selfish woman felt like a single parent, as shitty as that was to say, for having to do everything on her own.

But she pasted a smile on her weather numbed face and waited in line with her little girl, like a good mom. Lillie's holding her hand; squirming around like an electric eel in a frying pan. One step out of line and the people behind them would bumrush her out of their place in line. And Audrey really didn't want to have to punch someone in the face that day.

When it was finally their turn, store employee elves hurried Lillie onto Santa's lap, pausing them for pictures. It took Audrey's most embarrassing efforts to get her toddler to cooperate with Santa long enough to snap the picture. The little girl rattled off a lengthy list, appropriately creative for a girl her age. She hopped off of his lap and was given a candy cane.

She thanked him and turned around to leave.

"And what would *you* like for Christmas this year Mommy?" 'Santa' asked; stopping Audrey in her tracks.

As this happened, Lille dropped her freshly unwrapped candy cane on the floor, initiating a siren of tears. The man playing Santa still stared at the mother expectantly despite the display. Didn't he see how badly she wanted to leave? There were a lot of people behind them and Audrey could already hear the sighs of annoyance.

An unknown voice from towards the back of the line drifted towards them.

"See Bobby? Naughty children don't get presents from Santa. Don't be like that little girl okay hunny?"

Jesus H. Christ...

"Alright Santa." Audrey sputtered through my unkempt hair as Lille pulled at it in rage as her mother lifted her to carry her out. "You know what I want? I wanna wake up in the morning in silence, if only for ten minutes. I want to go sit on the toilet in peace...without interruption, I want to sleep in until noon like I did before I had kids, I want to have a life. Satisfied? Do ya think you can do that for me Santa?"

She left without waiting for an answer.

Christmas morning, Audrey was surprised to find the sun shining through her bedroom window when she woke. Lillie must have been sleeping in, her mother thought. Normally she was tearing through the house before the sun came up.

The clock on the stove read *11:17AM.*

She ran to Lillie's room, only to find a storage room. The presents her and Kevan had put under the tree for her the night before were gone. No milk and cookie tray sat on the fireplace next to the tree. What's worse, every single handmade ornament they had made with Lillie was gone.

Audrey ran, sobbing, to her bedroom. She threw open the door and shook her husband awake.

"Kevan!" She shouted. "Where's my baby? What happened to Lillie?!?"

Her husband stared at her through sleepy eyes. His lips held a tone of concern as her asked her.

"Babe, whose Lillie?"

THE OLDER TRADITIONS

By Donna Cuttress

My brother and I had to spend the holidays with my Grandfather, who lived in a small village. Just before Christmas he sent us to search for a Yule log. We headed into the nearby woods with our torches and stayed on the path as instructed.

"How long have we been walking?"

My feet were numb with cold. Jonah shone his torch in my face.

"Not long. Keep looking!"

As the sky darkened, we came to a small copse. There were lots of broken branches but nothing suitable. The timber had to be thick enough to burn for a long time, the embers had to be raked and a piece saved to light the Yuletide fire next year.

"What are you two boys doing out in this weather?"

I gasped, falling backward. A tall man barred our way. He stared at us from behind a pair of dark snow goggles. A thick scarf covered the rest of his face, yet his voice was clear. My brother stood between myself and him.

"We're looking for a Yule Log. Our grandfather believes in tradition."

He took a step near us. We took a step back. Large flakes of snow fell silently around us. We stood in silence. This stranger fascinated and terrified me.

"I thought no one practised the older traditions anymore ... Try by the church. The trees are sheltered and stronger."

Something growled behind us, we looked, but could see nothing. When we turned back, the stranger had disappeared, leaving no footprints.

My brother grabbed my hand.

"Let's find this stupid log and get back."

His hand shook through his glove as we ran. I pointed ahead to the church. A single candlelight burned within and we followed it like it was a star. The gates to the churchyard were padlocked, so we searched the tree line by the border wall.

"This is perfect!" I cried.

The log was thick enough to burn and sure to keep Grandad happy. Back home, he rested it by the hearth to dry.

On Christmas Eve he placed the Yule log in the grate, then whispered to us, "Some say, the burning signifies the return of the sun after the darkness. Remember, we must keep a small part to light next year's fire."

He reached into his jacket pocket and took out a small piece of wood. It ignited quickly from a burning candle. He held it to the paper packed around the Yule log. Soon we could smell fresh wood burning.

"Where did you find this?" Grandad asked.

"Outside the church grounds, the gates were locked."

We explained about the stranger, as the log burned fiercely. Grandad grabbed the poker and pulled the Yule log from the grate.

"That was a demon! A trickster! That ancient ground belongs to those who could not be buried in consecrated soil ... The evil and possessed!"

We thought he had gone crazy.

"Those trees grow from cursed bones ..."

The log hissed and spit, as violent flames erupted. I swear I saw a face in them! Something demonic. It's hate filled eyes as red as blood. Sparks exploded! I felt something fly through me, burning and scalding everything it touched within! Grandad kicked the log outside into the snow. Jonah said the flames screamed with pain.

I felt so well the next morning, different somehow. Instead of unwrapping my Christmas gifts, I cleaned the house. Brushing out the grate, I noticed something underneath grandfather's chair. A sliver of wood. I hid it in my pocket. I need it ... to light the Yuletide fire next year.

LIGHTS OUT
By Lynne Conrad

"Laura, how do you like the lights?" Scott called out. Laura peeked around the corner from the kitchen.

"Awesome." Laura admired the colored string lights that Scott had strung around the doors and along the floor moldings. "Are those new lights?" She couldn't remember buying them.

"I found them in the attic."

"They really look good."

"Thanks. Is supper ready?"

"Yeah." Scott followed Laura to the kitchen. After eating, they retired to the living room to watch a movie.

"What do you want to watch?" Laura asked.

"I really don't care."

"How about 'A Christmas Carol'?"

"I guess I can sit through Jacob Marley haunting Scrooge," Scott laughed. Laura tossed a throw at him and then they settled down to watch the movie. When the credits begin to roll, Laura yawned and announced she was going to bed.

"Are you coming?" she asked.

"No I think I'll watch another movie."

"Okay. Suit yourself." She left him on the couch, remote in hand, surfing the stations.

Dozing off, Laura rolled over and opened one eye and then the other and frowned. What was he watching that had all that screaming? And why did he have it turned up so loud?

"Scott, turn the TV down," she shouted, but the loud screaming continued. "Blast it."

She got out of bed, jerked open the bedroom door and huffed down the hallway into the living room.

"Scott!" Laura screamed and backed away from the door when she saw him. Scott lay writhing in the floor, the new strands of flashing colored lights wrapped around his body like a large snake.

"Laura, help me," he begged. He was tugging at the lights around his neck that were beginning to tighten up.

Laura ran to her husband and jerked on the lights, but to no avail. She watched as Scott was squeezed and choked to death, finally taking his last breath. She backed away when she saw one of the strands of light snake toward her. She jumped up and ran to the bedroom, slamming the door shut behind her.

Leaping up on the bed, she leaned toward the edge on her knees, watching the door. She could hear the clack of the lights on the wooden floor as the strands of lights slithered toward the bedroom. She could see the colored lights flashing under the door and looked around for a weapon, but all she could find was her grandfather's hiking stick in the corner.

Bounding across the floor, she grabbed the stick and leapt back on the bed as the lights slipped under the door. Flashing reds, greens and blues lit up the room.

"Stay away from me!" she screamed out, raising the stick, but the lights, reaching the bed, began to slink up the blanket. When the first lights peeked over the edge, she swung the stick, whacking the lights. Instead of smacking the lights across the room, they wrapped themselves around the stick and wound around it until they reached her hands. She tried to pitch it away, but it was too late. The lights had wrapped themselves around her arms. They wound themselves around her until she was bound head to foot. She closed her eyes as the last of her breath left her body and the flashing lights went off.

BEFORE THEIR TIME

By Anthony Giordano

Ice cubes clinked as they melted in scotch.

Tinny, hollow Christmas muzak piped through the speakers.

Ryan Desmond stared blankly out the 58th floor window of Desmond Tower, oblivious to the festive colors of the Dallas landscape.

I'm the third richest man in America, he thought. And it amounts to nothing now.

Desmond's fortunes hadn't been enough to save Esther and Victoria. The tidal wave of holiday profits amassed by Desmond's 5,000 stores was a poor solace for the despair of burying a wife and a daughter in the span of two weeks.

Poor Victoria. Perhaps it had been a foregone conclusion. She was always a troubled girl; her inner demons consistently resistant to therapy and pharmacological approach. But to think she would mutilate her own beautiful body.

And yet, she was found with no less than two dozen small, vicious cuts across her lithe form; inflicted before she had sliced her arm open from wrist to crook.

Eight days later, despondent over their daughter's suicide; Esther replicated the act.

His father's words echoed in his head - "All the money in the world can't buy family."

I'm alone now.

Desmond's stupor was broken by the chime of a small bell. Spinning, he beheld a diminutive form unfolding from the shadowed corner. It strode toward him; jangling from bells on its hat and shoes. No more than three feet tall; Desmond thought - hoped - that it was some practical joke, one of the company's animatronic holiday dolls.

No. The figure approached with a bizarre, organic gait; nothing like the cheap wares which occupied Des-Mart shelves.

The figure walked into focus, stopped. Desmond appraised the being before him. Short, with a round, cherubic face, sharply pointed ears. Its clothing was an unholy marriage of reds, greens, and whites. Triangular fringe. Candy-cane striping. Those damn little bells, tinkling away.

"Y-y-you're a-" Desmond started.

"A shame, really. Taken before their time." the elf responded. Its voice was a bizarre contradiction - basso profondo hopped up on helium.

"Wh-what?"

"Your wife and daughter." Icicles formed in Desmond's stomach at their mention. "Taken before their time. Goes against the order of things, you know."

Desmond's mind ran a gamut of emotions. Rage, at this creature's flippant nature. Also, fear, curiosity.

The elf reached behind its back, threw a manila folder atop the desk. Photos scattered. Pictures of Des-Mart store shelves; filled with Christmas goods. Next to Thanksgiving goods. Next to Halloween costumes. Next to back-to-school displays and endcaps.

Desmond recovered. His fist slammed the desk. "Just what the hell is the meaning of this?"

The elf sneered. There was no jovial aspect to its rotund face. The smile was cruel; eyes hard, uncaring. "There is an Accord; to guarantee no one holiday supplants another. Your holdings set a precedent in your society; but your actions have caused disarray in ours."

"I-I don't understand..." Desmond stammered.

With a hissing swish, a wicked, curved blade appeared. Perfect for inflicting small, vicious cuts. The elf waved it menacingly. "Every year, you widen the overlap of Christmas on the other holidays! Have you no idea of the consequences of such actions?"

"And for that you murdered my family?" Desmond bellowed, cocking his foot to punt the tiny messenger. Just then, he sighted more darting flashes in the shadows.The malicious glint of murderous eyes; the evil flicker of tiny blades in the dark.

The elf cackled. "You think you have nothing more to lose, Ryan Desmond. But you are so wrong. We can always find new ways to make you weep."

"Remember, to each holiday their time, and not before."

HE SEES YOU WHEN YOU'RE NAUGHTY!

By Marcus Cook

Wyndrk Nazwoski was seven foot four inches and weighed four hundred and fifteen pounds. He was dressed in a Santa Claus outfit when he entered his mountain cabin. As he closed and bolted the door shut, the stench of rotted meat, cabbage, and beer didn't seem to bother him as he took two long strides to the fireplace. The fire had gone out. Grabbing some logs piled in the corner, he built a new fire. He then placed a single coal in a pot hanging over the flames.

He glanced at the mirror that hung over the mantel and chuckled. He had remembered Sister O' Cassidy telling him that Santa believed all orphans were naughty and that's why he had gotten no presents.

Last year, he learned that shopping malls hired Santa's helpers to listen to what children want for Christmas.

When Wyndrk applied, the store was excited about his size and hired him on the spot.

Once they gave Wyndrk his specially ordered Santa suit. He never returned.

The giant pulled up his chair to the side of the fireplace and pushed play on his cd player. The Beatles "Wonderful Christmas Time" began to play. Wyndrk loved the Beatles and as a child imagined he was their drummer.

"Now who is here to see Santa Claus today?" Wyndrk bellowed as he stepped into the connecting room. There a young woman locked in a large dog cage.

"Please, sir let me go." the girl begged.

"Oh, you would like Santa to let you go. Wouldn't you?" Wyndrk asked as he unlocked the cage door.

"More then anything!" she pleaded with tears rolling down her face.

Her capture easily wrapped his hand around her neck. Gently he pulled her from the cage.

"Come with Santa." Wyndrk said as he gently guided her by the shoulders into the living room.

The girl's body quivered as Wyndrk sat on his chair. He then yanked the woman up and sat her in his lap.

"Now tell Santa what it is you would like for Christmas." Wyndrk said in his best Santa impression.

The girl noticed how his suit was covered in dried blood, "I want to go home."

"That is what every girl wants when she sits on my lap. Now tell me. Have you been naughty or nice this year?" Wyndrk asked as he released his grip.

"Nice!" she screamed.

"No..No...No. You have been naughty! I saw you dancing without your clothes. I saw men give you money as you touched them on their manhood. I watched as you led them to the other room. " Wyndrk disproved.

The girl started to cry louder, "It's just to get me through college. I promise you; it is not a career choice." The girl wept.

"Sister O' Cassidy would whip me if I touched my manhood, she would tell me only my wife shall touch me there." Wyndrk preached.

"Then punish the men who pay me to touch them!" She screamed.

"They will be punished in time. Now I must give you your gift." Wyndrk announced as he tossed the girl to the ground. The girl froze in fear as she watched Wydryk pull out a hot coal from the fireplace.

"Naughty girls get coal." He grabbed the girl and forced open her mouth, "Ho-Ho-Ho"

Before she could scream, he jammed it down her throat. The girl's throat glowed red and blood poured from her nostrils and eyes. She never let out a last breath as her body went limp.

Wyndrk smiled as he sat back in his chair. Sister O'Cassidy would have been proud.

THE CANDY CANES
By Gabriella Balcom

"Drop that!" Lynette snapped at her sister, who was nine.

Cara began unwrapping the candy cane instead, prompting the seventeen-year-old to knock it out of her hands. "Hey!" the younger girl protested. "I was going to eat it."

"Get away!" Lynette said to the woman who'd given Cara the treat, grimacing as if she'd tasted something vile. Bristles protruded from the warts on the old crone's face and her clothes were tattered and dirty.

"She's a nasty hag," the teenager told her sister. "Her candy would've made you sick."

"But I'm hungry," Cara complained. "You spent all the money Mom gave us for lunch on makeup."

"Quit whining." Lynette turned away to answer her cell, chattering a hundred miles a minute.

Cara stared longingly at the cane on the ground, which was covered in multi-colored swirls and shiny flecks. She'd never seen one like it, but bet it was delicious.

Edging closer, the old woman raised one gnarled finger to her lips, and opened her other hand.

Seeing the candy canes she held, Cara's eyes widened.

The woman placed them in the girl's hand, winked, then hobbled away.

Cara stuffed them in her purse with a giggle.

When the sisters got home, Cara darted into a bathroom, and fished a candy cane out of her purse. She turned it every which way, admiring the colors and how it gleamed before eating it. It tasted so amazing, she had another gone within seconds.

At supper, she stuffed herself with dinner and pie. Still craving sweets, she went to her room to enjoy another cane from her secret stash. She hung the three that remained on the Christmas spruce tree in the front room before heading to bed.

Hours later, the lights on the tree went out.

Dorrie, the family's calico cat, raised her head from where she'd been napping on the carpet, sniffed, and padded toward the spruce. Batting the lower ornaments, she knocked two down before squeezing between presents, leaving the tip of her tail sticking out.

A candy cane fell to the floor with a thump, and the cat hissed, whirling around. She slunk toward it, tapping it with a paw. The treat suddenly moved, and Dorrie somersaulted backward through the air, fleeing down the hall.

One of the shiny flecks on the cane twisted open. Something slender extended from the tiny hole, then a second thing, and another. A spider hoisted itself out, its eyes glowing green. More spiders appeared, and the other two canes fell to the floor beside the first.

The carpet became a dark, flowing stream as dozens and dozens of arachnids scurried across the room and up the stairs. Crawling under Cara's door, they surrounded her bed. One raised a leg, pointing upward, and cookies appeared beside the child. Other spiders raised their appendages and chocolates and other goodies materialized.

The arachnids left, passing her parents' door and entering Lynette's bedroom. They swarmed her, crawling into her nose and ears. She woke, shrieking and flailing around, but the spiders poured into her mouth, choking her cries. Her eyes rolled back in their sockets until only white showed.

For a few moments, she lay motionless. Then her eyes opened, glowing green.

∩ANA'S BROKEN MAN

By DeBickel

When leaves crumbled in the yard and the local grocery spat carols at the doors, the Holdens knew Nana's was then the place to go: an aching wooden home obscured by pines and bookended by apartments, it seasonally abstained from its ordinarily somber presence for strings of colorful primary lights, faux reindeer, and a pine wreath at the door.

Sammy Holden explored its many rooms as Nana excitedly chittered to his cousins, parents, and holiday-sweater-enthusiast Uncle Ben in the kitchen, where he could smell the turkey cooking. He bounced through the dining room with the over-burdened Christmas tree and up the wooden stairs with its worn paisley thread carpets, poking his head in every bedroom. He came to the strange closet-like room at the far end of the hall: Nana's sewing room.

The room was a colorful barrage of textile delights, from long sheers to crocheted granny squares, from patched jeans to enviable needlepoint works. He loved it all. Then, *it* caught his eyes: an aging popcorn tin in a drawer large enough to be a drum, decorated with fading labels and cityscapes of London. It bore deep fractures along its sides as though it had been shattered porcelain, but all the cracks were seamed together with thin, delicate colorful threads.

Sammy turned it in his hands, observing it with awe: the threads were so meticulous, careful, and tight. They held all the pieces in place; he couldn't even see the holes they vanished into. Some stitches were simple, and others bloomed in various flowers with shiny golden linings. Though, something felt inherently sinister about what could be inside.

He ran to the kitchen with the tin squeezed tight in his arms, wanting to ask how Nana had made it.

"Mom!" Sammy showed the old tin, shaking it to hear no sound. "Look! Why's it made
like this?"

"I don't know." His mother answered. "Put it back, Sam."

"But I wanna ask Nana!"

"Ask me what?" Nana turned from where she rested in the corner rocking chair, where

she liked to watch Uncle Ben to finish cooking. Feeble lines along Nana's brow tightened, the

holiday chair unusually exempt from her answer. "Sometimes things we think won't break, will;

and we've got to help put it back together."

"But it's tin." Sammy protested as would any child denying tall tales. "Why not tape?"

"Tape lacks a mother's touch." Nana set the cookies nearby as she turned back. "Please

put it away, Sammy."

He pouted but complied. He thumped upstairs with it tight in his arms only to stumble on the landing. Sammy fell forward, the tin rolled backward, bouncing down each individual stair until he heard a clatter akin to porcelain. Paling, Sammy turned back to see two of the pieces dangling from broken threads and the lid askew, various salts and dried plants spilling over. A dark puff he hardly discerned dissipated in with dust.

"Sammy?" Uncle Ben's voice called.

He shamefully picked up the pieces and returned to the kitchen to apologize. But something felt different. His parents sat quietly at the table and the turkey smelled unusually

plain. Nana, in her rocking chair, seemed sadder; and the room, emptier.

Sammy, forgetting his apology, asked, "Where's Uncle Ben?"

Nana scratched the side of her chair. She looked to be reflecting on something she

couldn't do anything for. Sammy followed her gaze to an old photo left on the wall—the newest

among them—and saw a younger man's smiling, pained face. Uncle Ben's.

"He had a lot of pain when he was younger, Sammy. He was ... broken."

A REAL TREE
By Charlotte O'Farrell

All of us in Apartment 154A were Christmas fanatics. Living hundreds of miles from home in a big, anonymous city, something about "doing Christmas properly" felt comforting.

Every year at the start of December, the three of us would pull the decorations from their dusty boxes. After five years, they were starting to look their age.

"The tree," said Sadie solemnly, "has seen better days."

She lifted the spindly plastic thing out of its coffin-like box and held it at a distance, as if it stunk. Some of its branches were completely naked now.

"I've been saying it for years. We need a real tree," said Sven, not looking up from the ungodly tangle of flashing lights he was unpicking.

For the first time since Sven had started his annual festive tradition of lobbying for a genuine tree, Sadie and I didn't argue. Our apartment wasn't spacious but this played to its advantage in December, giving it the air of a colourful, cosy little den of tinsel. We were planning to adopt a cat in January, who would no doubt scratch and swing from our decorations in years to come, so this felt like the right time to add that final special touch to proceedings.

We bought the real tree home the next day. Getting it up three flights of stairs wasn't fun but we managed it, panting and leaving behind a trail of green needles in our wake.

I had to hand it to Sven: it certainly looked and smelt Christmassy. Nestled in the corner of our small lounge, it was quite magnificent.

We decorated it straight away. As I was hanging a bauble, I felt something stab me. I pulled my bleeding hand away.

"It – bit me!" I shouted, holding the puncture wound on my finger. Both Sven and Sadie laughed.

"Bit early for mulled wine, isn't it?" joked Sadie. "You've just caught it on a spiky needle.
Rinse it off and put a plaster on it."

Too shaken to argue, I went to the kitchen to do as she said. I was halfway through washing it when I heard the screams.

Dashing back, I was stopped in my tracks by an awful sight. Sven's legs were suspended in the air, his body wedged into the tree. He was slowly disappearing into its depths – which looked red inside, like the innards of a Venus fly trap. The tree was making disgusting digestion sounds. I heard some loud snapping noises from his bones as he was pulled in deeper.

Sadie was pulling on his ankles but she was no match for the monstrous eating machine.

As I watched, Sven's skull – stripped of eyes, hair, and all skin – dropped out of the bottom of the tree. It sat underneath like a macabre Christmas present.

My legs gave way under me. I'll never celebrate Christmas again.

LITTLE BROTHER

By George Alan Bradley

"Another one!"

I had been aware of it - the way any six-year-old kid is about presents - but figured the one at the back, near the wall among loose pine-needles, had to be Dad's. Dad was slow when it came to presents. Slower even than Momma, and she was slow as a three-legged tortoise. Theirs were still mostly wrapped, while they were busy in the kitchen.

"I'll get it!" Amy scooched in her pajamas, dragging it out. Unlike the rest, its paper was not colorful but brown. Like the kind that regular packages get sent in.

"Oh weird," she said.

"What?"

She showed me. It didn't have a label, somebody had just written on the brown paper in a scrawling black ink. I took it from her. I was better at reading.

"What's it say, Tommy?"

"It says, 'Little Brother'."

"Oh." She looked at me, disappointed. "Must be yours."

"I'm your big brother, dummy."

"Well, 'snot from me," she said, folding her arms. Duh, I thought. We didn't get presents for each other, that was Momma and Dad's job. And Santa's, though I didn't believe in him much anymore.

"Who's it from?"

"Maybe Grandpa?" I stared at it, "Maybe he forgot I was...older?" This seemed possible, Grandpa was old and forgot things.

"Open it!"

I started peeling. It was tough, almost like it wasn't supposed to be opened. The paper was thick. Sharp.

"Well?"

"Some...doll."

Amy leaned in excitedly

"But..." I hesitated. It was a doll, but not like any doll I'd seen.

"UGH!" She recoiled sharply, "Tommy, whys it stink?"

It was a good question. The smell was bad, like the fridge when something spilled and got left in there too long.

The smell seemed to seep from its shriveled skin, skin that was dark brown, like the burned skin of a roast turkey.

"It has a note." I touched the clumped hoof. A loop of string was tied to a tag. This one was harder to read. I'd started to sound it out when footsteps came.

"Done with presents?"

I quickly pulled the weird doll behind the paper. Turning, we nodded in solemn silence. Momma was sipping coffee.

"Alrighty," she smiled. "Just gonna run to the bathroom, then it's dinnertime."

"Okay."

When Momma left, I tried to give the doll to Amy, but she pushed it away. "Yours," she said.

"I don't want it!"

"Too bad, so sad." She stood, wrinkling her nose, and ran off. "Have fun with your doll, Tommy!"

When she was gone, I looked at the brown paper again. Little Brother. It was hard to believe Grandpa really had got it for me. I looked at the note attached to its foot again.

"Yo...u..." I read, haltingly, "...won...t...re...place...me."

I shoved it back in the paper. Pushed it all back under the tree, right up to the wall.

Scrubbing my hands on my pajamas, I could still smell the rotten food smell. It followed me to the kitchen.

"Ready!"

Momma came back in, all smiles. She went over to Dad, whispering in his ear, kissing his cheek.

Dad's eyes lit up.

"Got some news, guys." Momma sat, her cheeks glowing. Her hand brushed at her belly softly. "Your daddy and I...we decided to..."

"What?" Amy asked, worried.

"Try again," Dad said, taking her hand, smiling.

Try again.

Suddenly, I remembered. Last Christmas. The same table. The same news.

Little Brother.

Momma talked excitedly across the table, but I wasn't listening. Out in the living room, I heard the soft rustling of paper coming from under the tree. The putrid smell wafting from my stained legs.

You won't replace me, I heard the brown doll whisper. *You won't replace me.*

THE TWELVE DAYS OF CHRISTMAS

By Stephanie Levy

I should have smelled trouble.

Most students go home for Christmas break—well, holiday break as it's called now, which made the notes on my pillow every morning all the more strange. Each one was a different color—red, green, or white—and each had a different scent—cinnamon, holly, or pine.

"I" was all the note said on that first day—December the 12 th . "Know" was the word on the second day.

Since almost the moment classes ended, my roommates had all left. The only person here I knew, besides faculty, was Britt. We'd been a couple since Halloween, and I wondered if she was the one writing the notes?

When I asked her, she seemed puzzled. "Erin, why would I do that?" She shrugged and gave me a hug. "I have no reason to tease you."

I really thought it was a prank—Britt trying to be cute.

On the third day, I received a piece of green folded paper and the word "what" in glitter.

Each day, this became less cute.

I keep my window and door locked. But each day, there was another note, another word.

By the sixth day, the message became clear. "I know what you really are."

I panicked. Only Britt knew, or so I thought. The colorful Christmas paper and holiday scent did little to dampen the threat in those six simple words. At this point, I told campus security, who brushed me off as paranoid. They filed their reports, kept examples of the notes, and suggested I was being hazed by sorority sisters.

Ludicrous! I wasn't pledging. That wasn't my kind of thing.

I hoped if I stayed awake after that, I'd catch the culprit in the act. But, no matter how hard I tried, no matter how much coffee I drank, my mind wandered and I'd drift off to sleep.

Five more nights and five more words. "Meet me in the Forest."

On Christmas Eve morning, the note said, "Tonight."

Britt begged me not to go; something in her bones told her it wouldn't be safe.

"I'm not weak," I told her sternly. "I can handle myself. I will not become someone else's prey."

It was Christmas Eve and families happily shared meals filled laughter. Tonight was a time for cheer. Just not for me.

The snow-filled skies darkened and there was barely any visibility. The nearly full moon peeked behind drifting clouds, and I felt the wolf inside me stir. I saw the flakes clearly and heard the snow crunch under my feet.

My paws...

I smiled, only now it was the smile of a wolf. I'd shifted, changed. My snout elongated and my teeth grew sharp in my muzzle.

That's when I heard the howl and caught the scent. Realization sunk into the pit of my stomach and now it all made sense.

A rival pack had found me and flushed me out. Those stupid notes; I was like some dumb deer—weak and naïve. I crouched, tensing for what I knew would be a fight for my life.

As they circled from all sides, I thought of Britt—her smile, her smell, her touch, and her kiss. I would make it home to her!

I should have smelled trouble...

FROSTY

By Dan McKeithan

The kids from the block gathered outside in the newly fallen snow. It was the start of that magical season. Christmas was in the air and snow was fresh on the ground.

Christopher watched from the window as the other boys and girls all threw snowballs and made snowmen. They never invited him out to play with them. They barely acknowledged his existence on a normal day. Why would they include him on a special day like this?

Bruce and his brother Jimmy had watched as Christopher moved into the last house in the development this past July. They came over to see him. Once they realized he wasn't normal—he didn't play sports—watch baseball—join Boy Scouts—they stopped talking to him.

It was just as if he wasn't there.

They ignored him in school and when all the kids gathered for Halloween—they didn't include him in their trick or treat games. He'd dressed as a ghost and they treated him like one—invisible.

Christopher watched as Bruce rolled a large snowball into a larger one and made the base of a giant snowman. Darla and some of the other kids added the second ball with the stick arms and rock buttons. Jimmy made the head with the carrot nose and coal eyes. Then all the kids stood and looked at their creation. They held hands and danced in a circle around the snowman.

Christopher waited until it was dusk, and all the kids had been called in for supper. His grandma wouldn't be home for another hour or more. He'd been reading up on spells and magic. He thought with a little luck he might be able to make the snowman live. A real life Frosty.

It was dark and the cold wind blew through the empty street. Christopher snuck out into the road. He had his spell papers from the computer. This street needed a jolt of Christmas magic. And he knew exactly which spell to use.

He took a razor blade from his pocket and cut a little gash on his hand. Blood mixed with the snow on the head of the snowman. Then Christopher pulled out some of his longer hairs. He sprinkled them over the snowman. He chanted the Latin verse. And spit three times on the ground. Nothing.

Even the internet was conspiring against him.

He watched headlights come over the hill and down toward his house. His grandmother was almost home. It was time to go back inside.

That night something magical happened. The snowman came to life. He skipped about town and called to all the little boys and girls. They all left their homes and followed him.

Christopher woke the next day to find the snowman gone along with all the kids. They were never seen again.

CHRISTMAS COOKIES

By Tony Logan

Vivien pushed the needle into the elderly dog's leg. Rukus lived a happy life of eighteen years. The newest Euthasol was incredibly potent. After securing her Vet locker in the closet, she walked into the bathroom to compose herself.

She wished her husband were here. Only her third Christmas since his car accident. On the mirror under her baggy eyes and reddened face, sat a green blob drawn in crayon.

A Christmas tree.

Another subtle hint from her son, Kevin.

Vivien wrapped Rukus in a large faded towel, then moved him to the garage. She would bury him tomorrow night.

Kevin stood close, staring at the lump. "Is he in heaven with daddy?"

She replied softly. "Yes, sweetheart. I'm sure they're playing fetch together."

Kevin wiped his eyes.

She patted his head. "Let's drive into the city and shop for presents."

They wandered the mall for hours as Kevin added more toys to his growing list. She chose his present last month, before she knew Rukus was ill.

A new puppy.

Leaving the toy shop, Kevin yanked his mom's arm. He pointed at a man covered with frayed blankets.

"Is he hurt, Mommy?"

"I don't know, honey. I think he's homeless."

"What's that mean?"

"Some people have problems that become too much. They end up without a place to go."

"He's suffering?"

"How about we give him some money?"

Kevin nodded.

She handed a few bills to the man. "Merry Christmas."

The ride home Kevin asked questions about homeless people. As they pulled into the driveway, Kevin declared he would make cookies for all the homeless. Vivien figured they could make a couple dozen and pass them out tomorrow before they picked up the new dog.

The day had been an emotional rollercoaster, and she opened a bottle of Cabernet.

Making cookies from store-bought dough required little supervision.

Kevin plopped small dough globs onto foil.

Moving toward Kevin, she wobbled. She looked back at the half-empty bottle.

"Are you okay, Mommy?"

"Yes, just tired."

"It's okay. I'll finish the cookies."

After she shut off the oven, Vivien pulled the trays out and placed them on the counter.

"Let them cool. Don't touch them."

Vivien fell back on the couch and laid her head on a pillow. Minutes later, she fell asleep.

Vivien woke up. She panicked until she saw Kevin in the living room chair. She stretched and stood; her head filled with pinpricks of pain.

On the table sat a shoebox.

Inside were twelve plastic baggies. Each contained two cookies.

So persnickety, just like his father.

A half-voice half-yawn rose from behind her. "Don't eat any, mommy. They're for the homeless!"

"Okay. Okay. I won't"

The next day they drove around and handed the bags. Kevin made sure he searched every street as they drove past. Not one bag wasted.

The end of the trip brought them to the animal shelter.

The staff walked out a tiny beagle. Kevin gasped. The puppy charged him, and licked his face.

Kevin hugged his mom. "Can we name him Cookie?"

Vivien loaded the new puppy supplies and headed home. Kevin played in the back seat with Cookie while they waited in traffic. Once Vivian got around the ambulances and police vehicles, it was a straight shot home.

Kevin and Cookie chased each other around the house, and Vivien put on the TV.

She hung her coat in the closet and began to close the door when she noticed her Vet locker was open.

She traced her thoughts back.

I know I closed and locked it.

She looked inside and everything was there.

Except the euthanasia meds.

Vivien stormed into the living room. But as did, she saw the TV played a news story.

"Investigators are puzzled by what killed all these homeless people."

Vivien's bottom lip quivered.

"Sweetheart...Did you put anything on those cookies you made?"

Kevin rolled Cookie on his belly. "Yeah. That stuff that sends people to heaven with Rukus and Daddy."

TINY TOTS WITH THEIR EYES ALL AGLOW

By Matthew A. St. Cyr

It was five miles to the next exit when the low fuel light chimed on the dashboard. Dan's eyes flicked down to the bright orange image of a gas pump that sat in the semi circle made by his speedometer.

"Come on baby, just a few more miles." Dan said while rubbing the steering wheel like a magic lamp. "I'm sorry that I didn't fuel you up when I should have."

There were few other cars on the highway, which was not surprising for six-thirty on Christmas Eve. Most everyone else was already with their families and having turkey dinners and eggnog.

Brilliants dots of moonlight reflected off the soft white blanket that covered farmland to his right. Every once in a while, he'd catch an extra bright light in the corner of his eye.

After a couple of white knuckled miles, Dan reached the exit and was delighted to find that the gas station was literally right at the turn-off. Pulling into the station on little more than fumes, he was even more excited to find that it was a full-service station.

Pulling in front of the pumps, he waited for several moments. No attendant in sight. No other cars at the pumps on in the lot, but all the lights were on in the mini-mart, so Dan decided to go in. Perhaps the attendant was dozing off. Something felt wrong, but he couldn't quite put his finger on it.

Inside the mini-mart Dan recoiled at the horror displayed before him. Several employees lay on the floor in pools of blood. A man dressed as Santa was hanging by his neck from several strands of garland that were attached to the ceiling.

Turning to run back out the door, he froze in his tracks. Several children, varying in ages from toddler to pre-teen stood before him. Each had a candy cane danging from their mouths and each had glowing white eyes.

The Christmas music piping through the store's intercom was interrupted by the tones of the Emergency Broadcast System.

"This is not a test," a deep voice intoned. "Officials are urging all residents to stay inside their homes and watch their children carefully. Officials report an epidemic of children, of varying ages, displaying extremely hostile behavior. Secondary reports state that affected children's eyes are turning bioluminescent after ingesting candy canes. Officials believe we may be under a biological attack, but do not know from whom."

The children blocking the door stared blankly at Dan, sugary red drool hanging from their lips.

"This epidemic is apparently confined to the New England area, though there have been reports of other anomaly in North Dakota, Oregon, California and Tennessee. If you witness any children displaying the aforementioned behaviors, contact your local authorities immediately."

Dan reached for his phone with a shaking hand, but the children were upon him in an instant. His cries were cut short as one bit through his larynx, spraying a holiday red across the front window.

THE DIFFICULTY WITH SNOW ANGELS

By Nicholas Rud

Snow came three days late for Christmas to the town of Ashland. This failed to dampen Nathan Jennings' excitement or, by extension, his puppy, Tulip, as they raced to Hiddleston Park. Since they had first met on that Christmas morning, the two had been inseparable. His parents, Amanda and Mathew, followed behind him in a lazy pursuit, laughing at the pair's shared eagerness. They waved as they passed Nathan playing on the frozen jungle gym with Tulip nipping at his boots before continuing down the path. Nathan dropped to the ground and clambered after them.

A nature trail connected Hiddleston to its sister park, Gehl. The trail passed through a valley between by a steep embankment to the east and a pre-existing hill backed by a thin forest leading down into wetlands on the west. For the most part, the hill was overlooked by most of the kids in favor of the eastern embankment, which was viewed as the superior spot for sledding.

From the top small hill, Nathan called out to his mom, which gained him the attention of a small crowd in addition to his parents. He stood with his arms outstretched like he was a gymnast who had just stuck the landing. "Watch this" he cried before squatting down and jumping backwards into the snow. Tulip seemed confused by this action and followed him to where he fell, sniffing the ground as she went. When she reached the edge of the child shaped crater she started barking, then ran back yelping. Amanda and Mathew came running with a small group of parents following behind. There was an impression left in the snow where Nathan had landed that lead all the way to the grass.

Some of the parents stayed behind to help with the search while the rest escorted the kids over to Gehl Park. Tulip stayed by the imprint in the snow and continued to howl. After several attempts to calm her down, Mathew took her to the car. A patrol car arrived some time later, along with one of the park keepers. Over the next couple of weeks multiple search parties were formed going past the tree line and into the wetlands, each coming back empty handed. No trace of Nathan was found outside of the imprint in the snow.

Eight months after Nathan's disappearance, Mathew and Amanda filed for a divorce.

Following their split, gossip started circulating around Ashland that Mathew had been an abusive husband and father. This was denied by Amanda; however, Mathew's move upstate caused the rumor to spread further. Amanda continued to live in the area for some time, before moving away in 2011. A section of fencing was added to the back of the hill where Nathan vanished preventing access to the wetlands along with a small memorial to him. At the top of the hill a section of dead grass can be found in the outline of a snow angel.

MITTEN TREE

By Vonnie Winslow Crist

In December, when she moved into a charming house in a picket-fence neighborhood, Drucilla Darkwander decided to set aside her witchy ways. Only one day passed before her neighbors, the Testermans, tested her resolve.

"Sorry about your flowers," said one of the girls on day two as a group of Testermans smashed her herbs while retrieving their soccer ball.

"Hm," replied Drucilla.

"Too bad about your fence," called a Testerman boy on day three after he crashed his minibike into the pickets.

"Hm," murmured Drucilla.

On day four, after she'd shooed her neighbor's dogs away from her roses, a spell popped into Drucilla's mind. She ignore it until Lila, the matriarch of the ill-mannered Testerman clan, quipped, "Dogs will be dogs," before dragging the hounds home.

"I must do something," she whispered as the magic in her veins burned hotter than a Christmas pudding. "But what?" she said to her cat.

Shadow tugged a yarn ball from her knitting bag and mewed.

"Mittens!" exclaimed the witchy woman who'd decided to embrace magic one last time.

Drucilla searched her pattern drawer, located directions for mittens, grabbed worsted- weight yarn from her stash, picked up a pair of needles, then cast on twenty-three stitches. Next, she knitted four rows of stockinette stitch for the cuff.

"Time for hair," she told Shadow who had positioned himself on the window sill where he could monitor the Testermans, balls of yarn, and Drucilla.

She retrieved her hairbrush from the bathroom. "Plenty of hair for our needs."

Shadow groomed his shoulder.

Placing a strand of her hair alongside the yarn, Drucilla knitted it into the remainder of the cuff while chanting a binding spell. Once her hair was woven tightly into the fabric of the mitten, she continued knitting until the mitten was completed. Knowing she could complete more mittens with another pinch of magic, Drucilla spoke a speed spell and her needles clicked in double-time.

Throughout December, the Testermans annoyed Drucilla by trespassing, damaging her gardens, kicking balls against the side of her house, and allowing their dogs to dig in her lawn. If they apologized, Drucilla acknowledged them with a forced smile.

For days, as she chanted binding spells, Drucilla knitted mittens in various sizes and colors—each with one of her hairs stitched into it. On Christmas Eve, Shadow purred as she tied the pairs together with red-as-blood yarn and loaded them into a bag.

"Our problems are nearly solved," she told him when she stepped outside.

Shadow jumped to his favorite spot and peered through the windowpane.

Quick as a needle poke, Drucilla tied the mittens onto a fir tree located on her front lawn.

Next, she walked to the Testermans' front door and knocked.

"Ms. Darkwander," said Lila Testerman as she opened the door.

"I've made mittens for your family. Won't you all come over and pick a pair from my mitten tree."

"How nice!" exclaimed Lila before shouting for her brood.

Like a cackle of hyenas, the Testermans raced to the fir, arguing over who got what, stripped the mitten tree, then clamored back to their house with nary a "Thank you" from the bunch.

Chuckling, Drucilla Darkwander walked inside her cozy house. Now that they possessed enchanted mittens with a part of her woven into them, Drucilla could possess the Testermans.

She picked up her knitting needles, wondered what sharp things the wretched Testermans would receive for Christmas, and considered exactly what, or who, she'd tell them to stab in the morning.

MERRY CHRISTMAS, AVERY

By Mama Creep

It's 2019 and I find Christmas celebration ridiculous. The older I get, the pointless the jolly holiday gets. This seething hatred came from the time I was a young child.

Years before I was sent to live with my estranged grandmother. Years before I lost both my parents on Christmas Eve. Years before, I unknowingly committed a sin.

Growing up, it has always been me and my mommy. She's nice in the sense that she provides the basic needs of a child to survive but her presence lacks feelings. There was never a connection made between us. I believe that she just had me because her religion prevents her from having an abortion. I guess I can thank her for that.

As for daddy? I grew up believing that he was this white-bearded old man, wearing a red coat with a fur collar, red trousers, and black leather boots. He was the type of man who was busy all year 'round to keep track of naughty and good children. He can only visit me once a year to bring presents and that is on Christmas Eve at least that's what mother told me. But in 10 years leading up to their death, I never saw him. Not even once.

A few days before that awful night, I was cutting the hedges on my neighbor's yard for quick cash. Mother rarely gives me money and I need one to buy ingredients for the cookies I'm going to make for daddy.

Mom and I went grocery shopping for Christmas. For once, I saw a hint of happiness in her face. She even bought me new clothes and helped me make the cookies. I had to add the special ingredient to make daddy sleepy and stay for a little while when mommy's not looking.

Just like how rats fall asleep when mommy uses rat poison.

Eight o'clock rolled around and mother tucked me to bed. She planted a soft kiss on my forehead apologized for neglecting me.

"I promise you, everything is different now. We'll start a new life together. A happy one." she said as she smiled at me and I lovingly stared at her. This warm fuzzy feeling in my heart made me smile too.

I slept soundly that night, expecting to see both my parents in the morning. When I woke up the next morning, I hurried downstairs expecting my dad sleeping on the couch except, there was no daddy, only mommy. There's mommy lying lifeless down on the floor with white dried liquid on the corner of her mouth.

AS THE HOLIDAYS APPROACH

BY KIMBERLY REI

Snow fell gently as James climbed out of the car. He was grateful it hadn't started until he arrived home. The reports called for a wicked storm and he had no interest in driving through a blizzard. He paused to take in the view. His house, keeping his wife and two kids safe. The lights, merry and bright as was proper for the season. The lawn display was new this year. The boys had begged for the garish Santa with his sleigh. James had thought the snowman trio a little ominous looking, but Nell laughed him off. She even sang Frosty the Snowman to him, "With two eyes made out of coal." Well and good in the daytime, he had told her, but downright creepy at night.

He sighed, joy and satisfaction with his life made visible for a moment in the cold- captured wisps of breath hanging in the air. The back of his neck tingled as he walked past the decorations. He scratched at the hairs and opened the door, ignoring the snowmen.

The next night, when he took the trash out, he stopped to stare.

"Nell? Honey, did you move the lawn snowmen?"

Confused laughter spilled from the den, "Why would I do that?"

His eyes shifted to the freshly fallen snow. No footprints.

"Never mind. I'm seeing things."

But two days later, in the bright winter sun, he wasn't so sure. The sleigh was closer. Wasn't it?

The week leading up to Christmas was too busy to notice much of anything. Between holiday commitments and long hours at work to prepare for the extended break, James was lucky he remembered where his bed was located. The sense of doom kept tickling his neck, though.

Every time he crossed the front yard.

On Christmas Eve, the boys wanted to leave sparkling feed for Santa's reindeer. Nell bundled them up against the howling winds and opened the front door.

"James? James, someone is playing a prank."

That tingle became a grip as he stood beside her. Three black-eyed snowmen blocked the path. The boys shoved their way between their parents.

"Momma, why is Santa climbing out of the sleigh?"

On Christmas Day, the house was dark and silent. Neighbors assumed the family had left on vacation. By New Year's Day, people were starting to talk. Their town was small enough for gossip to spread fast and worry to settle in.

By Spring, the family was declared missing. Their personal effects were packed up and placed in storage. The rest was put up for public auction. Most of the town turned out for the auction. They were all sure the family would return, and they would return the furniture and dishware when that happened, kept safe and treasured.

The auctioneer hid his surprise at the turnout, "Well, it certainly is good to see all you folks. Let's begin with the holiday decorations. First up, lawn sets. A sleigh with twelve reindeer, three snowmen, and a family of carolers to include two adults and two children."

CHRISTMAS CLAMATO

By Della Sullivan

In a tiny red house, beside a gorge full of hulking dark evergreens, four children were nestled warm in their beds. Outside, another group of young'uns tossed and turned beside the dwindling firepit all shivery in their sleeping bags. Two couples in the wee dwelling guzzled mulled wine and danced drunkenly together as carols played around and around on the same music disc. On every rotation past the blinking Christmas tree, they grabbed a cookie from the plate of goodies put out for Santa.

Outside, four older ones crawled out of their sleeping bags and stomped their feet for warmth. They tore apart the snowmen made earlier by their progeny, ate hunks of snow to wet their mauls of mouths and grumbled as the hour crept close to midnight. They looked almost human with only one percent of difference in their genealogy, but it made a world of difference.

Their skin shone like tinsel and their mouths protruded from their face, with jaws that could clamp down as tight as this world's largest clam.

Their life on a planet in a separate galaxy had eroded and shrunk until only these eight remained. A dash of this and a comet away, they had descended from the heavens tonight. They needed pure human DNA ingredients to restart their tribes.

There were deer in the forest and magical antlered reindeer in the air. The delicate deer stepped cautiously around the fire ring, while the animals in the air could almost be heard, jingling merrily along. It would soon be time for the big man to arrive with his bag of presents and candy canes galore. The others outside waited impatiently for the gore to begin.

The grandfather clock stuck twelve, each bong steady and sure. As the last note echoed in the air, the adults in the house heard shuffling and pawing that seemed to come from the roof. They looked up at first and then at each other, knowing it really could not be the big elf. Perhaps a relative was playing a joke on them.

Their welcoming smiles froze on their faces as four large creatures with silver and gold complexions streamed through the front door. Leaving leaves, muck and dirt in their wake, the outside others each grabbed a human partner and a parody of dancing continued as the holiday music played on. The melancholy sound of 'I'll be home for Christmas' rolled through the air as the two groups, one human, one not, grappled with each other.

The four humans screamed as mouths as big as Tridacna Gigas clams devoured them arm by arm and leg by leg. Soon, only a pearlized shimmer shone in the air and hunks of human hair decorated the muddy floor. The others belched and burped with satisfaction. It seemed an entire human was a bit much for their digestion to handle, but even so, it felt wonderful as they glowed with good health. With the yuletide gift of the precious seed of humanity already growing in their bellies, they ransacked the kitchen putting the raw turkey and Christmas pudding in knapsacks for the celebration dinner they would later share with their children.

Then these four not quite humans turned their attention to the stairs. Upstairs where the children slept. Their leader crept stealthily up, one step, two steps, three steps, and then paused. He put his finger alongside his lips and whispered, "We have taken enough for our needs. In the spirit of the season, and with everlasting good will, we will return to our space ship and wave a cheery goodnight to all as we fly out of sight."

FEASTING

By Gabriella Balcom

Strolling from one of the banquet tables to another, Gary surveyed the wide array of foods. Members of this church prepared a Christmas feast for the homeless every year. So did several other congregations in town. He had a nice home and wasn't anywhere close to being needy, but the idea of free food appealed to him, so he always went wherever it was offered.

After filling his plate, he grabbed a chair, deciding to eat outside.

A black cat padded up to him within moments, mewling plaintively.

"Quit begging and go catch something," he snapped. Not a fan of felines—of any living creature, really—Gary kicked it and it fled.

He was considering going back for seconds when the animal reappeared, walking toward him across the grass. Scowling, he went for the BB gun he kept in his truck, then chased his target across the church's lawn and into a meadow.

When he shot the cat, it flinched. After he fired a second time, it yowled loudly, and dozens of felines emerged from the nearby forest.

Gary aimed at another animal, pulling the trigger. He frowned when it acted as if nothing had occurred.

The cats slunk in his direction, surrounding him and ignoring his continued shots at them. Their bodies shimmered and they began growing larger, soon looming over him. One raked him with its claws, drawing blood. Another bit him.

Yelling for help, Gary tried to run away, but the animals batted his legs out from under him, continuing their attack.

He was still screaming as the felines drug him into the woods. There, they ripped his body apart, feasting on it, piece by piece.

SANTA'S LAPSE

By Corey Lamb

The mall never looked so dead.

"Santa...Santa..." a shrill voice rang as fingers snapped the haze into rigid clarity.

For the first time in years, the line of children struggled to reach the Christmas ficus at the edge of Santa's Workshop. Hell, it wasn't so much a line as it was a remainder, and Santa had all but lost his holiday cheer, which meant the Cymbalta had finally kicked in.

A hand yanked the tail of Santa's elastic beard.

"Santa!"

It was that damned Elf again, his gaze searing through Santa's plastic half-moon spectacles like roasting chestnuts. His pointed nose sharpened as he whispered, *Get it together, Claus.*

Santa shoved the Elf aside and forced a smile as his eyes fell to the next child waiting at the candy cane archway. He was a small boy, maybe eight years old.

"Ho, ho, ho," Santa choked, coughing a near fit at the third *ho* as he patted his knee, beckoning the child closer.

Hesitating, the boy approached the winter throne, glancing back to the remaining children.

There, beyond the bunch, stood a woman Santa hadn't noticed before. She was thin—no, thin wasn't right. Where thin could be healthy, this woman stood haggard and gaunt—her black gown hanging from her bones like wet tissue.

The Elf gestured for the boy to hop onto Santa's lap as he steadied the tripod, but the boy stood fixed on the woman. *His grandmother*, Santa thought. *Or, God forbid, his mother.*

"Go on, tell Santa what you want," the Elf urged from behind the camera. A few of the other children giggled.

Santa nudged the boy with his boot, and he jumped. "Well?"

The boy inched closer but avoided Santa's lap.

"You're not the real one, are you?" The boy asked, looking back to the woman in black, who stood closer since Santa had last checked, clutching a large purse at her waist.

"Of course I am," the old Claus growled as he sat upright. "Don't be silly."

Then... the boy whispered, peering back into Claus's eyes. *"Can you make her go away?"*

Santa looked from the boy to his grandmother, now standing inside the gates of the North Pole, just behind the Elf. How had she moved so quickly?

Make...who go away? He whispered back.

The boy closed his eyes and shook his head.

Your...grandmother?

"She's not my grandmother," the boy spat.

Oh... Santa said, frowning. *Your mother?*

The boy shook his head.

Santa glanced at the woman looming in front of the Elf. It wasn't a purse. It was a black burlap sack.

He raised a shaky hand to her.

"Just a moment," Santa grumbled, but something pulled at his insides. Though Santa had looked away, the woman lingered in his mind—only, the image was warped and disfigured. Like an animal on hind legs.

Please, the boy begged. His eyelids squeezed tight.

A sudden cold gripped Santa's chest.

Please, the boy cried, *don't let her take me.*

Santa reached for the boy's shoulder, but something beat him there. A wrinkled, sickly hand dressed in black at the wrist. For a moment, Santa couldn't breathe. For one tortuous, infinite second, he couldn't move.

"Santa!" a shrill voice rang, and fingers snapped. "Santa!"

The Elf clapped, and Santa turned to his side—to the boy—but he wasn't there. Instead, a younger girl sat on his lap, pawing at the fake beard.

"W—what? Huh?" Santa grumbled, scanning the North Pole for the woman in black.

Alas, there was no such woman.

Jesus, the elf whispered, scowling at the sweaty Saint Nick. *Get it together, Claus.*

DON'T MAKE THE YULETIDE BRIGHT

by Tim J. Finn

The watch captain tightened the rope binding Cyril Knox's hands when he saw him grin while the expanse of buildings burned.

"Try smiling at your hanging, Master Knox. The verdict will be swift."

"I die righteous," Knox said. "Heathen cavorting on sacred Christmas Eve. My township's sins will forever taste hellfire."

"That craziness lost you the colonial rights," the captain said. "You'll find it difficult to spread those outmoded Puritanical ideas molding in your righteous grave."

Knox laughed at his words

Monica and Jeremy Stanton embraced as they watched the Star Shower lights dance across their house. Jeremy scowled when an Accord halted at the curb. Kelly Hanson leaned out the passenger's windows while her husband fidgeted at the wheel.

"She insisted on another try," Brian Hanson said.

Monica pinched Jeremy when he mouthed a silent epithet.

"There's enough rooms reserved for the night." Kelly said.

"We're stick in the muds," Monica said. "First Christmas in our own house and all. Next year maybe."

Brian shook his head.

"You tried, Kell."

"Turn the lights off at least," Kelly said. "Maybe he'll... I can't say, not after last time." Brian floored the Accord as she started to cry.

"Weird ass tradition," Jeremy said. "The whole community spends Christmas Eve at a hotel party. Let's start our tradition, babe."

They French kissed under the sprig of mistletoe hung above the doorway casement as they returned to the house.

Scraps of tattered clothing and rancid, putrefied flesh dropped from the rotting corpse as it shuffled up the walkway to the Stanton house. The cadaver growled at the Star Shower and wrenched the gadget from the ground. The carcass cupped its hands around the device and squeezed.

Blue flame that reeked of Sulphur engulfed the Star Shower and charred it to plastic and metallic cinders. The stiff trod up the stairs to the Stanton's porch. The body groaned when bones cracked, and sinew snapped as it ascended the steps. The corpse's left eye glowed a red bright enough to also light up the empty right socket when it spied the mistletoe. The sprig incinerated when the cadaver touched the twig with a skeletal finger.

Monica stopped sorting ornaments and Jeremy ceased tree decorating when a decayed corpse strode into their living room. Worms slithered around its blackened tongue as the body addressed them in a croaky voice.

"Long time since profaners called me from my grave. I guess lessons still must be learned."

The cadaver entranced them with the glow from its eye. The body raised its smoldering hands as they walked to it. The corpse grasped each of the Stantons by the throat.

Smoke wafted from their mouths, followed by a vomit of ash and steaming embers. The corpse dropped them and watched them convulse on the floor for a few seconds.

"The house can stand this time. Perhaps the next tenants will heed warnings and let me rest in peace."

The body sighed as it exited the house and shuffled down the walkway.

THE GINGERBREAD ELF

By Jeannie Warner

Death looked around the room's carnage. He found the ghost hiding and tucked it into his cloak.

It was heavy for being small.

Normally, children were light due to a lack of life experiences. But this child was different, the soul edgy and faded already. With time, it might have healed. Or, as happens occasionally, it could have grown worse. He found a penciled note.

Dear ~~Satan~~ Santa,

It's hard to be gud. I ben trying but I still make my brother cry. I don't understand what gud is. I know we can't have a pet because of me, but I'd really like a stuffed kitten for Xmas I can love

and teach how to be gud so I can lern it too until
I can have a real one agin.
Milo

He read the letter, then looked at the ghost huddled in his cloak. "I see. I know just what to do with you."

The journey north was quick, a whisper of wind lost in the arctic breeze that blew ice needles into the unprotected skin. The destination was a house on a ranch with multiple workshops and a barn.

Death knocked upon the door, which was answered by an old woman with bright red cheeks and kind eyes. "Oh! Oh my, what an honor to have you visit! Do come in."

"I don't feel the storm."

"Well, yes or no, it's got to bother the ones you carry. Can I fetch you a cocoa?"

"That would be kind."

Death watched as she puttered about the kitchen. "I apologize for not coming to visit socially, but it has been a busy season."

"Yes, I know." Her voice was sad.

"But it's your busy season too. I've come to offer you another helper."

She looked up from the kettle, alert. "Oh. We'll need the gingerbread then."

He nodded, and the woman wiped her hands in her apron and set to work. Perhaps an hour and two cups of cocoa later, she pulled a large gingerbread man from the oven and set it before Death.

With great care, Death pulled the tiny ghost out of his cloak. It clung to the folds, whimpering slightly, but he soothed it. "There now. I've got you a sweeter home." Gently he pulled the spirit loose and pressed it into the gingerbread, which started into motion under his hands. It lifted itself off the pan and Death stepped back. "He is all yours."

The old woman leaned forward and kissed the ginger head. Immediately, it plumped out into something rounder, gaining color and substance until a small, naked creature stood on the table that blinked about the kitchen in confusion.

"Where am I?" the newborn asked Death as the woman bustled off to find some small clothing.

"You're at the North Pole,"

"I'm not a little boy anymore, am I?"

"You're an elf now. You have an important job to do. You're going to make stuffed animals for Santa to deliver."

The smile on the elf's face broke like the dawn. "Truly?"

Death nodded. "Making things for people will teach you how to be good, and the other elves will teach you how to live among people without hurting them."

"I would like that. Then no one will cry."

"No one ever cries here." Death nodded respectfully to Mrs. Claus who returned with a holiday suit, then turned to leave. "Madam, thank you."

Mrs. Claus smiled. "We are here when you need us. Come for the cocoa."

"I'd like that," Death replied, and vanished into the blizzard.

THE 12 DEATHS OF CHRISTMAS
By Marcus Cook

"Good Evening. I'm Charlie St. Graham and this is our top story. The sixth victim has been found and appears to be from the Christmas Killer. 46-year-old Martin Gacho was found dead in his bed with a hard-boiled goose egg jammed in is esophagus......"

The television screen went black and a wiry man wearing a nutcracker mask stepped out of the shadow. He walked over to the edge of an abandoned high school pool. His newest kidnap victim was chained to the pool floor and the water level stopped at her neck.

"Christmas Killer? That is the name they are giving me!" the man started to pace from edge to edge of the pool, "I mean Son of Sam, The Zodiac Killer, Jack the Ripper. These were GREAT names given to unknown killers. I'm given the Christmas Killer."

The woman noticed he was very upset and was worried this would set him off and kill her quickly, "What do you want to be called?"

"The Nutcracker, duh!" he pointed to his mask. "Only problem is I haven't revealed myself yet. I mean I am the only serial killer taking on a holiday theme. There was the St. Valentines Massacre, but that was a hit not a murder. "

The woman started to cry and shiver.

"My deaths even took some time to be suspected of being connected. The first victim was a homeless man I stabbed with a branch of a pear tree. The second victim was a woman I killed wearing two doves on her sweater."

The woman noticed the killer's pace quicken as she tried to follow him with her eyes.

"I know, I know, so lame. The third one started to take notice because he was a farmer whose eyes were pecked out in his hen coup. It took the jewelry store owner who was choked to death by five golden rings to finally make the police notice they had a serial killer. It wasn't exactly like the movie Seven, but that had better material to work with."

"So, it seems they named you off of what they had to work with." The woman said as she tried to slide her pruning hands out of her shackles.

"True. Once I reveal myself on the twelfth day, I'll get the name I deserve." He noticed her attempt to break free, "Seeing you'll be dead, let me share the surprise. I plan on being a part of the Christmas Parade. I'll be drumming down the street and when we hit the Main Square I'll stop. Turn to the crowd and announce who I am. I will then shout, "God Bless us everyone! Then Boom!"

"You are sick! You'll kill hundreds of people on Christmas!" the woman shouted.

"Starting with you!" The killer pulled out a nest attached to a kickboard. He placed it in the water and pushed it toward her.

The woman appeared confused, until she heard the flapping of wings. She struggled to turn her head and saw three black swans angrily heading toward her.

The Nutcracker turned away as her screams and the honking of the swans echoed around.

Softly, he started to sing, *"Six Swans a swimming."*

DARKENED NUTCRACKER

By Thomas Sturgeon Jr.

Julie's mother had brought her a nutcracker doll for Christmas. The toy had been worn out from excessive use and Julie had grumbled when she had opened the present. She wasn't thankful for what she had been given from her own mother who was at that time trying to make ends meet. Her mother was trying hard to keep the power on and the water running so that they could take baths.

"That nutcracker there was once my toy when I was growing up. My mother gave that to me when she was working two dead end jobs and I guess I showed her that I didn't appreciate what she'd done for me just like you didn't the gift I gave to you. You see that nutcracker has sentimental value now that I think about it." Julie's mother told her as she was washing the dishes after the guest's had left earlier that morning.

Julie took the nutcracker up to her bedroom and closed the door quietly behind her. As she threw the nutcracker into the garbage can that was sitting next to her bed.

The garbage can started smoking as flames erupted out of the trash can as Julie cried out in surprise as the nutcracker grinned its toothy grin and pointed its finger at her.

"Don't ever do that again!" the nutcracker said.

Julie shook with fright as her mother rushed in and looked Julie in the eyes just after looking at the smoldering trash can, and cried out, "Didn't I tell you to be thankful?!?" as Julie's mother cradled the nutcracker in her arms as she sobbed.

Julie never wanted to see another nutcracker again after that.

SANTA CLAUSE

By Dan McKeithan

Gary waited for the maître'd to seat him. Alice was already at the table. It was nice to have a night out to themselves. Especially on the night before Christmas Eve. Alice had already ordered a bottle of the most expensive wine.

Gary sat down and placed his coat on the back of his chair. "Did Jennifer get there on time?"

"She was a little late. The kids were chomping at the bit waiting for her to arrive. I think they like her better than us," Alice said.

Gary handed the menu to the waiter. "I'll have prime rib with baked potato." The waiter nodded and left.

"How was work?" Alice asked.

"A bitch, to be honest. I had this asshole of a client today. I lost it with him and reported him to his boss. I heard that they may have let him go."

"Right at Christmas time? That's terrible."

"No, he deserved it. I think he's unbalanced or something. Enough about that, let's enjoy our time out."

Alice smiled and took a long slow sip of her wine. She removed her sandal and rubbed Gary's leg with her foot.

"How long have you been here?" he asked.

"I got here about ten minutes before you. Jennifer called and I had to turn around. Matt wanted pizza and I forgot to leave the money."

Gary took a sip of wine. "This must be powerful stuff then—"

Alice's cell lit up. She touched the screen and placed it to her ear. "No, it's fine—oh, really." She mouthed to Gary. "Santa's at the house."

Gary smirked. "Bob's an idiot. He must've gotten the nights mixed up. Tell Jennifer it's okay and we're on our way."

🔔🔔🔔

Gary and Alice pulled into the driveway. Jennifer met them at the door.

"Santa just left. He gave them some presents to open. He even brought a sucker for me," she said.

Gary took out his wallet. "How much do we owe you?"

"Don't worry about it. The night was called early and it's Christmas time," Jennifer said.

"We should pay you for your time, at least," Alice said.

Jennifer took out her sucker and opened it. "It's on the house."

She walked to her Honda, sitting in the drive, sucking on the sucker.

Gary and Alice watched as she backed out and drove off; then went inside.

Matt and Anne ran up to them. "Look at the presents we got from Santa," Matt said. He held a bow and arrow in one hand and a toy gun in the other. Anne had a Barbie doll and a horse.

"Santa did his research," Gary said.

"Alice leaned in close to Gary and whispered in his ear. "Did you give Bob those presents?"

Gary whispered back, "I haven't seen Bob in a couple of days. I was going to give him the presents to give out tomorrow."

The kitchen phone rang. Gary raced to grab it.

"Mr. Brooks? There is something wrong with my sucker," Jennifer said. "I'm sick, make sure the kids are not eating any of the candy."

Gary thanked her and hung up the phone. His cell rang at the same time.

Matt walked into the room holding his toy gun and pointing it at Alice.

"Hey, man—I can't make it tomorrow night. I'm down with the flu," Bob said.

Matt pulled the trigger of the toy.

BANG!

Alice slumped to the ground.

Gary dropped the cell.

SING FOR YOUR SUPPER

by Lisa Flanyak

Robert Forest knelt down and placed a log into the fireplace. He rubbed his hands together in front of the rising flames. As he stood up, something caught his eye outside the window. As he gazed out, the colorful lights from the Christmas tree next to him reflected off his face. The snow began to fall again.

Just beyond the end of the winding driveway, Robert could make out what appeared to be a group of carolers. The group glided down the sparsely populated street in the direction of the house.

"Honey! Come quick! We've got carolers!"

Frantic footsteps shuffled above him, then moved to the stairs and then to the hardwood floor in the foyer. His wife, Tasha, burst into the room.

"I found the mistletoe!"

Her eyes wide, like a child on Christmas morning seeing all the gifts under the tree. She rushed over to him and placed the mistletoe over his head. He planted a kiss on her glossed lips.

"Tastes like gingerbread," he replied as he smacked his lips together.

"For Christmas."

"I guess it could have been worse. Like eggnog," he shuddered at the thought.

Tasha tacked the mistletoe to the center of the arch above the room's entryway.

"I love you Robert Forest."

"I love you Tasha Forest."

"And I love our new house," she added.

"Speaking of which."

Robert stole another glance outside and watched the carolers make their way up the sidewalk. An eclectic group of about ten men and ten women. Each bundled up from the harsh cold. Some had rosy cheeks, some displayed bright red noses.

Robert chuckled and pointed outside. Tasha squeezed in to get a good look.

"I just love this time of year. I've always wanted to live in a town where they did this kind of stuff. We're living out our own Thomas Kinkade painting. They're coming to the door," he said.

The doorbell rang. Robert grabbed Tasha's hand and led her into the foyer. He flung open the door and they were flooded with the sounds of a joyful Christmas tune. It seemed like a magical scene out of a family holiday movie. The singing was so enchanting, melodic and almost hypnotic. The voices roared loud and in unison. Robert and Tasha both stood with huge grins on their faces and their arms around each other's waist.

"We wish you a bloody Christmas...."

Robert's grin flatlined and his face became distorted.

He looked over at his wife. Tasha's face said what he had been thinking. Those were not the lyrics!

"...and a deadly new year."

One man stretched out his arm and grabbed onto the front of Robert's snowman embroidered sweater which caused the carrot nose to fall off. The man yanked Robert into the group and a few of the carolers swarmed around him. Before Tasha could react, a woman grabbed her by the hair and pulled her in. The group of harmonious singers turned inward and the sound of bones crunching and flesh ripping replaced any warm peaceful melody that was there just moments before.

Moments later, the group composed itself and re-formed. No one spoke a word. The members straightened up their clothes and some wiped their mouths with their scarves. One member of the group pulled the door shut. The singers then turned away from the house and walked back down the sidewalk. They began to hum another Christmas tune.

The only evidence of Robert and Tasha Forest's existence was a red stain on the snow- covered sidewalk.

THE MOUSE KING'S REVENGE

By R.C. Mulhare

The previous Christmas, the Stahlbaum girl had protected her Nutcracker Prince and defeated the Mouse King, striking their lord and ruler with her slipper.

But this year, the girl had grown closer to womanhood and disappeared from the house, going to a charm school in Vienna. Frau Stahlbaum ordered the maids to pack away the toys remaining in the girl's room, including a number of French dolls and the Nutcracker she had fawned over, then had the houseboy bring the boxes to the attic. The toys sat there, through the autumn and into the winter. The mice, smelling the Nutcracker Prince within one box, chewed at the thin wood, trying to worry a hole into it.

On Christmas Eve, when ghosts lie still, animals speak and playthings move about, the Nutcracker Prince awakened, twitching his limbs, finding himself hemmed in by the china faces and limbs and silken skirts of the French dolls. He wanted to tip his shako to them, but of course, he could not move a joint.

The lavender gowned lady beside him rose. He stretched, intending to greet the lady, but the lady had not stood on her own.

Two huge gray rats tossed the lady aside. They seized the Nutcracker, flinging him to the floorboards.

The Nutcracker looked for his wooden sword, as he pulled himself to his feet, but it remained in the box. He ran for it, but two more rats armed with forks leapt from the shadows, joining the first two, surrounding the Nutcracker.

"You haven't a girl with a slipper to defend you now," the largest growled. And the rats closed in, two grabbing the Nutcracker by his shoulders. He kicked at the second pair. More rats, armed with forks and knives and a horde of brown mice, armed with bone toothpicks, closed in, weapons lowered.

"Soldiers! My tin comrades! To arms!" the Nutcracker called.

"There's no soldiers up here to come at your call, and the trap door is latched tight," the largest rat growled, and stabbed the Nutcracker's knee, wedging the point of his knife between the halves of the joint and levering it. Another rat leaned in to bite the Nutcracker's shoulder, one ear brushing his face.

The Nutcracker clamped down his jaws on the ear. The rat squalled and jumped back, ear bleeding. But another took their place, wedging a fork's tines through the Nutcracker's other knee. The Nutcracker raised his arms to strike the rats, but the mice stabbed his elbows and shoulder joints, jamming them.

Two especially enterprising mice levered their toothpicks, loosening one shoulder, til the pins holding it together bent. His arm dropped off, clattering to the floor. A young mouse ran up, grabbing the arm, waving it about. Emboldened, the beasts dragged their prisoner across the floor, toward a hole in the wall. They pushed him into the maw, as far as his wide, blocky head.

The largest rat brandished a carving knife. "We can take that in hand." He thrust the point under the Nutcracker's jaw, wedging it shut before pushing in deeper. One mouse, clenching a lavender silken slipper in its paw, ran up, slapping the Nutcracker's forehead.

"That is for the Mouse-King, my father!" the mouse squeaked.

"And this for our lord and ruler," the rat leader snarled, levering the knife. The Nutcracker's head broke loose, and rolled across the floor...

First the maids, then Herr Stahlbaum himself had to knock on Clara's door, to rouse her. She shuffled into the drawing room, when the year before she had dashed toward the Christmas tree laden with baubles and surrounded by wrapped parcels.

"Shall I open Clara's presents for her?" asked her little brother Fritz.

"I might need your help. I could not sleep a wink. The mice were dragging something heavy across the ceiling," Clara said.

"Maybe they dragged one of your silly old dolls?" Fritz asked.

BEST CHRISTMAS EVER

By Michelle River

I watched the light of the early dawn as it flickered through my window, casting the room in a warm pink glow of Christmas morning. I had been up for hours, anxiously waiting for my bedside clock to read 8:00 a.m., Mom and Dad's Christmas morning rule. When it finally did I leapt from bed and yelled "It's Christmas" at the top of my lungs, rushing downstairs to the massive Christmas tree which now exploded with gifts.

I skipped to the fireplace and the overfilled stockings and grabbed mine from the hook. I looked down at the empty plate of cookies and milk I had left out for Santa and smiled. Looks like Santa got my treat.

"Shelly, is your Dad down there already?"

Grabbing the small square box from the top of the stocking, I gingerly began unwrapping it. "No, I haven't seen him."

Mom made her way down the stairs, pillow creases still fresh on her cheek and smiled, kissing me on my forehead. "Merry Christmas my love."

"Merry Christmas," I said as she walked toward the kitchen to make some tea.

The indistinguishable scent of chocolate and orange wafted up at me as I finished unwrapping the first of my gifts when I heard mom scream.

"Shelly, call 911." I heard my mom's frantic cries as I bolted into the kitchen. She was kneeling over my dad; his body still and silent, lips a pale blue, the same colour as the tile he rested on. I ran to the counter, grabbing the phone and with shaking hands dialed 911. I put the phone on speaker, another one of mom and dad's rules, as I watched mom start CPR compressions.

I hurried to them, stepping on a half-eaten cookie I had baked or Santa just last night. Confused I moved closer. In my dad's clenched hand was the other half of the cookie, and on his chest and around his mouth were crumbs.

"Mom," I screamed. "Why does Dad have a cookie I baked for Santa?"

"911 all of our lines are busy please hold,"

"What?"

I pointed to the crumbled cookie.

"Dad ate the cookies I made for Santa. That wasn't for him. It was for Santa. You told me only Santa eats the cookies. That was the rule. YOU SAID IT WAS A RULE."

"911 operator what is your emergency,"

Her eyes went wide and her face paled as she stopped the compressions and grabbed my hands, the cold phone between us.

"Baby, what are you saying. Did you put something in the cookies Daddy ate? What did you put in the cookies?"

"911 operator what is your emergency,"

"You told me they were for Santa," I cried. "I asked Santa for a kitty cat last year and I didn't get one. You told me Santa said I wasn't ready for a kitten but I was! I wanted to make him sick, get him back for ruining Christmas. They were supposed to be for Santa!"

"This is 911 operator, we are sending an ambulance to your location."

"Baby what was in the cookies." She screamed but I didn't hear her. Something else had caught my attention, in the corner of the kitchen, tucked away beside the table was a box I had never seen before. It was wrapped in shiny red paper with a big white bow with holes cut into the side.

I dropped the phone and ripped my hands from my mother's clutches, ran to the box as fast as I could. With trembling hands, I lifted the lid and giggled in glee. A perfect little kitten, soft and orange, was there waiting for me.

It was going to be a wonderful Christmas after all.

AUTHORS

DAN MCKEITHAN

completed his MFA in Creative Fiction from UC-Riverside in 2016 while fighting off cancer. Prior to that he attended UCLA in Professional Screenwriting in 2002 while working for Warner Bros Studios as security for the TV show EXTRA. Now his day job is running two nursing homes in North Carolina and when he's not at home or off in Russia with his wife's family, tries to get a little writing done.

KEVIN J KENNEDY is a

horror author & editor from Scotland. He is the co-author of You Only Get One Shot, Screechers and has a solo collection available called Dark Thoughts. He is also the publisher of several bestselling anthology series; Collected Horror Shorts,

100 Word Horrors & The Horror Collection, as well as the stand-alone anthology Carnival of Horror. His stories have been featured in many other notable books in the horror genre.

He lives in a small town in Scotland, with his wife and his two little cats, Carlito and Ariel.

Keep up to date with new releases or contact Kevin through his website: www.kevinjkennedy.co.uk

N.M. BROWN is an international

best-selling author from Florida. She's a happily married mother who sheds light on the dark corners of the mind that we like to keep hidden. Her other publications include stories in Sirens at Midnight, Calls From the Brighter Futures Suicide Hotline, the Scary Snippets Collections, Mother Ghost Grimm children's horror anthology, Dark Xmas, along with several others.

A.L. KING is an author of horror, fantasy,

science fiction, and poetry. As an avid fan of dark subjects from a young age, his earliest influences included R.L. Stine, Edgar Allan

Poe, Chuck Palahniuk, and Stephen King. He grew up in Sistersville, West Virginia, which he continues to call home. Facebook page:

https://www.facebook.com/alkauthor/

JAY LEVY is a devoted writer of genre

fiction and role-playing games, Jay spends much of his time reading stacks of

comic books, or taking walks with his lovely shield-maiden wife and dogs. His other works can be found

At: https://jaylevyswritingadventures.blogspot.com/

GABRIELLA BALCOM

lives in Texas with her family, loves reading and writing, and thinks she was born with a book in her hands. She works in a mental health field, and writes fantasy, horror/thriller, romance, children's stories, sci-fi, and more.

She likes traveling, music, good shows, photography, history, genealogy, interesting tales, and animals. Gabriella says she's a sucker for a great story and loves forests, mountains, and back roads which might lead who knows where. She has a weakness for lasagna, garlic bread, tacos, cheese, and chocolate, but not necessarily in that order.

You can check out her author page at: https://m.facebook.com/GabriellaBalcom.lonestarauthor

MAMA CREEP is a 25-year old

Filipina and an aspiring horror author.

She lives in the Philippines and is a full-time artist. She loves to dabble from crafting, illustration, book design, writing stories/poems and recording for her podcast. She can't seem to stop creating things so if you have time, visit her art page Hooman Error to know more about her antics.

KIMBERLY REI has

been writing for as long as she can remember. At five years old, her parents gifted her with a set of Children's Classics that she had no hope of reading. Yet. The potential alone sparked a love of words that has never wavered.

Kim has taught writing workshops and edited novels for Authors You May Recognize. She has published several short stories and now can't stop chasing paper dragons.

She currently lives in Tampa Bay, Florida with her wife and an abundance of gorgeous beaches to explore.

AARON MORRIS is an aspiring writer from Katy, Texas, and a lover of all things horror.

MATTHEW A. ST. CYR lives in Western Massachusetts with his wife and three cats. In addition to writing he is musician and former semi-professional magician. An avid cinephile, he is obsessed with cult/obscure/weird films as well as obscure music and bands from the 80's. All in all he's a strange guy.

DEAN KING'S work has appeared in Suicide House Publishing's *Scary Snippet Halloween*

Anthology, Kevin Kennedy's "*100 Woord Horrors 3*" - Blood Song Book's "*Forest of Fear*" and Reanimated Writers Press *100 Word Zombie Bites*. Additionally, my work has appeared in online and print venues, including *Teleport Magazine Science Fiction and Fantasy*, and *Dark Dossier Magazine* in both digital and print. My first novel "*Sarah's Cross*" is due out next year from Austin Macauley Publishers of London/New York.

A.L. KING is an author of horror, fantasy,

science fiction, and poetry. As an avid fan of dark subjects from a young age, his earliest influences included R.L. Stine, Edgar Allan Poe, Chuck Palahniuk, and Stephen King. He grew up in Sistersville, West Virginia, which he continues to call home.

Facebook page: https://www.facebook.com/alkauthor/

AMBER KEENER is a graduate

from Southern Illinois University with a B.A. in English. She lives with her husband, Jim and their rabbit Danger, bunny the beast of Caer Bannock. She's a geek that loves most things with magic, and when given the time, will often be playing video games.

JOHN KUJAWSKI has

interests that range from guitars to the Incredible Hulk. He was born and raised in St. Louis, Missouri and still lives there to this day.

STEPHANIE LEVY enjoys

reading tales of magic and mystery. Along with brewing wines and mead, she is an aspiring modern shield-maiden. She loves her dogs, her husband, and full-armor combat!

ALYSON FAYE lives in West

Yorkshire with her husband, teen son and four rescue animals. Her fiction has been published widely in print anthologies - *DeadCades*, *Women in Horror Annual 2*, *Trembling with Fear 1 &2*, *Coffin Bell Journal 1*, *Stories from Stone* and her own Yorkshire ghost stories, *Trio of Terror*; her debut collection of flash fiction, *Badlands* was published by Chapeltown Books. Her work has appeared in many ezines, (*Ellipsis, Horror Scribes*) but most often on the Horror Tree site, in *Siren's Call* and *The Casket of Fictional Delights*. In May 2019 *Night of the Rider,* was published by Demain in their Short Sharp Shocks! E book series and reached the amazon kindle top #10 best seller lists. Her work has been read on podcasts (e.g. Ladies of Horror), short-listed and placed in competitions and been published in charity anthologies.

She performs at open mics, teaches, edits and hangs out with her dog on the moor in all weathers. She enjoys swimming, crafting and singing.

https://alysonfayewordpress.wordpress.com/
Twitter @AlysonFaye2

ROBERT ALLEN LUPTON is retired and lives in New

Mexico where he is a
commercial hot air balloon pilot. Robert runs and writes every day, but not necessarily in that order. More than a hundred of his short stories have been published in several

anthologies including the New York Times best seller, "*Chicken Soup For the Soul – Running For Good*". His novel, Foxborn, was published in April 2017 and the sequel, Dragonborn, in June 2018. His first collection, *Running Into Trouble*,

was published in October 2017. His collection, "*Through a Wine Glass*

Darkly" was released in June 2019.

THOMAS STURGEON JR is a 33-year-old

author living in Chatsworth, Georgia. He's been published in eleven publications including Black Hare Press's "World's" "Monsters" and the upcoming "Apocalypse" anthology. He has a cat named Tigger. He loves to read and write.

THOMAS BAKER is a lover of

all things horror with a heavy emphasis on zombies, paranormal and things of the slasher variety! He grew up convincing his mom to let him watch all the scary movies he could get his hands on. He aims to keep his writing fast paced and fun. Thomas has upcoming stories to be featured in different anthologies but he is best known for his co-written "Outbreak Series" with his good friend and writing partner Robert Wagner. The series has reached trilogy status with the titles "Safe Haven", "Purgatory" and "Dead Of Winter" You can follow him on his 6K Press page on both Facebook and Twitter to stay up to date on the latest shenanigans that are afoot! Be warned, some parental advisory required! Facebook @ 6kpress / Twitter @6k_press

6kpress.com

AURORA M. LEWIS is

a retiree in her late sixties, having worked in finance for 40 years. In her fifties, she received a Certificate in Creative Writing-General Studies, with Honors from UCLA. Aurora's poems, short stories, and nonfiction have been accepted by The Literary Hatchet, Gemini Magazine, Jerry Jazz Musician,

The Blue Nib, Trembling in Fear, and Jitter Press to name a few.

Social media links are FaceBook, Aurora M. Lewis, and Twitter, @auroralewis5

● ● ●

W. H. GILBERT is a writer from Texas who was once mortally afraid of Santa Claus and is a returning contributor to Scary Snippets. He has other short stories that can be found in Scary Snippets Halloween Edition, Road Kill Volume 2 from Eakin Press, Road Kill Volume 4 and The Toilet Zone from Hellbound Books, and has several more on the way.

DONNA CUTTRESS is a short story writer from Liverpool, U.K. This is her second piece published for Suicide House Publishing, her previous appeared in 'Scary Snippets

Halloween'. Her work has been published by Crooked Cat, FoF Publishing and Black

Hare Press. She has had work published by Sirens Call as part of Women in Horror

Month and been included in Flame Tree Publishings, Chilling Ghost Short Stories.

Her work for 'The Patchwork Raven's' 'Twelve Days is also available as an art book.

She is currently completing her first novel, and has been a speaker at the London

Book Fair.

@Hederah (twitter)

donnacuttress.wordpress.com

MICHAEL BORGE is a Writer, Voice Actor, and overall sporadic artist who enjoys pop culture and other nerdy material. You can find his voice acting talents at the Scarecrow Tales Podcast. He also appears in Suicide House Publishing's *Death and Butterflies Anthology* to be released in early 2020.

MARCUS COOK lives in

Cleveland, Ohio with his inspirational wife and cat. Ever since he saw, "Star Wars" at the age of four, Marcus has loved science-fiction. He is also inspired by Timothy Zahn, Kevin J. Anderson, Kevin Smith, Luc Besson, Ernest Cline, and Elmore Leonard.

Other stories Marcus has written include;

"Ava Edison and the Burning Man." Found in "Burning an anthology of short thrillers". Published by

Burning Chair Press. 2018

"Not my Ship." Found in "Worlds: Dark Drabbles #1" published by Black Hare Press.

"Cherish Salazar" found in "Storm Area 51" published by Black Hare Press.

You can contact and follow Marcus on his Facebook page: ReadMarcusCook

Or email him at readmarcuscook@gmail.com. He loves to hear from his fans.

DEBICKEL is a student of architecture

dabbling in writing. Twitter: https://twitter.com/debickel

GEORGE ALAN BRADLEY

lives in the Midwest with his wife, Lisa, son Everett and daughter, Evelyn, and a menagerie of peculiar pets. He is currently working on two debut novels while continuing to publish short stories. Website: WWW.GEORGEALANBRADLEY.COM Twitter: @GALANBRADLEY

NICHOLAS RUD

is a horror author from Bellingham, Washington. When he isn't at his desk, he can be found wandering about in the rain or tinkering with some small project

TIM J. FINN

was born in Boston and still calls the area home sweet home. He shares that home with a massive assembly of collectibles...his living room is a combination of library and museum.

Tim's non-writing jobs have included radio disc jockey, office temp, short order cook and receptionist. Tim is a member of the New England Horror Writers and earned a BA in English from Grinnell College. His work has been published in a number of anthologies and magazines. Please visit his website-www.authortimjfinn.net

DELLA SULLIVAN is a

writer of dark fiction and mysteries. She is a mother-of-four, owner of two enormous Maine Coon cats, and self-proclaimed voracious reader. Her Hallowe'en story, "A Romanian Tradition" was published in their latest Halloween edition.

NERISHA KEMRAJ -

resides in Durban, South Africa with her husband and two mischievous daughters.

She has work published/accepted in various publications - print and online.

She holds a Bachelor's degree in Communication Science, and a Post Graduate Certificate in Education from University of South Africa.

For more work, visit:

https://www.amazon.com/author/nerisha_kemraj

Visit her Facebook page:

https://www.facebook.com/pg/Nerishakemrajwriter/

Instagram: https://www.instagram.com/nerishakemraj

Jeannie Warner

spent her formative years in Colorado, Canada, and Southern California, and is not afraid to abandon even the most luxurious domestic environs for an opportunity to travel almost anywhere. She has a useless degree in musicology, a checkered career in computer security, and aspirations of world domination

Melody Grace is a writer of

all things terrifying and unsettling. She began her journey to the dark side at a very young age, as a way to bring her fears to life. As you read her stories, you will find that her dreams are now your nightmares, as she sweeps you into the dark realm of horror.

You can frequently find her work on Reddit's horror platform: NoSleep, along with many different podcasts. This year alone she has been published in many terrifying anthologies, as well as her very own: Nocturnal Nightmares.

Ann (without an "e") Wycoff

lives in Felton, California a few miles from Santa Cruz.
She spends much of her time plotting her next story as well as revenge against varied enemies,
both real and imagined. Since she moved to the California coast, *Sequoia sempervirens* has crept into her fiction and poetry with alarming regularity. You can find her easily enough on
Facebook and her website at annwycoff.wordpress.com.

Anthony Giordano was born and raised in NYC,

and has been adrift in Upstate New York for close to a decade.

He lives with his wife, four children, and two dogs.

When free time presents itself, he loves to read, review, and write.

MICHELLE RIVER hails

from Ontario, Canada where she is lives with her wonderful husband and fearless daughter. A lover of hot black coffee and everything dark and terrifying, she spends her nights writing horror and dreaming about all things that go bump in the night. Follow her on facebook.com/MichelleRiverAuthor/ and Twitter: MRiver_Writes

NICK MOORE is a lifelong lover of

horror. A believer that spiders are horrifying and the dog should always survive the story, Nick originally hails from New England and now lives in the Blue Ridge Mountains with his wife and rescue animals. His work can be found at www.nmwrites.com.

SCOTT McGREGOR is a new and emerging Canadian writer whose work has recently been featured in several anthologies, including the *Scary Snippets: Halloween* anthology

G.W. GRIM is a prolific author who specializes in horror and dark fiction. He is a very busy fellow who aspires to someday appear in a small cameo role in movie that no one wants to watch.

VONNIE WINSLOW CRIST is a member of the HWA, SFWA, and is the author of *The Enchanted Dagger, Owl Light, The Greener Forest, Murder on Marawa Prime,* and other award-winning books. Her fiction appears in *Amazing Stories, Killing It Softly 2, Chilling Ghost Short Stories, Potter's Field 4 & 5, Sea of Secrets, Midnight Masquerade, Monsters, Best Indie Speculative Fiction: 2018, Zombies for a Cure, Creep Anthology of Horror Stories,* and elsewhere. For more information: www.vonniewinslowcrist.com

DIANE ARRELLE,

(Dina Leacock) has more than 250 stories and two fiction collections, *Just A Drop In The Cup* and *Seasons On The Dark Side*, published. She edited the anthology *Crypt-Gnats* for Jersey Pines Ink.

www.arrellewrites.com   FaceBook: Diane Arrelle
www.jerseypinesink.com

LISA FLANYAK

developed a love for writing at an early age. Although she writes in all genres, she finds the most enjoyment in writing horror. Often when writing, she is fortunate to have the company of one or two of her feline friends, who always try to take over the keyboard to assist.

RADAR DEBOARD

is a horror movie and novel enthusiast who resides in the small town of Goddard, Kansas. He occasionally dabbles in writing and enjoys to make dark tales for people to enjoy. He has had drabbles and short stories published in various electronic magazines and anthologies.

CORY STEPHENS is a

husband to a lovely wife and father to a 12, 3, and 1 year old

boys. He writes in his spare time to keep himself sane after

getting yelled at by the 12-year-old over hair gel and seeing

Thomas the Train for the 12,000th time this week.

REDDIT

WEBSITE

K.M. BENNETT is a horror

author from the midwestern U.S. Her work has appeared on

The NoSleep Podcast and in various horror anthologies. She

lives with her husband, son, and Australian cattle dog. Find

out more at ThatKatieLady.com.

GINA PINEY sits in her hilltop home in Ontario, Canada releasing her stories to an unsuspecting world. Find her on Amazon or Facebook to see her latest projects.

DREW STARLING is an author of horror and dark fiction. His short stories have been featured in nearly a dozen published anthologies and his collaborative novel "*Storming Area 51: Horror at the Gate*" spent time ranked as Amazon's #1 Sci-Fi Anthology. You can find him on Twitter @ScaryStarling. His only rule of writing is the dog never dies.

CECELIA HOPKINS-DREWER is a speculative writer, poet and reviewer, who lives in Adelaide, South Australia. She has also written a Masters paper on H.P. Lovecraft, and a teenage vampire series that commences with "MYSTIC EVERMORE". Her poetry has been published in "*THE MENTOR*" a fanzine edited by Ron Clarke, and *SPECTRAL REALMS* (Edited by S.T.

Joshi). Cecelia has micro-fiction included in the Black Hare Press anthologies *WORLDS, ANGELS, MONSTERS, BEYOND, UNRAVEL and APOCALYPSE*. She is honoured to join the excellent group of authors in *SCARY SNIPPETS: HALLOWEEN EDITION* (Edited by N.M. Brown) and this exciting new Christmas volume.

TRICIA LOWTHER grew

up in Liverpool, England. Her work has appeared in numerous online and print venues, including *Writer's Forum Magazine, The No Sleep Podcast,* and *The Third Corona Book of Horror Stories*.

AKSHAY PATWARDHAN is a high school

senior attending Wando High School in Mount Pleasant, South Carolina. His hobbies and passions are reading and writing, and he specifically loves the horror genre. In college, he plans to major in English and minor in Creative Writing in order to follow his dream of becoming an author.

C.L. WILLIAMS is an

international bestselling author currently living in central Virginia. He has written eight poetry books, four novellas, one novel, and a contributor to a multitude of anthologies and magazines. His most recent poetry book *The Paradox Complex* features the poem "Sad Crying Clown" that was turned into a short film on YouTube by MMH Productions. C.L. Williams is currently working on his ninth poetry book *The Absolution* as well as *Bed Bugs*, a supplement book to the MMH Productions film of the same name. When not writing, C.L. Williams enjoys reading and sharing the works of other independent authors.

Facebook

Twitter

Instagram

STEVE ODEN is a retired newspaper

and magazine editor who now writes horror and speculative fiction. My work has appeared in Harbinger Press (Phantom

Stench) and is due to be published in Tales from the Canyons of the Damned (Toys and Monsters and the sequel, Blind in Battle). Several short stories will see publication in various venues next years.

ERIC NIRSCHEL graduated

from Temple University in Philadelphia with a Bachelor's in Interdepartmental Communications, which includes completed Associates tracks in Comparative Religions, Philosophy, Psychology, Magazine Journalism, and Marketing. A practicing witch of the eclectic variety, I've worked in a number of fields, including as the proprietor of a traditional bells, books, and candles style magic shop. As a longtime fan of horror in film, book, and game, I consider my work heavily influenced by Lovecraft, Koontz, Ito, and King, among others. Previous works of mine have appeared for Yahoo! News and 'The Dollar Stretcher.' More recently, my fiction has appeared in 'Beyond the Infinite: Tales from the Outer Reaches,' 'Scary Snippets,' and 'Monsters We Forgot.' Eric can be found on twitter at @ENirschel.

KATY LOHMAN is a quirky,

rather queer fantasy/horror writer and artist whose favorite questions are "What if?" and "Why?" She writes about the fae, dangerous angels, gods, demons and Things That Must Not Be Named. When not writing or drawing, she can be found researching various topics, reading, taking online classes, rolling dice, building decks and exploring rural Ohio. She has short stories published in Ugly Babies 3 and 47-16: Short Fiction and Poetry Inspired by David Bowie, Volume II. Her favorite angel is Raphael, her favorite god is Enki and her favorite comic characters are Wonder Woman (DC), Magneto (Marvel) and Skywise (ElfQuest, now of Dark Horse comics).

KIM PLASKET is a Jersey girl at heart relocated to sunny Florida. She enjoys writing mainly horror and paranormal stories and lives with her husband and 2 kids. When she is not slaving away at her day job, she can be found drinking coffee with fellow author Valerie Willis and planning the demise of some poor character. Currently, she has several short stories featured in anthologies such as 'Demonic Wildlife' and 'The Hunted', also has a story in an Anthology Titled Fireflies and Fairy dust she also has had a story featured in Shades of Santa. Also, the newly released DrabbleDark Anthology, Work of hearts magazine. She has stories in *Trembling With Fear, more tales from the tree*. Just released. The thrill of the Hunt: Buried Alive. Coming out later this year *Demonic Carnival: First Ticket's free.*

She also has several short stories and a post for Women in Horror Month on the website The Horror Tree.

Amazon

CHARLOTTE
O'FARRELL is a horror writer whose

work has appeared in many anthologies. She aims to share her love of the spooky, weird and wonderful with her readers.

She lives in Nottingham, UK with her husband, daughter and cat.

Twitter: @ChaOFarrell

Facebook: @AuthorCharlotteOFarrell

KYLE HARRISON is an award-winning author of sci fi and horror. He has written well over 500 stories and has been written several books including but not limited to: the 24 Hour Game, Door to Darkness and Tales From a Rookie Storm Chaser. He can be found primarily on Reddit at r/KyleHarrisonwrites

TOR ANDERS-ULVEN is a father, husband and horror fiction writer hailing from the cold mountains of Norway. He became known through his horror alter ego hyperobscure, primarily posting short stories on the vast writing subreddit of NoSleep. He has since had word published in several anthologies and will continue to expand his dark universe for as long as people dare to visit it.

Reddit:

TREVOR NEWTON is

a writer living in a rural area outside of Raleigh, North Carolina. When he isn't writing, he enjoys reading horror and true crime, as well as rummaging through thrift stores for old, forgotten horror films on VHS.

ALANNA ROBERTSON-WEBB,

known on Reddit as MythologyLovesHorror, is a sales account manager by day and a writer/editor by night. She has been writing since she was five years old and writing well since she was seventeen years old.

She lives with a fiancé and two cats, both of whom take up most of her bed space. She loves to L.A.R.P., and one day aspires to own a restaurant. She has a plethora of published short stories and is working (very slowly) on a novel.

LORENZO CRESCENTINI

was born in Forlì, and currently resides in Rome (Italy). His stories have been published in a number of collections and magazines including Clarkesworld, Weirdbook, ARTPOST magazine, Future Visions, Dream of Shadows among   others.

R.C. MULHARE

was born in Lowell, Massachusetts, growing up in a nearby town, in a hundred-year-old house near an old cemetery. Her interest in the mysterious started when she was young, when her mother read the Brothers' Grimm faery tales and quoted the poetry of Edgar Allan Poe to her, while her Irish storyteller father infused her with a fondness for strange characters and quirky situations. When she isn't writing, she moonlights in grocery retail. She's fond of hiking the White Mountains of New Hampshire and browsing antiques shops all over New England. A member of the New England Horror Writers two-time Amazon best-selling author and contributor to the Hugo Award-winning An Archive Of Our

Own, her work previously appeared with Atlantean Publishing, Macabre Maine, FunDead Publications, Deadman's Tome, and Weirdbook Magazine. She shares her home with her family, two small parrots, over seventeen hundred books and an unknown number of eldritch things rattling in the walls.

She's happy to have visitors to her on Facebook, on Instagram and GoodReads

Indiana author JAMES DORR's most recent book is a novel-in-stories from Elder Signs Press, *TOMBS: A CHRONICLE OF LATTER-DAY TIMES OF EARTH*. Working mostly in dark fantasy/horror with some forays into science fiction and mystery, his THE TEARS OF ISIS was a 2013 Bram Stoker Award® finalist for Superior Achievement in a Fiction Collection, while other books *include STRANGE MISTRESSES: TALES OF WONDER AND ROMANCE, DARKER LOVES: TALES OF MYSTERY AND REGRET, and his all-poetry VAMPS (A RETROSPECTIVE)*. He has also been a technical writer, an editor on a regional magazine, a full time non-fiction freelancer, and a semi-professional musician, and currently harbors a Goth cat named   Triana.

An Active Member of SFWA and HWA, Dorr invites readers to visit his <u>blog</u>

Ariana Ferrante

is a 21-year old college senior currently studying at the University of New Haven. Her main interests include reading and writing fantasy of all kinds, featuring heroes big and small getting into all sorts of trouble. She currently lives in Massachusetts, but travels often, both for college and leisure. You may find her on Twitter at @ariana_ferrante

Nicole Henning is a

book-a-holic who lives in a big-little town in Wisconsin. She surrounds herself with all things scary and bizarre and enjoys creating unique art. When she isn't writing she enjoys playing video games and spends a lot of time snuggling with her dog Allie aka Princess Prissy Pants. Reading, writing and horror are her biggest passions in life.

MATT HOFFMAN is a

small business owner living in New York City. He is an avid park-goer and loves to frequent and take walks around Central Park. He originally worked as a real estate agent but decided to switch things up and take a stab at running his own business. Matt is an avid reader, and a huge fan of anything horror.

LYNNE CONRAD lives in

Cookeville, Tn. where she works as a receptionist in the medical field. Along with writing, she enjoys reading, playing piano and traveling. Lynne has been published in *Sanitarium Magazine, Under the Bed, Heater* and am included in *Scary Stuff*, an anthology.

Made in the USA
Monee, IL
21 February 2020